SO-FQV-987

Denali Skies

A Seasonal Girl's Alaskan Odyssey

Danielle Rohr

To contact Wybear Press please visit:

https://denaliskies.wordpress.com/

e-mail :Wybearpres@aol.com

Third Edition: Denali Skies, *A Seasonal Girl's Alaskan Odyssey, Copyright* © 2018, Danielle Rohr, WyBear Press, Minden, Nevada

First Edition: Denali Skies, *A Seasonal Girl's Alaskan Odyssey Copyright* © 2013 by Danielle Rohr, All rights reserved.

ISBN-13: 978-0615768465 (Danielle Rohr)

ISBN-10: 0615768466

Cover Images and Design by: Evergreen Turtle Studios

Photo Title: Denali Skies in Polychrome, Denali National Park, Alaska

Copyright © 2006

Denali Bear by: Danielle Rohr © July 2013

While this story is inspired by Liz. This book is a work of fiction. Any resemblance to real events, places, and people is circumstantial, and are not actual representations of the actions or character, or likeness to real people, places or events.

This book is for Jon and "Move it or-Lose it Tuesdays".

Thanks for digging me out,

and keeping me out all these years.

A Record of Time

Monday, August 2002

"*R*ight here. Next to the river; what a wonderful way to spend the summer". The woman gestures to the big panoramic window in front of her table. "What school do you attend?"

Liz looks up at the ceiling for a moment, an involuntary tick that happens before she tells a lie. She moves her drink tray from the left hand to the right. This offers a slight distraction before she begins. "Umm, yes, I'll be back to UNR in the fall," delivered with a straight face, but sounding more like a question than an answer.

The woman with the thin white hair relaxes her face. Her eyes less discerning and more receptive. "Reno! We love Reno, don't we Frank?"

The quiet man turns his gaze away; he stares out the window in response to his wife.

Liz wishes she could too.

"Frank, this one goes to school in Reno." She claps her hands in approval.

Liz gives her a smile she hopes isn't too transparent. Tips are as ephemeral as the river, here in Denali.

"My grandparents own an RV park there. I stay with them." Another lie to frame the first. Liz knows it's good to answer slowly. People who tell lies tend to speak quickly. A dead giveaway.

"Oh we love RV Parks! We know Reno. Is it the Silver Dollar Club Park? Or maybe the Truckee River Sage Stop?"

This is no accident. There are no coincidences here. Just Liz, lying. Again. She bats her eyelashes and gives the guest a docile smile. "The park is called the Claim Jumper". She swivels to her left, and in usual fashion, clambers back to the third level of the restaurant to dart behind a server station to enter the lunch order for table Thirty-four.

"You did it again?" Gabe gives her a heavy look.

She steps in closer to the monitor and dials in a second order of crab cakes. She can't look at him. So, she looks at the screen. There's nothing left to enter.

"Liz, lying isn't nice. It's just, not you." He hovers just behind her right shoulder, watching the order flicker to a new image as she submits. Something she loves about the Tolkat; the close quarters and fast pace has given them permission to shed ideals of personal space. Always tangled in motion, or hunkered down for a few minutes in between orders, hiding in tight proximity behind the station partition. It's as simple as slipping behind the wall, but sure enough, all the customers are out of sight, and the servers can be who they need to be.

Jane interjects, "No Liz, it's funny, and the only way to get decent tips here. Reno, is a good touch. Old people love Reno." She cuts in front, extending her arm to grab three water goblets with one hand. The clinking of the glass is the sound of their world. Ten hour shifts, six days a week. The tourists arrive by train like clockwork.

"You're a bad influence Jane." Gabe steps back so he can give both women an amused look. The look that sends them both back out to the floor with stupid grins on their faces because he is so cute, and so right. A winning combination.

They both return to the server station simultaneously after retrieving paid bills and a few creamer caddies. The conversation picks up without skipping a beat.

Jane shoves a few dollar-bills into her apron, "You know what I'm tired of? Other than the question about being in school. For freaking sake, I've had my degree for two years now!" She locks eyes with Liz, "I love when they ask me how big the mountain is."

Liz nods in agreement. For some reason, Jane's tables frequently ask her about the mountain. She does have a stoic look, similar to a naturalist or a park ranger. Liz likes to think that's why she gets the mountain question so often.

"Watch, the next time they ask: I'm going to tell them it's shrinking."

"You wouldn't! They'll catch you. That's total BS. " Liz puts her drink tray down in preparation of heaving a big tray of china-plated crab cakes from the line.

"I'm also telling them I'm an Alaskan Native. It's the best way to make twenty percent."

"You, an Eskimo?" Liz pauses before making her dash back to the kitchen. A courtesy in case Jane wants to reply.

"Don't say Eskimo you tourist. That's rude."

"Rude like lying?"

"Rude like racist."

"Oh." Liz blushes at the suggestion. "I didn't realize". She would love for just one day where she isn't constantly schooled by her co-workers. She can feel her cheeks warming, so she darts through the double swinging doors and into the bright hum of the kitchen. The cakes aren't ready. She heads back into the dining room. She passes table Thirty-four, motioning to her busser to refill their drinks. Next, she pivots across the aisle to Thirty-six, a four-top. She unloads the water goblets. The leather-bound menus are lowered just a bit. Four grey-haired people turn their attention to her. It's difficult not to sigh before she begins.

"Good morning, I mean, good afternoon (it's only eleven thirty). Welcome to the Tolkat Restaurant. My name is Liz, and I'll be your server. Can I start anyone with drinks? Any appetizers?"

"The man sitting closest to her begins, "Hi there Liz. What's a nice California girl like you doing way out here in the middle of Alaska?" His gaze settles on her name tag. She hunches her shoulders in a little.

"Are you on a break from college?" He prompts.

She steadies her breath. The story has to be consistent in case table Thirty-four over-hears. She reminds herself to answer slowly. In her head, she can hear her answer before she speaks. The whole time, questioning what any of this has to do with their lunch. U-N-R. Ed-u-ca-tion. She wonders if everyone practices a lie in their head before speaking, or if this is something that is unique to only her. A quick gaze up to the ceiling before she begins. The story will match for Thirty-six. But for Liz, the story, the real reason she's here, the experience of this, is something entirely different.

Departure

Saturday, May 11th 2002

She's been anticipating this day for over a week. The day that shifts into the night when she will leave. It's his day; Eli's First Holy Communion. It's also Mother's Day. This is making Liz especially nostalgic given the fact that she's preparing to board a plane in less than twelve hours and will not see her little brother, or her mother for the next five months. None the less, the time is approaching and she is going.

"It's going to be fine, Mom. Really."

Her mom frowns.

"Think of all the interesting people I'll meet by waiting tables."

"That's what I'm afraid of." Her mom raises both eyebrows.

"Trust me." She takes her mother's arm as they enter through the second set of doors.

Growing up in the suburbs, in a developed metropolis of traffic, strip malls, the chronic artificiality, reveals more complacency than she's been comfortable with. Until this point, twenty two years into the world, the idea of having a real adventure somehow evaded the scope of her lifestyle.

That is, until she tipped. The scales that once balanced who she is had been tampered with. It started slowly, progressing from something from long ago, but over time, as time happens to serve us, the weight of her desire and a circumstance that left her empty helped to sway the direction of her personal trajectory. Like most forces of nature, the delicate balance has tumbled to chaos. A chaos that Liz hopes to enjoy. At the core of this tipping, she finds a pure sense of desperation. Desperation can make some feel uncomfortable, but being curious, she decides to move in closer to the emotion. It hurts to stay with the feeling, but in a good way. An escape is to take place. An escape that sends her catapulting into something so big, she doesn't even bother to fully prepare. Preparing would under-mind the point.

"How about this one?" Her father points to a pew, ten pews up from the altar. Liz slides in first, then her mother, then her father.

A few minutes later, her brother arrives, lifting his hat and sitting down in one fluid motion. "Hey".

"Hey."

Once in her seat, she ponders her choice. For years now she's been back and forth among the same kids she grew up with. Most of them finding satisfaction in drug addictions, or college, or both. She could spend all her days in this city. But there's a hunch. It's been there, nudging her silently. A dream of possibility. She always knew deep within, that she couldn't settle for the mundane. She just needs to know what she doesn't know. The promise of a job waiting tables in the National Park complete with a warm bed to sleep in and three square meals each day is a step towards personal progress.

This day, this prelude to her journey proves to bring more anxiety and angst than she can handle. Liz sits beside her mother and father on the hard wooden pew in the dim church. Sunlight filters through stained glass highlighting the background behind her very small, very solemn little brother. He steps forward, taking his turn to receive the body and blood of Christ. The priest lifts his hand in adoration.

"In the name of the Father, the Son, and the Holy Spirit," speaking both soft and loud at the same time.

Her heart heaves in response. She tightens her lungs to avoid an exhale that might include a waiver. She releases slow, her breath in control and discrete. Deep down, she's heartbroken to leave the cutest little second grader she knows. As a big sister, he's given her purpose for so long. He's growing up in front of them all, at the head of the church having his own experience. She keeps this vision of her innocent and overwhelmed little brother, tucking it away into her memory for a day when she needs connection. She's certain she will miss him the most.

Now, it's back to the family home for cake, coffee, and celebrating of all things Catholic. A Holy Communion celebration proper. Of course it's also a Mother's Day party, and a bon voyage party for Liz. It's layered like their emotions and grows complex as everyone comes together; trying to process it all.

Eli's Godmother sits across the oblong kitchen table. She and Liz are both clutching a mug of coffee. Liz's with two creams.

"So Beth," she begins, studying Liz's eyes, "Why are you going to Alaska?"

Liz wanted to say to her: "I always wanted more, and hated that I never felt truly satisfied with myself, and what I've been doing. The restlessness from being so distant from my own reality was finally screaming from within to go find out. I had to go find out anything, it didn't matter what."

Instead of sharing her true feelings, she takes a long sip of coffee and replies in a voice she isn't entirely used too, "All my life I have been attracted to the Alaskan allure, for no specific reason, it speaks to me."

Eli's Godmother is an intelligent woman, and Liz has always appreciated her perspective. She responds thoughtfully, "Be careful, stay safe, and make good choices."

Liz nods in recognition.

The Godmother laughs, "You Beth, are going to have some adventure!"

Liz laughs too.

Even though she hadn't quite understood, in a way, she had uncovered a deep buried fantasy to trek the Alaskan landscape. This realization is stunning and hard to comprehend. In her own mind, she always concluded that to go to Alaska there would need to be some validated purpose. If she were a scientist, or a fisherman, or a photographer, she would have a reason to go. It had never occurred to her that she could go to Alaska, simply to go.

The afternoon was a steady blur of cake, coffee, a beer, some Advil for her emerging headache, well wishes from aunts, uncles and family friends, and a late evening nap. Finally midnight arrives.

"Okay Beth, are we ready?" Her dad whispers. He's been riddled with his own anxiousness, but in good form, continues to focus on the logic of her journey. He's lingering in the foyer, her bag resting on the floor next to his foot.

The words spoken by her father solidify her choice.

"It's time so soon? Yeah Dad, I'm ready." She murmurs from a place that straddles dreams and coherent thought. She wants to try to stay there for a moment, hoping to give her subconscious one last opportunity to object. Nothing happens. There are no words of enlightenment or persuasion of instinct. It's so quiet, and the space between her and where her father stands, seems so large and so separate. She sits up, and squishes the couch cushion once, taking note that she will not return to this couch cushion for half a year.

"You have a two hour drive to the airport, plus the extra security check hours, you know, because of September Eleventh,." Her dad lifts her backpack over his shoulder and opens the front door with his free hand. Cool midnight air pushes into the room. Liz can feel it on her face and in her hair. She sniffs the valley at night, the smell that has been with her, her entire life. The scent of the jasmine vine near the front door and the cool mercy of the delta breeze are staples of her comings and goings at the Lungrin household. She can hear the faint croak of a frog nearby, and a delicate song from a bird who won't sleep. Her favorite is a sound she pretends are waves breaking on the ocean, but are actually semi-trucks speeding down Interstate Five, in the distance.

"Buckle your seatbelt." He turns the dial on the radio forward until he finds a classic rock station. She leans back, takes a breath. He leans back and takes a breath. The car pulls away from the curve.

Two hours and ten minutes later they pull into SFO. Dark shadows are the only things that seem to fill the hallowed terminal. Her dad helps Liz with her luggage. He watches her go check-in. The headache from before continues to develop and is now flaring up. This, paired with her nerves evoke times where she feels like she needs to hold onto things, or lean on objects to get by. Her body feels heavy. The minutes drag. Each step in the empty lobby makes an echo. The woman at the ticket counter is watching her struggle.

She checks-in. Boarding pass in hand.

It's time to separate. Her dad opens his arms wide. "I love you Beth, be careful."

As they release, she can see his lack of confidence in her. She shakes it off. "Goodbye Dad, I love you so much! Thanks for the ride, tell Mom I love her."

Simultaneously they turn away and do not look back.

She takes in her position, and evaluates what to do. Standing at the gate, so small and vulnerable. Dark jeans, her best black sweatshirt, layered over a fitted blue tee shirt, wearing her lucky trail boots since they would have taken up the most room in the blue duffel bag. Her backpack hangs from one shoulder. All color draining from her face. She squints with fatigue and emotion.

Only fifteen minutes had passed, but more travelers had arrived. Captivated by the buzzing, and whirring of fluorescent lights, and people silently moving about, she takes to her private moment. It's so peaceful. She's thankful to be left to herself. "I'm going to enjoy this." She thinks.

She wonders when the migraine might go away. Through the airport, she finds her gate, matching the number on her boarding pass with the gate three times, just to be sure. She finds a seat in a corner by the window. She can't remember ever being in an airport. Although, her mother promises she had flown on a plane one time, when she was very young.

Impulsive, with only a few small details about what she is doing, where she is going, and what waits for her during the next five months. It took fifteen minutes to fill-out an application, and two ten-minute phone calls that struck her unprepared and delightfully bewildered.

"Hi Elizabeth this is Samuel Donner from the Tundra Lodge, I just had a server on the morning shift cancel their contract. So I have a last minute spot available for you." Explained the deep enthusiastic voice. "Elizabeth, would you like to take the job? He pauses, allowing his words to settle.

She pauses with him, trusting the stranger's voice on the other end. In two beats of her heart the pause produces the answer they both want, the third beat of her heart pounds out the words. "Yes. I want the job."

The deep voice continues, "I need you to be here in ten days. Can you do that?" His words are pronounced clear and defined, they stand apart from the languid patterns of speech in California. The sound of his words are fresh, they offer a chance to have a new perspective. Without overthinking the direction; she replies, "Yes, I can be there to work in ten days."

Another phone call gave Liz her flight instructions (the company books these), and the rest has been a blur. Right now, from this point in time, this is what she knows; she is going to work for a famous vacation company that has a Tundra Lodge at the entrance of Denali National Park, Alaska. She knows that Denali National Park is home to Mt. McKinley, also known as Denali; the highest mountain in North America. She knows grizzly bears live there, wolves, caribou, and moose. She knows that she will be waiting tables in a fine dining restaurant, working for a wage and tips. She knows that they have lodging and meals for her at the Denali Tundra Lodge. She knows that her plane is leaving SFO, arriving in Fairbanks, Alaska, where someone will be waiting to pick her up to transport her to Denali. She has a list that she wrote down from the HR woman, after she had given Liz the flight confirmation. The list includes: three white, collared, button-shirts, three pairs of pants, black socks, black serving shoes, clips to put her hair up. That's it, that's all the information she has.

Sunday, May 12th 2002

Finally, it's time to board the plane. First, she gets to endure the post-September Eleventh bag search. It seems the process lives up to the hype broadcasted on National news.

"Please step to the side, Miss." A poised flight attendant instructs.

A well-groomed security officer rummages through her bulging grey backpack. She blushes and looks down at the ground while he pulls out two pairs of lime-green thong underwear. It's not that thongs are her thing, but when the next six months of her life are minimized into one carry-on, and a checked-bag, less fabric makes a lot of sense.

"Good morning to you too," She thinks, as her gaze searches for anywhere that can manage to avoid eye contact with him. When packing, she became obsessive-compulsive and started stashing extra panties in random compartments among her luggage. Not sure what to pack, she deduced she did not want to run out of underwear. After pulling out her ample supply of panties, he avoids eye contact. She appreciate this.

"You can go ahead Ma'am." He holds his arm out to let Liz pass.

As she enters the plane, she can hear the air pushing through the main cabin; it hums and her heart hums. She locates her seat, a spot by the window. She kicks her backpack under the seat. She squeezes it tight with her ankles. It's all she has now. She doesn't want to break contact with it for a second. Her attachment to the pack brings the same comfort a security blanket brings to an infant. There's plenty of room on the plane, and even better, she discovers a nice-looking boy flying alone, close to her age. He's sits in her row. She's glad for the empty seat that's shared between them.

"Hi," She does her best to offer a warm greeting.

"Hello." His answer lacks sincerity.

She's a little curious and completely terrified to fly. Soon, the plane goes into motion, slowly driving down the tarmac. The throbbing in her head courses through her entire body, including her stomach. An engine fires and a vibration is felt throughout the aircraft. She grabs for the puke bag. She throws-up.

The flight attendant appears. She signals to her partner who begins the safety talk before turning to Liz. "Oh, I'm sorry. Are you feeling okay?" She whispers in a matronly voice.

Liz nods and gives the flight attendant her best try at a smile. She holds out her slim delicate hand to accept the bag. Liz obediently hands it off to her. She gives Liz a wink, and disposes of it quickly. "Just try to relax dear, the flight will be over before you know it. When we get up in the sky, I'll stop by with some ginger ale for your stomach."

Liz nods to her. Everything she said, sounds good. She tries to look at the boy without seeming obvious. He definitely just saw her do that. He definitely saw the flight attendant take the bag of puke. He stares straight ahead, working hard to avoid an interaction with Liz. If he wasn't nervous about flying before, there's a good chance he's nervous now.

She slinks down in her seat, her gaze fixated on the sights out the deep-set window.

She pulls her brown hair back into a loose and messy bun. She can feel the cool air touch the back of her neck.

Instead of thinking ahead to what the near future holds in store for her, she can't help but let her thoughts wander back to a little nagging guilt. The guilt of doing something wrong. The guild that is pinching her stomach into a knot. She left without saying goodbye to someone. She couldn't say goodbye to someone because if she did, he wouldn't let her go. Still, she can reason that her own actions are justified. It's wrong how she did it, but necessary.

Her nerves are jumpy, her head throbs, and she's on her way.

The plane propels down the runway and lifts into the air. She tries not to blink. Distance between herself and California stretches until it's not even there anymore. She's in the clouds.

She has time. After all the preparation and activity, she finally has a few hours to sit and think. "What if it's horrible there? What if this is all a huge mistake? What if it's cold? What if it's too hard? What if the people in Alaska are rough and dangerous? What if this is no place for an inexperienced twenty-two year old California girl to be? It might just be the worst choice ever; after all I'm heading out into the middle of nowhere". Thoughts hang in the air, she hangs in the air with them, moving closer to their answers.

"What if it's the best place for an inexperienced twenty two year old California girl to be?" Nature is extreme; she wants to embody the same qualities. Thinking back to so many times, often depression spells, when she's caught in front of the television watching some PBS documentary on grizzly, eagles, and wolves scavenging and roaming in some far away, primitive land. A place concisely uncivilized. She thinks about her former self (pre-flight).She never thought it would be possible to go there, to the places in the shows, to exist on that plain, to be there among the elements of nature, to tempt the danger. For Liz, is just a mediocre valley girl from California, who's never really been anywhere, never thought to go. Well maybe she thought to go, but not really go. Not really do it. To go see it for herself.

She manages to negotiate the transfer in Seattle without a hitch. Soon she's back on a plane, up in the air, visualizing her arrival as her travel continues.

The pilot gets on the intercom; "Hello this is your Captain speaking, we are now flying over Denali National Park, if you look to the left, you can see Mt. McKinley."

Liz is sitting on the left side of the plane. She peers out the window, there are so many clouds.

This is her first glimpse of her new home for the next five months. She has no preconception of what she's about to see, but when she peeks over and down towards the earth, what she sees strikes her with surprise and fear. This truly is the Alaska she's seen on television and books, with no towns, or people, or signs of development.

What Liz can see are massive twisting glaciers, spilling over a vast landscape, contorted and pushed upon by jagged snow covered peaks. Then Denali herself, rising up from under a blanket of clouds. She couldn't easily be described, but the traditional mountain words can suffice; like majestic, and untamed. She stands so tall, above everything else; bearing witness to Liz's journey.

"Here I am. You called me here Denali. I heard your quiet voice beckon me from a place of darkness so far, far away. Now, I am here. I found you, and am humble before you, ready to pay homage to the one who speaks to my soul." Liz can't help but pray, she suspects this isn't unusual, and perhaps others, the truest of those who go to her, pray too. Not in spite of God, but because of God.

The plane passes over her tallest peak, and Liz is once again concerned with the cumbersome and unstable looking rivers of ice, dirt and rock. 'How exactly am I to live in this sort of environment? This is certainly my greatest challenge, but has definitely spiked my curiosity. The kind deep voice believes I can do this, the helpful woman in HR, instructed me to bring pressed white shirts in preparation, not mountaineering boots. Why not believe them?"

Soon, everyone buckles-in, and braces for the landing. Whooshing steady through the thick clouds, and bumping down onto the Fairbanks runway. Liz realizes she's gripping another puke bag, she smooths the wrinkle in the paper and carefully pushes it back into the pocket of the seat.

Thursday, May 2nd 2002

It's so ominous in the open and inadmissible as the frost holds fast to the ground. Even though it's dark and early morning, hunger persuades her to go forward, out into the open beyond the protection and comfort of her den. As she moves through the freezing mist that hangs outside their entrance, she shakes off the stale scent and dirt that coats her heavy fur. She's been asleep for so long, that even now; she's not sure if she's dreaming or awake.

Then with the growl of her stomach, and a painfully ravenous hunger she's once again, aware; she's wide awake and standing on the outside. There is no time to stay and ponder her first trip out into the open, and without a second to spare she continues on, into the low hanging fog that curls and bends around her. Even though it's still dark, the presence of the sun is making itself known. A soft glow grows and shimmers off in the distance. The cold frozen earth is softening and evaporates to creep around the spectral form.

Her once strong and steady legs are now unstable and sore. The pads of her feet no longer grip the slick rocks, but slide and slip along, and sometimes she's pitched sideways, resembling an awkward young cub. At that, she's reminded of the twins and her Mama back in the den. They were asleep when she left them.

She hates the cubs, and wishes they would leave. She wants to have her Mama to herself. Many times during their slumber, she would push them away from her, and

15

curl up beside the soft warmth. Sometimes she would stretch out, and try to smother them underneath her. It felt good to have the little soft, squishy things act as a warm cushion between her body and the frozen earth beneath. Despite her best efforts, they are resilient, hearty little Denali cubs, who will have to endure even bigger threats and risks by the summer's end.

She shakes her body and head from side to side, trying to wake up her nerves, and help the blood flow throughout her long, sleeping extremities. Shaking harder, as if to shake off the thought of the twins. It works.

She continues on, down the slate rock filled slope, because down takes less effort than up, and she is weak. So desperate for a meal. Navigating for food down in the river basin, filled with a strange mist, makes the prospect of eating evasive. All she can smell is the wetness, and decomposition of the damp earth.

When she focuses in on the scent of the land, she moves on with her nose down to the river floor; taking in short motivated sniffs. Finally, she locates the mold and nut smell of last year's roots that have died, and were buried under glacial deposits and water. With some slow and precise cuts into the ground, she pushes and tears away the dirt, to reveal a small mouthful of thin, wispy, grass roots. She scoops them up with her tongue and can feel them in her mouth. She quickly gulps the single bite, and it is gone. The taste and flavor dissolve on her tongue, and mingle with the roots tannin smell. She rolls her eyes back in pure enjoyment of the single mouthful.

After swallowing the bite, her enjoyment is replaced by more hunger, intense hunger. As if she's going to surely die, if she doesn't eat right now.

She lifts her head up not to look, but to smell the air, to detect something, anything. She drops her head again in irritation. She detects nothing, and as she scans the active and steadfast moving river, she wonders if she's the only creature in this whole big place. The expanse of land so humble, and open, she feels as though it owes her a meal. This is her place, and she is the only thing existing in it. She must be sustained. Dropping her nose to the ground, she continues to smell for roots, once trying to eat a dried branch from a tundra bush, only to spit it out, and go back to digging. She discovers more roots closer to the base of the hillside, and further from the water.

Smell, dig, and bite, after bite, until she feels strong enough to locate different, better food. This is the hunger that kills, and she's a yearling bear, who will remember this hunger, and do whatever she can to avoid this condition at all costs.

Explore

Sunday, May 12ᵗʰ 2002

Liz's eyes open wide, absorbing her first impression of Alaska, and her first time visiting

the Fairbanks airport. It isn't like SFO or Seattle. She got to leave the plane from the landing strip. The terminal looks like an airplane hangar. She approaches a desk where a few people happen to be checking-in. She's interrupted by a hissing sound, that's followed by the groan of a motor. A creaky belt begins to move. Luggage starts a slow transition from the plane to their owners. She's satisfied. She's now found someplace unfamiliar. This is encouraging.

She puts on a "she means business," expression and heads over to a small group of people watching for their bags to appear on the carousel.

"Denali Tundra Lodge? Liz swings around to locate the source of the voice. It's a boy. He has a carryon, too.

He continues to talk before she's turned to face him completely. "My name's Diego." His smile is genuine. This eases tensions she isn't entirely aware of.

"I am. I mean, yes. I mean, you're going there too?"

"Nervous? You're going to be okay." She's embarrassed, he can see she's struggling through her process. "It will be my third season working at the Tundra Lodge. I think you'll like it there. It's great. What's your name?"

Liz begins to think he's older than he looks. She decides he's a good person. He's safe. She now has one safe person here. She now knows someone here. Someone who will be in Denali.

"Oh, sorry, I'm Liz." She hates that she's introducing herself as an apology. Something her former self would do. Something she plans to correct. She looks around the room a little more, curious if there are others. She puts her hand out to shake. He pushes his pack onto his shoulder more, and reaches for her hand. "I'm from California." She adds.

"I saw you on the plane. I had a feeling you were going to the Tundra Lodge."

Liz is surprised that she was being watched during the flight. She was completely unaware. She smiles and hopes to think of something to say to keep the momentum of formalities rolling, anything to avoid an awkward silence. A bold and charming older man walks up. He already knows Diego.

"Diego, my man! I'm glad to see you back this year. How have you been?" His Southern Drawl is rich like honey and a delicacy in Liz's world. The tall gentleman with salt and pepper hair extends his arm, he wraps it around Diego, giving him a sideways man-hug.

Diego beams with pleasure. "Hi, Ray. I didn't know if I'd see you!"

"I've got nothing better to do, no place better to be. Laura's here too."

"That's great, Ray."

It doesn't take long before Ray greets Liz. "You must be Elizabeth. Welcome!" Liz loves the way he pronounces her name. He hits all the syllables an octave higher. He extends his hand. She gives him hers and he pumps the handshake as he talks. "I'm Ray. I will be driving you and Diego back to Denali, but before you get too excited, I have to warn you; we have a four hour drive ahead of us. I know, not the best news after your long flight, but believe me, it's a beautiful drive."

She pulls her hand back gently. "So, it's just the two of us you're picking up?

Her duffle bag creaks around the turn. She reaches to retrieve it, but Ray beats her to it. "Thankyou."

"I've got it, and yes. You and Diego are my only passengers. Everyone else arrived last week."

"Oh." Her headache weakens her ability to converse. She's grateful for the intimate group and she's eager to climb into the passenger van. All she wants right now is to pull down her sunglasses and try her best to rest. The migraine and her body are ready to give way from all the stress, excitement, and flight. On the bright side, she's sure once she gets to her housing and settles in, finds a bed to lie down in, the recovery from the migraine will be quick and simple. She trails behind Diego and Ray. It's lovely to board the van. She takes this time to contemplate the introduction; such nice people; they've worked for this company in the past. This is a promising sign that wherever she's going; must be okay, since these two men are returning for another season.

Ray starts the engine and shifts into drive. Soon, she's in motion again. Closing her eyes and resting before their arrival sounds good, but she can't. There's too much to see, and so much to analyze. She can't figure this place out. Fairbanks is nothing like she pictured. She imagined something out of the television show "Northern Exposure", but it actually reminds her of the cities in the valley of California, only with more trees, and a sapphire blue sky filled with clouds, but still quite flat. Diego takes a seat in the front beside Ray. They have their own conversation happening. Diego seems to know Liz isn't feeling well. She thinks he took the job of Ray's co-pilot so she would have the opportunity to retreat to the back of the van. She decides he's a thoughtful person. Her spot in the van is cozy. The road to Denali is mostly straight with a few bends. It's broken by river crossings every hour or so. Liz is inspired to look out over the many miles without any sign of people.

A flex of her stomach reminds her that it must be close to dinner time. They roll into the driveway at the Denali Tundra Lodge. "Just follow me, Elizabeth. Don't worry about your bags. I've got them covered. This is it!" He gestures to the scenery around them. Just beyond the sprawl of the hotel structures and a restaurant, is a dramatic drop into a river canyon, and behind the canyon she can see an endless range of trees and mountains. A cool wind blows against her brow. Liz closes her eyes and lets the cool temperature settle on the surface of her skin. This slightly appeases the headache.

"Okay." He gestures again. "I've got to go check-in and introduce you to HR." First Diego goes, then Liz follows right behind. She focuses on the task at hand as she climbs a narrow staircase up to the little reception area.

Ray introduces her, "Karen, I have Elizabeth and Diego here, we made it back from Fairbanks safe and sound!"

The woman sets down her gold-plated corporate pen, "Thank you Ray."

He turns to Liz, "It was very nice to meet you Elizabeth, you're going to have a wonderful time here, and I would like to be the first to welcome you to the lodge." Ray turns, high fives Diego, then vanishes out of sight.

The woman at the desk has sculpted short brown hair, librarian-style glasses, and a stiff white collared shirt. "Hi Elizabeth, my name is Karen, it's good to meet you. We spoke on the phone. I run the human resource department here at the Denali Wilderness Lodge.". She continues. "If you and Diego would please follow me this way. Hello Diego. Welcome back." She greets over her shoulder.

"It's good to see you, Karen. Thanks for having me back." Diego steps to the side so Liz can go ahead of him. They follow her into a room filled with bookshelves, file cabinets, and a large mahogany desk. "Okay, this is the part where I'll need to make copies of your identifications, social security cards, and have you sign your contracts."

Diego pulls out the first chair for Liz. "Thank you," She whispers.

Right here, in the human resource office she realizes she's reaching a point of exhaustion. She wants so badly for her introduction with Karen to go well. She can barely manage to make eye contact with Karen as she speaks. "K-Karen, I'm not feeling good . . . I have a terrible migraine headache, I'm doing my best to get rid of it before I start my new job . . ."

Karen interrupts, "Oh, I understand Elizabeth, we will get you up to your room to rest very soon. Traveling can be tiring."

Her efficient demeanor seems so representative of the company. Liz takes this as a good sign. The comfort of Karen's assurance is enough to support her through the final moment before she has a chance to lie down.

Karen lays out a few details; "Did you bring your uniform?"

"Yes, I have everything that was listed in my hiring contract."

Karen smiles and reaches into a storage box near her desk, "Here are two bow ties to go with it, and three black aprons. You are expected to come to work each day with a clean pressed uniform."

Pausing to check in that her instructions are being understood, she continues, "The washing machines are at the end of the hall in the employee housing building. Employee housing is that long brown building in the middle of the property. The girls are on the top floor, and the boys are on the bottom floor. Beside that building is the employee restaurant and bar, this is where Denali employees eat. Breakfast is from six am to nine, lunch is from twelve to two, and dinner is between four and six. If you don't like the employee dinner, employees have an option of grabbing a slice of pizza and salad from the Wolverine Pizza Parlor at the north end of the property. Housing and meals are automatically deducted from your paycheck as one lump sum."

She reaches into another storage container opposite of her desk. "Here are the keys to your room. For now, the room is all yours. But, you will be assigned a roommate later this week." Liz reaches out and accepts the two keys. Hearing of her room, is easily the best news she's heard today.

Diego is handed his keys. He stands up first and is on his way, but not before giving Liz a big welcome hug. "It was nice to meet you, Elizabeth. If you need anything just come and find me. Don't be nervous. You'll get used to everything soon."

"It was nice to meet you too, Diego. I'll see you around."

Karen watches the exchange in approval. It's a personal value of hers that her employees support one another. She stands up and smooths a crease in her pants. "I'll walk you to your room Elizabeth. I want to make sure it was cleaned properly." Her kindness alleviates some of Liz's doubts and concerns. Back down the stairs they find her luggage waiting for her in a heap on the curb. "How about I carry this for you? We're going just over here." Karen swings the person-sized duffel bag over her shoulder and muscles it all the way up the stairs of a long brown building, to room 117.

Room 117 is in the center of the long upstairs walkway that wraps around the housing structure. Karen waits for Liz to work the key into the lock. The door swings open.

"Make sure you report to training tomorrow. Eight sharp, bright tomorrow morning at the Tolkat Summit Restaurant. The Tolkat is right there," she points out the door across the way, close to the HR office. Don't forget to change your watch." She warns with a scrutinizing tone. She leaves before Liz has a chance to respond.

Now, it's time to take the remainder of the day and night to try to nurse herself back to health before the long day tomorrow. The shades are pulled, two beds are neatly made. Two modest dressers are resting neatly against the far wall. It's gloriously dark inside. Liz makes her way to the bed with a great deal of enthusiasm. She made it. Despite the welcoming and friendliness during her brief interactions, she feels all alone and so small in this odd place. Her migraine defeats her. On her own, all she has is herself to count on, and she can't help but confront the irony that her own body remains against her. She kneels to the floor, glad to be unzipping her duffel. The Advil were resting on the top of the duffel's contents. She reaches for the bottle of Dr. Pepper she picked up before leaving the airport. She sips just enough of the warm sweetness to pass a few pills down her throat. Instead of standing up, she crawls to the bed beside the window. She pulls herself up, and tucks her legs beneath the stiff blanket. Pressing her face into the pillow.

Twenty minutes pass. Her mind won't settle. Hunger reminds her that it's dinner time. She didn't realize how shy she'd feel. The idea of walking into the employee dining room alone with dozens of new faces is a little terrifying. All of the sudden she can hear sounds in the room next room. Where her bathroom is; is a door that's locked. It connects to someone's room on the other side of the building. The soft melody of a familiar song drifts into Liz's room. The presence of someone on the other side of the door reminds her of possibility. It's just enough to know they are there. It soothes her heartache from the hard goodbyes yesterday, and relieves the fear of tomorrow's introductions. Because, although she's alone, someone in a room next to hers is playing one of her favorite artists. Someone close by has something in common with her. Someone is good, and okay. Too sick to be social, she closes her eyes and sleeps, all the way through dinner and into the next morning.

Monday, May 13th 2002

"Oh my God." Liz whispers to herself in the dark room. New sounds and smells overwhelm her senses before she registers she's waking up in Alaska. She pulls the scratchy covers up around her throat to trap the heat around her. She lays still, listening. Sounds of people talking on the balcony outside her room are what must have woken her. She turns to her side to angle her ear so she can detect the words. There's laughter, and bustle. She thinks, "It's morning. I slept until morning!"

Hunger pains push for Liz to get out of bed. She sits up and ties her hair into a bun with the hair band that's been on her wrist since yesterday. She peeks out the window, hiding behind the heavy mustard-colored drapes with caution as she does. She can see the door to the employee dining room. Two girls exit the dining room. One is blonde, the other brunette. They look spry and more importantly, comfortable. Liz hopes she can look the same when she makes her appearance at her new job today. This morning, she feels reclusive. Too embarrassed to walk into the dining room alone, she leaves her bed to forage for snacks in her duffel bag.

With great disappointment, the headache remains. It hurts, and is even more intense, as it recoils on her; angry about all the traveling she put it through. "I should have had water before I passed out last night". She murmurs, "Oh," she moans, realizing she talked out loud to herself.

She manages a shower, a quick application of makeup, and some fresh clothes.

Liz counts to three in her head, then steps out the door and onto the balcony. She turns to her right, she can see the restaurant about forty paces away. Her head throbs a little faster. She pulls on the sides of her new beanie, then slips on her sunglasses. One step after the next, she goes to work.

Climbing down to the first level, she gets her first glimpse of people milling around. A few there, a few here, on their way to assigned places. Housekeepers report to the rooms. The front desk girls report to the lobby. The baristas to the coffee house, and the servers to the restaurants.

The Tolkat Restaurant has a beautiful knotted spruce entrance. She pulls on the custom door handle just a little, then a bit more, she gets it halfway open and slips in. Inside, there's so much to see. The restaurant is grand, decked out in polished wood and overlooking the river, which is big, murky, and full of glacial deposit. Liz takes a few more steps inside. It's gorgeous. She moves toward an elegant front desk. The morning light shines in and gives the room a gold accent. She moves through the lounge and into the restaurant. She sucks in her breath, taking note that every table has a view of the National Park, four levels all together, with the first level offering seating right beside the floor to ceiling windows. The recollection of reading on the company's website; that on a clear day; it's possible to see the mountain from the restaurant, comes to mind. All she can see today, are clouds. Before she has a chance to ponder the mystery of the view, someone interrupts.

"Are you looking for me?"

Liz swivels to her right and spots the body that projected the voice. Her small frame hides behind the bar. She's emptying crates of wine alongside two warehouse men. One of the men pauses to give Liz a lingering stare. He grins in approval. Liz looks down, then up in embarrassment. The man who looks to barely be of drinking age sets a bottle of wine on the bar and holds his hand up to give her a wave.

"Hi. Claire?"

"Since the last time I checked." Claire hands off a box of liquor to the man and steps out from behind the bar.

Liz, tries to pardon the cliché joke and continue. First impressions are so important. She decides to come clean and just disclose everything to Claire. "I'm Elizabeth, I just arrived last night. I might seem a little distracted today. I'm not feeling very well. I have a migraine." She barely gets the sentence out before she stumbles over her words. Words she had practiced in her head on the walk over.

Claire half smiles, visually inspecting her. "I'm sorry to hear your feeling poorly. Migraines can be awful. Try to take it easy today. Karen told me all about you. She also told me about your headache. I'm from California too. Welcome Elizabeth, come on in and join us." She takes a large box from the counter, then turns back to

Liz. "Elizabeth if there is anything I can do for you, just let me know." This time looking more serious.

"I will Claire. It's so nice to meet you, and thanks for being so understanding."

She turns to join the group of servers, then stops. "Claire?"

Claire has her attention to the warehouse guys who are pulling bottles from one of the boxes. "Yes, Elizabeth?"

"I just want you to know that I'm really happy to be here, and you can call me Liz."

Claire laughs. "Liz, we're happy you're here too. This is us, over at the table." She points to two tables that contain a leisurely, but social crowd. A couple of them seem to be watching Liz with curiosity.

She takes a shallow breath and adjusts her posture. She goes to join a group of approximately twenty people who are lounging in chairs set along banquet sized tables.

"You missed orientation." A man with a shaved head gives her a soft smile, "Hi I'm Robert." He extends his hand for a shake. "Actually, you missed a lot, my dear."

"Hi Robert. It's good to meet you. My name is Liz." She pulls a chair out and sits down next to him.

"Breakfast or Dinner?"

"Ummm, what?" She squints her eyes. Her headache pulses a little harder. She blinks to suppress the pain.

"Oh, sorry. Let me explain, are you a breakfast server or a dinner server?"

"Oh, yes, of course." Liz lifts her hand to her head and pushes on her temple as she answers, "I'm a breakfast server."

"Well, I'm pleased to meet you, my dear. Unfortunately, we'll be working opposite of each other this season. I might see you in passing, but probably not that often here at work. That's okay. I'm still very happy to meet you. Welcome to Denali."

Hearing him welcome her to Denali, strikes a chord with Liz. She sits up and flashes an inspired smile. A smile that fades quickly as she realizes everyone at the table is watching her. She turns to Robert in hopes of seeming normal. Like she walks into restaurants in the middle of the interior of Alaska all the time to work. No big deal.

Hi Liz, I'm Connor. A new hand extends in front of Robert to shake Liz's. .

"Dinner." He shares, emphasizing there wouldn't be anything more to discuss.

Liz nods to him. She's beginning to suspect that opposites extend beyond schedules and shifts. Her sunglasses are still pulled down. She pushes them back.

She's quick to learn these gentlemen, along with the other hip, and well-polished, but ever so slightly hung-over crowd are what are known as: "The Dinner Shift". The less fancy kids down at the other end of the table are her coworkers, "The Breakfast-Lunch Crew."

"Okay kids, Kent and I are ready to begin. Breakfast, you're with me over in the bistro. Dinner, go with Kent to the deck. It's beautiful outside. Take advantage."

Moans from the group cause Claire to snap back, "Those of you with hangovers: I don't want to see you in my restaurant in bad shape. I'll send you straight home. One way ticket back to wherever you came from! Now go get some sunshine, Sunshines."

She follows the breakfast-lunch servers to bistro.

"Morning everyone. Closer, closer." Claire says, while scooting her chair into the table.

Liz moves in. The whole time she keeps her eyes on the floor to baby the headache. Her coworkers nod hello, but, seem intensely competitive as they size her up. By this time, she has a proper introduction formed, and has answered the same questions many times. "Hi, my name is Liz. I am from California, and I am a breakfast server."

"I'm Marvin. I'm from Idaho. Want to sit with me?" Liz can't help but notice his round green eyes. More importantly, kind eyes. Relief floods through her, comforted to meet those to whom she belongs. "This is my group, appointed to me by the higher ups. I have found my place among the ranks of food servers," she thinks.

As the training begins, Liz can't help but find distraction in every detail of the space. The building inspires her, and she's thrilled to be working here.

The group moves through the restaurant side of the building to memorize the table sections. During the day's training session, Liz and the other servers enter the kitchen. She's intrigued. She's never seen anything like it before. It's huge, white, and shining in stainless steel everything.

Claire calls to one of the chefs. "Morgan, can you come here for a second?"

"Busy, Claire!"

"Don't give me slack man! Just come out." She shouts back.

A tall man with an even taller hat in a crisp white uniform walks over and gives the group a wave and a smile. He turns and winks at Claire. "I'm here babe."

Claire continues, "This is Morgan, he's our full time Sous Chef. If you have any questions about the food or the menu, he knows the answer." She pauses, "He's also my husband."

"I actually have you penciled in after lunch today. I'm going to discuss proper storage. Who knows the safety range for meat temps?" He glances at the crowd of servers. Everyone is still. Liz wishes she knew the answer. "Okay, keep that in your head, I'm going to give you the answer this afternoon."

In the kitchen, a big counter divides the front of the house from the back of the house. The kitchen goes back for miles. There are plenty of cooks to fill this space. Chefs, lead cooks, assistant cooks, pantry cooks, cold lines, hot lines, prep cooks, expediters. And on the bottom, the dish washers. The cooks are fresh out of culinary school and wear white smocks, big crisp hats, and flared chef pants. Liz is intrigued.

Claire turns to her staff, "This counter of division is sacred. The cooks do not cross onto the server's side, and the servers do not go into theirs". Claire leads her group out of the kitchen, and the training commences. The day passes. Everyone's dismissed. The restaurant clears out. Most of the staff are going to the employee café for dinner. No one bothers to invite Liz.

She takes her time walking back to her little room on the second floor. While she walks, she looks out at the property. During the second week of May, the Tundra Lodge isn't open. Right now, the only population on property are the employees. These employees are not your average seasonal laborer. This population represents the best the hospitality industry has to offer. In other words, everyplace she goes, Liz is greeted, encouraged, and welcomed by people like never before in her life. Everyone is considerate, kind, and detail oriented. It reminds her of the erratic moving objects that dance and sing around the Beast's castle. The combination of the headache and her shyness directs her back to her room; for rest and snacks out of her suitcase. Once inside she pulls her journal from her duffel. She writes, *"I find myself front and center of my own life, standing amidst the backdrop of an old classic Disney cartoon, merged with a Bob Ross painting, and an episode of Wild America. I have one word that can describe this, cool"*.

In the sanctuary of her own dark space, she thinks about her day. Her headache has faded to a slight lull. The breakfast shift; she's not so sure about. Or, they're not so sure about her, to be precise. She recalls acting oblivious to their strange reception; instead her eyes were skimming over the menu, with great interest. Not only will she see Alaska. Liz will get to taste Alaska. Thank goodness for the tasting course, otherwise Liz would have crashed from starvation. Alongside the standard breakfast fare, are items like: reindeer sausage, lingon berry butter sauce, wild Alaskan blueberry pancakes, sourdough pancakes, crab eggs benedict, fresh halibut, salmon burgers, and other yummy treats.

. She goes to the mirror to give herself a long, critical look. "How did I seem to them? What is it that people find distasteful?" With interest she starts by comparing herself from the top down. Liz sighs, uncertain. She turns sideways and checks her profile, once with her stomach sucked in, and once with her stomach relaxed.

Part of her wants to go see the café. Too excited to sleep, she lies in the shadows, euphoric and light. As she lies there, she quizzes herself on the names and faces of the breakfast shift. There's Marvin, who has to make a joke or a funny observation at least every fifteen minutes. She likes sitting next to him. He's short like her, this makes her feel comfortable.

There are the two friends: One is Jane with her reddish brown curls, and the other is Lauren with the platinum blonde that cascades all the way down her back. Liz avoided them most of the day, and based on their behavior; she suspects this avoidance is reciprocated. The poised women sat together. They seem capable and confident in their serving ability, and she's certain that they suspect, she's the complete opposite; lacking in both experience and technique.

She recalls her conversation with Lauren earlier in the day.

"Where are you from?" Lauren asked, looking coy and guilty of something. Followed by more "Why did you come to Alaska?" and "Where did you wait tables before?"

After answering several questions, it felt less like a conversation and more like an interrogation. Liz had the impression Lauren wasn't asking because she wanted to make friends.

There's Mark and Sarah, the twenty year old married Mormon couple who are extremely nice.

Saving the person who causes Liz to feel happy she's come to Alaska. His name is Gabe. He stands out from the rest of the breakfast lunch shift because he's so tall and handsome. He has a very natural style, as if he's been out surfing in the ocean all day.

Liz recalls when Samuel Donner made a surprise appearance in the afternoon. He singled Gabe out; "You're Gabe, right?"

Gabe extended his hand. "Hey Boss, that's me. It's good to meet you in person. Your voice is even better than how it sounds on the phone."

Samuel Donner relaxes his posture. "Sure, sure Gabe, but what are we going to do about that hair?"

Gabe flipped his head back and shook his hair side to side. "You don't like it?"

In Samuel's deep musical voice; he replies, "Well Gabe, I don't want to hurt your feelings, but such a handsome guy like yourself should have a nice-looking haircut. This doesn't meet Tundra Lodge standards. You have to think of the guests and your appearance."

Gabe looked conflicted, thanked Mr. Donner for his suggestion, and whispered to Liz, "No way, I'm cutting my hair."

Thinking of Gabe, confronts her with an insecurity. She admits, for the first time to herself, "It would be amazing to meet someone to fall in love with here. Someone like me, who travels and works. Someone who will take away the heavy reality of feeling so alone. I'm so alone here."

She shifts her thoughts away from her romantic wish, Gabe's polar opposite; Chris, who sends Liz the same negative vibes as Lauren and Jane, fully believes he's a star server. She caught him rolling his eyes at her twice today during times when was she asking Claire questions.

She closes her eyes, looking forward to what tomorrow will bring, hopefully a big breakfast and the ability to win over some friends. Dinner tonight; trail mix.

She rolls to one side. Before she finds her trail mix, she falls asleep.

"I'm hungry. What time is it? Where the hell am I?"

In her stark, bare room, she can hear rain. It's raining. This brings her into focus. The clock shows ten thirty at night.

"Let's see . . . I must have fallen asleep around six, and now it's only ten thirty. I can't go to sleep. I hear voices outside, laughing, yelling, music, fun."

From her window, is the second-floor wrap around hallway, she can see the corner building: that contains the employee bar and café. The back door is open, and it's just a downward flight of stairs away. Food, a bar, other employees entice her to climb out of bed. She reasons with herself. "I could go down for a beer. Shit, I'm too shy."

She grabs her bag of trail mix and slinks back into bed, pulls the scratchy hotel cover over her chest and rolls over.

"Please sleep, come quick. Why are things always so difficult for me?"

Tuesday May 14ᵗʰ 2002

They're traversing a high and sparse slope that rises to the glaciers ahead. She's off to the side, and quite a ways away from Mama, while the twins are right under her feet. She's a distance from them not by choice, but because Mama lately, has been keeping her there. When she tries to get too close to Mama and the twins, her mother snorts, and gives her a flash of big white teeth. Her mother points her head directly at her with ears pinned back. She hates when Mama looks at her with her ears pressed down like that. She knows why she's treating her this way. It's the twins. She hates them, and their dumb, squirmy, little play. Always playing and finding trouble. Sometimes they tangle in the bramble and willow; sometimes they fall into the water, and get washed down the creek. Today is no different, and right this moment the twins have invited trouble their way.

High on the rocky slope, with no place to hide, they managed to tease an intimidating and very large eagle. He's hovering above, circling, and watching, and then diving; flexing his sharp talons. The twins love it, as he swoops in on point, with surgical speed. They often roll over, and expose their soft bellies to him, while Mama tries to swipe the raptor away with her great, broad paws.

The eagle finds her very interesting, since she's away from the others revealing her vulnerability. She hates the way he hovers, and passes slowly above, determining whether he wants to hurt her.

Mama is constantly forging forward looking for food, moving the cubs, and chasing her away. She watches for threats, while keeping the twins out of trouble the whole time. Tired of the game of tag with the aggressive eagle, she lies down, practically on top of the twins, who crawl up and stretch out; pressing into her great bear physique.

She wants to be close, and snuggle in, and rest with Mama too. She knows her mother may not let her, so she slowly approaches, trying to appear as submissive and twin like as she can be. As she gets closer, Mama raises her head up, ears back. Her Mama huffs big lungful's of air.

She steps back, but she doesn't leave. She just stands there; looking at Mama, trying to reason with her, or at least convince her mother that she's too tired to deal with her, so she can slink a little closer to sleep with the family. A strong Eastern gust blows right in between them, bringing new faraway smells. The wind is strong and loud enough that it interrupts their activity. That's when she notices the eagle is still above them, this time doing great wide circles, only passing their heads every couple minutes. She can smell the eagle when it passes; a potpourri of dried blood, beetle parts, and decayed feathers that are ready to shed. Their eyes lock and he almost seems to smile a menacing grin for her.

She hasn't backed away, and now Mama is standing up, shaking aside the milk hungry twins. She's still huffing, and has squared her shoulders.

She remains, standing firm.

Mama walks towards her, with slow wide steps, her head is down, and her eyes seem to stare at her chest. The only time she's seen Mama do this, is when threats occur. This is how she makes the bad things that chase them and hunt them, stop.

She steps back with fear. Mama looks scary right now.

Stepping backwards, she almost loses her footing. She backs down the steep incline. Mama lunges towards her. She pushes off the loose rock with her feet, trying her best to get out of the way.

Another pass from the eagle, who seems to be enjoying the demonstration of grizzly family affairs. Even though the twins are a short distance from them, Mama seems so scary that even the eagle avoids the young cubs.

After regaining her footing, and looking at Mama, her mother turns her back and slowly walks to the twins.

All of the sudden with one step, Mama pivots around and runs straight at her, opening her mouth as wide as she can, lips curled back; showing fierce whites before biting into her shoulder, hard. She screams out in pain, and recoils, backing away.

She runs. When she turns her back on Mama and the twins, she begins to descend the steep slope. She doesn't look back, distracted by the throbbing, pulsing pain in her shoulder.

Tuesday, May 14ᵗʰ 2002

Sunlight slips through the gap between the curtain panels in her room. Liz yawns. More rest than necessary coaxes her out of bed and into a spell of enthusiasm. She's glad to be up and expected somewhere, where she can be with other people. "Today, I'm going to make friends. Today, I will eat an employee meal!" Affirmations and a promise, but still nervous.

Liz goes to her wardrobe and takes her white blouse from the hanger. She takes off the shirt and shorts she had slept in and pulls on each piece of her black and white ensemble. Looking in the mirror she can visually see the transformation. Before her stands a woman who looks professional, complete with black vest and bow tie. She ties up her long hair in a special accessory she picked up before leaving California. Servers are expected to dress in uniform, and not stand out, yet sometimes the small polished touches can evoke patrons to reach deeper into pockets and tip more. In this case, the accessory is a small pearl cluster ponytail holder. Perfectly white, matching the uniform and tying the long wisps of hair up and away. She stays with her reflection, her only company since yesterday.

After a few minutes, it's time to go. She practically skips down the steps and across the property to the restaurant. She can't wait to pour herself a hot cup of coffee with two creams. She hopes at some point this morning she'll cross paths with some breakfast.

This morning there are less people in the restaurant. It seems only the breakfast and lunch crew are in. The dinner shift will arrive later for their turn. The group is much smaller, and the space seems even bigger. Upon reuniting with her group, she notices she's the only one looking rested and chipper. She wonders if she might have missed a pretty great party last night; the Season Kickoff Party. More mingling, introductions, and now everyone, everyplace knows one another, with the exception of Liz. She has her identity. "Apparently, I'm the lodge loner". Looking around at her co-workers, she thinks, "Out of everyone here, no one, not one of them thought to invite me to go?" She lowers her head, embarrassed for not having been included.

The Mormon couple sit down next to Liz at a table near the kitchen. Liz looks up from the cup of coffee. "Hi, good morning."

"Liz, we were just talking about you." Sarah says. They both watch the cup of coffee with a disapproving glare.

"You were?"

Sarah looks fresh. She's not hungover like the others. "Yup, we have a friend coming next week from our church. There's a chance she might be your roommate."

"My roommate? Really? Is she nice?"

"Well, we like her. You two will get along great. You're both really nice." Her husband comments while he puts his arm around his new bride, moving his fingers questionably close to her breast. Liz turns her gaze away, trying to not notice that she notices.

"How old are you, Liz?" Sarah asks.

"I'm twenty-two. How old are you guys?"

"I'm twenty," the husband shares.

"I'm nineteen".

Marvin interrupts. "Refill? Have to get into practice. Tomorrow's the opener." Marvin tops off Liz's coffee.

She looks up and grins.

"I can tell, you're not a one cup kind of gal." He walks off, to fill other cups.

Gabe comes over to the table. He takes the empty seat next to Liz. "So what do you think?"

Liz slinks down into her chair. "Ummm, good?"

"Right answer." He pops back out of his chair and goes to join the large group of hangovers.

Claire enters from the kitchen. "If this were tomorrow, you'd all be screwed. Nothing's set up. You're all a disaster. Where are the menus? The tray jacks aren't ready. Where are the sugar caddies? They're going to need Splenda. Let's do a line up. Everyone over there."

The group hustles to the long table in the back. Liz stays right behind Sarah and her moussed-up curls.

"Okay. Good. Yes. Good. Okay." Claire checks each uniform. "Liz, black socks tomorrow. Gabe, loose the watch. Good. Okay." She walks up to Jane and Lauren. "Nice girls."

"Who's hungry? Today we are working in teams. Hmmm, let's see. Boys, you're team Caribou. Girl's, you're team Ptarmigan. Caribou, you'll wait on ptarmigan. Ptarmigan, order anything you want from the menu. You haven't had breakfast yet, right?"

Jane and Lauren follow Liz and Sarah to a nice table by the window. They moan at the thought of ordering food. Liz and Sarah have blueberry pancakes and crab benedict.

"Okay Lauren, you need to eat something. Don't pretend like I didn't notice you only had an apple for dinner last night". Gabe calls out Lauren, when he's supposed to be role playing that she's a guest.

Lauren squares back her shoulders, "Why wouldn't I order something? I want oatmeal with raisins and dry wheat toast".

Jane looks on, using her expression to communicate agreement with Gabe's suggestion.

"I'll be back with your breakfast, ladies." Gabe turns, giving a generalized wink meant for all the women at the table. "Thank you for being our guest at the Tolkat."

By lunch time, the serving crew is released by Claire. She informs them; "This is your time to regroup and get your bearings, so go explore and enjoy the park before tomorrow. When the train arrives and we get to serve lunch for the first time of many times, kicking off this wonder they call Tourist Season, you're going to need to hang on and keep up. It doesn't stop kids, not for months. Liz, I'm glad you're feeling better."

A few servers snap sideways to inspect Liz. They didn't know she was sick. Liz blushes.

Jane leans in, "you were sick?"

"Yes. Migraine. Nothing big."

"Oh, wow. We just thought you were an alcoholic, super hungover on your first day of work." Jane giggles. "Sorry about that."

"It's okay".

"Now, go." Claire waves good bye to her break-lunch crew.

Liz watches Jane and Lauren dash to the bistro to say hello to Kent the dinner shift manager. Liz can see those two have angles they like to work. Brennan and Adam the breakfast-lunch bussers coax the girls away from Kent. They're discussing a trip into the park for the afternoon. It sounds like fun. Liz lingers as long as she can without seeming strange, hoping for an invite. Her efforts yield nothing. The bussers and servers leave. Liz regrets the awkward effort to make friends.

Why Did You Come?

Tuesday, May 14th 2002 (still)

In the late afternoon, she's still too nervous to enter into the employee pub, so Liz opts for her other option. Employees can get a slice of pizza and a small salad from the pizza place for lunch or dinner, instead of the employee café meals.

She makes her plan from the cramped space of her room. "All I have to do is go get the pizza and carry it back up to my room, to eat in peace. Peace? How reclusive do I need to be?" She rolls her eyes, discouraged.

With that, she puts on a plum-colored sweater, braids her hair, and heads down the short flight of stairs and across the grass to the pub. She blinks her eyes to adjust to the darkness inside. It's an off hour. There aren't many people. Scanning the bar, she summons the courage to approach. Everyone else in the building is sitting and chatting with at least someone. She has no one. This is hard.

It's not raining, but the gray clouds cast long shadows and give the light a murky tone. This fits her mood perfectly. She makes her way to an empty bar stool.

She thinks, "This is appropriate, lonely weirdoes' should sit at the bar, not at tables designed for groups, and couples".

Liz gives her best effort to climb onto the stool gracefully. Being short has its challenges, including climbing onto bar stools. She around the room, hoping no one notices her awkward ascent and wiggle to stabilize herself once perched on the seat.

A tall, broad statured guy walks over and introduces himself. "Hi, my name is Drew, what's your name?" He's confident.

"I'm Liz. Ummm," she scans the drafts behind him, "Guinness!"

"Hey Liz Guinness, nice to meet you." He waits for her to laugh at that awkward joke.

Liz laughs a little too much. She's trying too hard. "Oh, I'm sorry Drew. It's been a confusing couple of days."

"I haven't seen you before. Do you work for Tundra?" He turns to pour her drink. "I usually avoid Guinness because it's so heavy, it's like drinking Thanksgiving dinner in a glass."

Liz likes him immediately. "I do. I just got here. Just the other day. I'm a Tolkat server."

She can tell he figures she's a good tipper, since upon saying this, he arches one eyebrow. "Oh, okay. You're with Robert and them?" He sets a coaster and a pint of beer on the bar in front of Liz.

"No, the other group. Breakfast and Lunch."

"Oh, okay. Jane and Lauren. I love those girls."

Liz nods. Not thrilled to have to talk about the snobby girls that snubbed her at work two days in a row.

He watches her with discretion, noting that she's all alone. He wants to stay, maybe to help. She looks so sad.

She sips the drink, thankful for the calories and alcohol, then permits herself to watch drew, taking note of his masculine features, catching herself delayed by the copper flecks in his eyes. He looks like he was either the high school football player, or the high school stoner, or maybe both.

As she sips, they chat in between his pours of drinks and greeting new customers. "Where are you from Drew?"

"I grew up just outside of Portland."

"How do you like it so far? Have you been to any of the bonfires yet?"

Liz takes a drink, avoiding an answer.

Drew leans over the bar closer to her. "So Liz, how am I doing? I've never bartended before."

Flattered that he wants her opinion, she replies: "You're perfect Drew." Which causes her to blush and stare off into a random corner of the bar.

Within the hour the bar gets busy, and she takes her second drink; a pint of Alaskan Amber (Drew's recommendation) over to a small table against the wall. She's glad she came here, and isn't alone in her room tonight. She's glad she hasn't bumped into anyone from work. She's not ready for them to see her drinking alone in a bar.

"Can I join you?"

Liz looks up. The question belongs to a man who looks like he could be a tall twelve year old.

"Sure."

He pulls out the chair across from her. He doesn't have a drink in his hand.

"I'm Tony."

"Liz." She sips her ale.

After introductions, he asks the question. "Okay Liz, tell me why you wanted to come to work at the Tundra Lodge?"

Feeling a little tipsy from two drinks, she takes a moment to think on his question. Ready to respond with something fresh, authentic. "What should I say? Should I explain the long story about how I was too cowardly to break it off with a bad boyfriend? Should I tell him I needed an adventure? That I'm here because I'm lonely. Should I tell him it is my destiny to come here?" After a pause, she confidently answers, "I came, because I wanted to see Denali." Which is the shortest version of the truth.

He looks at her kind of confused. "You want to see Denali? Have you seen Denali, yet?"

Something becomes lost in translation. To Liz, she's at Denali. The whole area, and surrounding area she considers Denali. Denali National Park. To him, an actual

40

Alaskan; she suggests she flew out here from California by herself, because she wants to see a mountain.

She shakes her head with uncertainty.

He thinks for a moment, and then answers with a question. "Would you like to see Denali?"

Again, things are not translating well. She just stares at him, not sure what he's suggesting. He tries again; "My truck is parked right outside; I can drive you to see Denali, right now." He gestures to a truck outside the bar.

Her whole face lifts with excitement. This, she understands.

"Yes, I would love to go see Denali with you right now, more than anything!" She tips her glass back to catch the last bit of ale still in her cup. She slams it down.

"Come on then." Tony slides out from the table and reaches to open the door for Liz.

They load up into his Alaskan-proper, beater pickup truck, which is sort of blue, but mostly mud colored. They take off down the Parks Highway, until they reach the road that turns off into the National Park. It's May around seven or eight, and the sun is still out. It bathes everything in a pink and gold light, casting long lucid shadows. It's cold, but Liz doesn't mind.

"I can drive us to Savage River. Inside the Park." He states, in between shifting gears.

Liz asks him questions, pretending to be interested. It's not that she doesn't mean to not be interested, it's just, she's going to see Denali. Looking out the window is stifling in a good way. She has a panoramic view of mountains. White and brown, the contrast of the taiga and tundra.

The car slows down once it turns onto another road. A road inside of the gates of Denali National Park. He points to a mountain saddle between two snow covered peaks that are much more defined than the Sierra mountain range back home. "Between that saddle, and up the ridge to the right of the mountain behind them, is where you can see Denali, if the clouds weren't hiding her. Denali is so big, that the mountain can create it's own weather. Usually cloudy weather".

She looks at the empty void where Denali hides. So here Liz is, processing the fact that she's within visual miles of the tallest mountain in North America, only to be informed that it is common for her to hide within her own clouds. She is now acquainted with one of the many enigmas to be found folded within the Brooks and the Alaska Range.

She looks at him with a grateful smile; "Thank you so much, now that we are here, I . . . it means a lot to me." Emotion starts to surface. He notices her lips tighten to try to hold back big feelings. She's there with him. She's also caught someplace else, her heart has been hooked like a Chinook salmon and perhaps she should fight it, but the line is tight and pulls her regardless. The truck, the twelve year old looking boy who happens to cook at the pizza place sort of fade for a moment. All of the sudden life fills her lungs, electrifies her cells; her feet start to sink into the earth underfoot. In this moment, she experiences her first encounter with Denali National Park, and no word, photograph, painting, or song will ever truly capture this singular expression of humility and sacredness that overtakes her being. Her eyes are afraid to blink, in fear she may miss the smallest detail; a blade of grass bent over from the melting snow, or a low hanging cloud curling around a twisted peak. The trails etched into hilltops by sheep so far away that they look like small white blemishes. Gold, greens, browns, blues, whites, and the greys of glacial stones all seem to choreograph into some deep ancient dance, orchestrated by the lord himself. The earth here moves. Tectonic power, hydraulic power, and glacial force push and pull the geology, spreading it to its absolute limit, yet layered and rich with hues of darkness, immortality, and mysteries not meant for men.

She pulls back, it's too much. She's completely captivated by this wilderness; this Alaska before her. She realizes she's holding onto the car door for support, and let's go, only to find her balance is completely absent. Her eyes follow the park road past the gate barrier. It winds around a rocky slope and up into the horizon. The sun lowers and shadows reach. It's cool, and desolate out here. Her new friend and driver shares this quiet space with her. He seems to understand what it must be like for someone who has never been acquainted with Alaska, and allows it to unfold for her. She does her best to keep up, while taking it all in, remembering and interpreting everything that she's looking at.

Tony checks his watch after twenty minutes of uninterrupted silence. "It's close to half past nine, and close to another half an hour back to the property. So Liz, we should head back". He's been watching her.

She feels close to him, even though they've only spoken of trivial things. She's learned that he's in college in Fairbanks, and not much else. They make their way back for the big opening day tomorrow. She can't remember what they talked about during the drive back, but she knows it was friendly; and that she was dreaming while awake, because her dreams were real.

Back in her room, she writes in her journal, *"I did it. I went to the bar and a I made a friend. How appropriate for an actual Alaskan to facilitate this first experience, away from the buzz of the tourism. Who was this funny boy, who just seemed to show up at the right time, and bring a rainbow of color to my black and white thinking? This is a moment of clarity; I realize that I have important work to do here. That important work will be done here. All I have to do is submit and trust in the transition. This evening I'm so happy to lie in my bed, close my eyes, and imagine the park. I made it. This little common California valley girl made it, and this place delivers. This place provides everything I had hoped, and more. I can't wait to go back to the park; the first chance I get".*

As she starts to drift to sleep, she's at peace, because she no longer feels alone. Not because she made a friend, but because she has Denali. She can spend all her free time in the park, completely happy and busy. She has a purpose in this place and it's not to wait tables.

She ends her journal entry with a final thought, *"Here in this place I have nothing to lose, and everything to gain, because I was already lost. I came here to find myself again, to know my potential, and this life and the landscape that cradles it. Denali, your ways are powerful and intoxicating. How can I be like you?"*

Monday May 15th 2002

The metallic clang of her Hello Kitty alarm clock rings throughout the room. It's a surreal sound at four in the morning. Back to reality. The melancholy feeling from last night has left her heart, and is now replaced by a more militant and direct sort of sensation. Liz isn't a morning person. She rises, and sort of sleep walks through putting on her uniform. White bra, black panties, black socks, black pants, white collar shirt, button the cuffs, black vest, black tie, and finally the black apron. She slaps on a conservative amount of makeup. A gold eye shadow to make her green eyes stand out against the black and whiteness, and her light brown hair tied up, and jumbled into a floppy, but secure bun.

While she dresses, she speaks out loud, rehearsing and memorizing lines. "How would you like you're eggs with the Minor's Claim Breakfast? What kind of toast would you like with the Lynx Special? We have wheat, white, rye, sourdough, or an English muffin." At this point, she barely has five minutes to stumble across the property to show up for her first day of actual work.

Liz makes her way through the dark morning, as she goes, she's collected into the group. They all ascend up the hill towards the restaurant. Greeting each other, and sharing in the euphoria of being awake and in a bow tie at four in the morning. This is a circumstance that has only been shared by the few elite, who have called themselves breakfast servers. To rise to the day, before the guests, armed with weapons of choice to battle the crowds. Namely hot strong coffee and a freshly baked bread basket. Clad in full battle uniform, the ties tight around their necks, like dogs wearing choke collars. Yes, they were the dogs, collared and ready to work, happy to obey the masters. Fetching the coffee, and breakfast meats. To do tricks, beg, sit, stay, and smile for tips.

It's interesting how comforting being together up this early, and dressed the same can be in such a scenario as this. Liz turns to Marvin; "Morning Marvin, you're lookin' good!"

Marvin shoots her a smile full of freshly brushed teeth. "You're not so bad yourself." He dishes back.

The realization that this is going to be the standard for the next five months washes over her. Liz's life opens up before her, and it is a series of four am morning shifts, complete with uncomfortable uniforms.

"Oh God, I'm so tired, why is it so early?" Jane cries and laughs at the same time.

Gabe puts his arm around her. "Suck it up sister, it's game day!"

The first day was nothing. It came and went, and all she has in the end, is a nice chunk of money and sore feet. Those tiered rows of tables she thought were so classy, turned out to be killers on the ankles and knees.

Saturday, June 1rst 2002

Descend the steps, swivel-turn, and back down the aisle. She balances great big trays of Alaskan portioned food served up on heavy grade white china. When the trains arrive, the guests come in waves, and these waves are hungry. As they step inside; they try to direct the host, pointing and objecting for their favored window seat.

"We would like a table by the window." They command in a tired, often delusional voice.

When lunch time peaks, every table at her station is fills all at once. She has to run from table to table, taking orders, placing orders in the computer, picking up orders from the window, juggling the drinks, and appetizers, and bread baskets.

At the Tundra Lodge; they do not call them customers, they are the guests, and the breakfast-lunch crew honors them, and fusses over them accordingly. But these guests are actually old people. Tidal waves of elderly. The tide comes in once in the morning for the old people who have spent the night, and again at noon. When the noon train arrives, the old people have nothing to do but come in and eat lunch while they wait for the bellhops to bring their luggage to their rooms. Liz has never seen so many old middle and upper class white people concentrated into one location in her life. It's the cruising culture designed for the retired.

Monday, June 3rd 2002

She's been alone for many days and nights now, and it's been a struggle without Mama to follow. She finds herself walking directionless, and uninspired. Her only motivation is to seek out food, which is easy. She can spend entire days digging up roots and napping. There are wonderful bugs, and she's acquired a taste for mosquito larvae, which are juicy and fresh tasting. She also enjoys the long ones, with all the wiggle legs; they crunch, and are fun to find. After many days of wandering, she's discovered a territory that suits her well. Down hidden in thick taiga, which hides an abundant and diverse spectrum of food, she lingers here.

The dense wooded places, decorated with long thick willow and soft pliable earth is peaceful. She adores lying down on this ground, and she's pleased to stumble upon this territory without any help from Mama. The mosquitos are starting to hum in great numbers, and they never stop harassing her, day and night. The fungus and lichen and bugs are plentiful, but she's growing sick from the constant moisture and mosquito bites. It's a wonder that something so small as a mosquito is able to defeat something as large and devastating as a bear. It's time to leave this territory.

Wednesday, June 13th 2002

A month into waiting tables and the breakfast lunch crew have accepted that regardless of their opinion; Liz is holding her own, carrying her weight, and indeed, she's not leaving anytime soon. Despite her own ideals, shattered, the mirror that would refuse to reflect who she wished to see, it's evident there's a lift in her step and a sparkle in her eyes.

Lauren corners Liz behind the server station during a lull in the breakfast shift, "Where did you say you waited tables before?"

The question isn't friendly. Liz looks up and can see Jane pretending to watch her tables just outside of the station. "Ummm, I worked at a Donny's back in California."

"Donny's?"

"Yep." Liz grabs a tray and heads out to drop off a couple of checks. Ignoring the catty ways of her co-workers feels like the best option. Liz thinks, "I do belong here. These are my tables, this is my job, truly none of their business."

The next day, Liz can sense more tension. In the heat of a rush, Liz who was second in line grabbed the last available coffee carafe, filling it feverishly to return to the floor. She turns to hurry through the kitchen doors when Chris steps in front of her with a frown. This causes her to stop short, grabbing the carafe with both her hands so not to spill or drop.

"That's my coffee." He holds his hand out in command.

Liz pulls the carafe into the crook of her arm, keeping both hands on it. She shakes her head and tries to maneuver around him. Another day, a different rush, she might have handed it to him without an argument. But, she waited for the carafe. Her guests are waiting for her. It's not about her, it's about taking care of her tables.

Chris slides over two inches, blocking Liz. "Are you kidding me?" His voice is reactive and loud. So much, that the other four servers stopped filling their bread baskets and trays to watch the confrontation.

Tears begin to well in Liz's eyes. She wants to abandon her post, run and hide. He won't let her.

"You know what? I can't even figure what you're doing here. You're a joke. I'm sorry for you! Why don't you go back to Donny's? Screw it!" He throws his tray that flies past her head and slams with a pop against the walk-in door behind her. Keep it. I'll just lose tips, and my guests will lose coffee, because someone doesn't know how a restaurant works. Someone doesn't belong here." He shakes his head and turns to go back into the dining room.

Liz is still clutching the carafe, tears want to come. She knows there are many eyes on her back in the kitchen. He said those things in front of everyone. Liz knows he's not the only one that feels that way about her.

"Hi. Okay?" Gabe strides over to her, leaving her path wide open. "Look, two carafes just came back. I'll fill this one and run it out to that jerk. It's him, not you. You know that, right?"

Liz nods her head.

Gabe turns to fill the carafe, giving her a minute. The other servers and cooks pick-up the dropped pace of the back of the house. He turns and opens the swinging door to let Liz go before him. He gives her a smile. "Quite a rush this morning, your killing it! Go get'em."

All Liz can do is take his direction. Pushing back some tears, she lifts her face into a smile and heads down to her section to top-off some cups of coffee.

Walking into her room at the end of the day is the relief she'd been wishing for, for hours. The first thing she sees is her roommate's perfectly made bed. She turns, to see her own bed, blankets jumbled, and sheets hanging off the mattress sideways. She tugs her bow tie loose. She collapses into the bed. Ready to have a private moment. A time to cry. It doesn't happen. Overexposed, undefined. Chris is wrong. The part that makes her most sad, is that she's so happy to be here, in Alaska, on this property.

As much as she doesn't want too, she enters the Tolkat for another long day of serving.

"Hey, Liz. So, you know my boyfriend back in Minnesota's thinking about visiting me . . . only I'm not sure I want him too. I've been hanging out with this guy. Just hanging out," she stresses. I just want some space, you know? It's good here. Right?"

Liz grins. It's the first time Lauren's spoke to her about things that have nothing to do with work.

"Morning Babe, I put out your creamers and sweeteners for you." Jane calls, as she passes Lauren and Liz.

"Thanks." Liz calls back.

Jane reappears, taking a spot next to Lauren. "Hey. We want to say, don't take to heart the stupid remarks from Chris. We don't feel that way about you. You're a good server. Look, you've made it to week number four. This work isn't easy. We're all doing fabulous."

Liz nods. The morning flows with more support and encouragement. By the afternoon, even Chris becomes infected by the love for Liz.

"Liz, can I talk to you? He catches her, after she puts in a lunch order to the back for herself. They happen to be in the same spot as the confrontation from yesterday. He looks different. His expression serious, but not the same as yesterday. "I want to apologize."

"Oh, it's okay. It's nothing. Really."

"No Liz, that was out of line. I'm so sorry. I like you a lot. You're funny, and nice, and you treat your tables good." He shifts his weight to his other foot. "Can I give you a hug?"

Liz nods. They're the only servers in the kitchen at the moment, the chefs are busy breaking down the line to notice the heart to heart.

He reaches out and pulls Liz in. He wraps her up in a hug. He holds her there for a minute. He smells like the lunch shift. "Come on." They walk into the dining room with his arm around her. When they get to the back table, he pulls out a chair for her.

"Thank you." Liz sits for the first time since she left her room over ten hours ago. Feeling desperate for acceptance, she genuinely forgives Chris. "Beer's on me tonight," he smiles.

It's time to sit down, eat food and count their dough.

Gabe leans in and eyes the pile of tips in front of Liz. He looks worried, "Are you pitching appetizers to them?"

"Yes," she squeaks. Looking away.

"Tomorrow, I'm going to help you. Will you let me help you?"

She nods.

Lauren and Jane are the most vocal about their views. "Don't you want to make money?"

Liz just shrugs her shoulders. "For me just surviving the double shift is my victory."

Three weeks later, two new servers arrive, and Liz is relieved to not be the "new guy" anymore. Doug, an interesting man in his late forties who looks like he enjoys his drink, and Kendall, the girlfriend of all the girls on the crew's favorite server: Gabe.

Gabe, along with the Mormon bus boys turned out to be wonderful flirts, and keep the girls on the morning shift feeling zealous and distracted throughout the long days. The busboys always take the lead from Jane and Lauren, and within their clique really aren't that interested in anything beyond a working relationship with Liz. But, when it comes to Gabe, she must confess; he compensates for their snobbish attitudes.

"Hey Liz, are you having fun yet?" He teases, during a trying lunchtime rush.

With so many of the other servers still keeping her at a distance, she likes to focus on her relationship with him. He really goes out of his way to get to know her. It's genuine and kind, and is exactly what she needs to feel okay about splintered environment.

In the kitchen, high above the white grained wall paper and stainless steel, is a poster just above the big metal door that opens into the walk-in fridge. The poster has a hand making the "okay" sign. Three fingers out, and the thumb and index pointer making an "O". In the background, behind the hand gesture are pictures of food items; a fish, some lettuce, an animated graphic of a rib eye steak. Above the hand are the words "Proper Storage". Liz loves this poster, and decides it will make the perfect name for a band.

She catches him counting some ketchup bottles for his station. She leans against the partition, closing-in to his space. "Gabe, do you want to be in my band?"

This invitation grabs his attention "You're starting a band Liz?" He looks at her; assuming she's serious.

"Yes it's a restaurant band named after my favorite poster: Proper Storage." She points, and gestures to the poster on the far wall. She makes the okay gesture with her fingers at him.

He looks at her, and then at the poster, and then back at Liz.

He starts nodding his head. "Yes, yes Liz, I'm all about your band!"

This new project keeps them both distracted for several weeks during the comings and goings of the long shifts. Of course there is the brand song that has the band's name in the title. *"When I say proper, you say storage! Proper – Storage! Proper-Storage!"* With all songs sung in a British rock sort of accent. Gabe creates one called: "Sour Dough, in San Francisco". This song is reserved for times when they find themselves serving sourdough bread bowls, sourdough pancakes or anything else sourdough.

One day Gabe walks up to Liz and declares, "Liz, I want to help you make money. You're going to sell some deserts today!"

She rolls her eyes in her usual laziness, not interested in having someone push her to work harder than she already is. Even if that somebody; is Gabe.

"I know," He mutters, looking inspired and smiling at her. He grabs the dessert tray that some of the servers constructed out of a regular food tray. He holds it out in front of himself with both hands. "I'm going to dance a jig with the cheesecake down the aisle."

"Gabe if you do that, I will respect you on a whole new level!"

Gabe dances a jig down the aisle of the bottom rows of tables during lunch, as soon as every table is filled. The sight of the tall, gawking young man, holding out a tray of pie and cake, jigging past each table, bobbing his head from side to side, hair flopping around, looking like a total ass, makes her laugh so hard; she has tears. Gabe is her sunshine. The other girls on their crew are equally smitten with him, and he keeps their days smooth and productive.

Poor Kendall, upon her arrival the females on the crew are already annoyed, and disappointed. The dancing, joking, and flirting are reduced to a small fraction of what they had once been. But, as Liz's affection for Gabe is more fun than anything, and she really did appreciate seeing him so happy to have his girlfriend back in his life, the change in the crew feels okay.

After all, Kendall is wonderful. Gabe had told her how much fun Liz is, so Kendall is completely ready to laugh and joke with her, like they're already friends. Liz can definitely use some friends on the breakfast-lunch crew. Kendall is funny, but not as funny as Liz. She tries hard to match her antics, and Liz encourages her. She finds herself watching Kendall, trying to study what types of features and qualities Gabe finds attractive. Kendall wears her hair in a high pitched pony tail every day, dusted with stiff hairspray. She wears neutral shades of makeup, but likes to add a generous layer of mascara to her long lashes.

Jane would joke; "Do you know why Mormon girls wear their hair so high? So they can be closer to God!"

Liz turns to inspect the pony tail fastened at the highest point on the top of Kendall's head. She laughs, not because the line is funny, but because Jane is hysterical when she tells a joke. So now they have two couples on the crew, the young married couple: Mark and Sarah, and Gabe and Kendall. So be it. The new distance from Gabe is okay. The Tolkat hired a new expediter.

Looking as uncomfortable as a wet cat, Susan stands in the center of the kitchen, in front of the line. Chef and his wife are reconsidering her uniform; the black and white chef pants and a white smock drip from lack of shape off her small frame. She looks like she's going to a slumber party. Susan interrupts the couple, "Ummm, so what is my job?"

Chef and his wife stop. They stand gawking at the confused girl before Claire gives her a tactful smile and returns to her side of the restaurant leaving Chef to train his brand new expediter. "You're an expediter".

She stares at him, then at the cooks on the line, then at the servers stocking their trays. Chef scratches his head, "Okay, it's easy. We'll do some together until you get the hang of this. Liz, Jane, Chris, Marvin come here".

"Sorry, no time". Marvin vanishes, while the other servers are amazed he just snubbed Claire's husband, Lord of The Back of The House.

"Okay. You three, this is the new system. Beginning next week, our lodge is at maximum capacity. Meaning, we are going to need to pick-up the pace. We've brought in some help for you. This is Susan your expeditor. I want you to explain to the rest of your crew my rules. Susan, any of these penguins break my rules, let me know. Her job is to take a ticket, read it, place it on a tray, and then call the server forward to take the food out to the guests. No one takes a plate from the line from this point forward. Only Susan. You mess with the orders, it slows everyone down". He gives the servers a sincere look they won't soon forget. "Okay Susan, let's begin. He pulls the ticket, "Right to left". He reads to her the dishes and they begin to assemble a tray. "Always in order".

Susan often finds herself right in the middle of the firing line, the cooks on one side, the servers on the other, and they all need her to keep up. They shout things at her, like: "That's my order right there, let me take it!"

Many of the servers dislike Susan, and the rest of the bunch seem to barely tolerate her. Liz discovers she enjoys spending more time in the back of the house, near Susan. After the first day, Susan begins to sing songs. Not silly songs like she and Gabe, but beautiful songs. A friendship is kindled, mutual, and for the first time, Liz has someone to eat dinner with, and take walks with, and have conversations. They're no longer awkward misfits at work, because they have a common interest in one another. Liz has a partner, someone who understands.

Susan's room is four doors down. After work, Liz shimmies out of her uniform, throws on some jeans and a thermal shirt and knocks on the same brown door that hangs in her own room.

"Come in, girl," Susan calls.

Liz opens the door just wide enough for her to fit through. Her eyes blink as she adjusts to the darkness inside. "Is this a new one?" Liz approaches a water color image, leaning against the headboard that Susan's been using as an easel. "I love this." She takes in the image of the girl running in the painting. "Woah, are these pastels under the shadow?"

"I'm always using pastels." Susan mumbles.

"Oh my God, I need some now."

Susan's bed is like Liz's, but exponentially worse. She has a mountain of clothes stacked on one end, and a little nest of blankets where she sleeps on the other end. Her art supplies have taken over her headboard, and some snacks are opened and half eaten on top of her dresser. The bed across from Susan is neat and orderly.

"Susan. Do you have a Morman roommate?"

Susan watches Liz stare at the perfect bed. They both start laughing.

"Come on, we're going to meet the coffee shop girls for Chai". Susan is bold and outgoing. She's met more people around the property in the short week she arrived, than Liz had met over the last month.

Susan, Liz, and the girls who work at the coffee shop: Denver and Rebecca; move their tired bodies across the street to collapse in the comfy couches at the locally owned coffee house for relaxation and gossip. They all order big steamy cups of chai tea with nutmeg sprinkled on top.

"Oh ladies, I'm so freaking tired." Susan whines, flexing her feet. "There's no way I'm going to make it to the end of the season. I miss Washington."

"You two are miserable at the Tolkat, why don't you come work with us at the coffee shop?" Empathizes Rebecca.

"I'm seriously going to consider that, my dear." Liz answers in between sips of tea.

"Bar tonight?" Chirps Denver.

"Do you want too?" Susan turns to Liz.

"Really?" Liz is in disbelief. She's been fantasizing about participating in the Denali night life.

"Nine O'clock shuttle?" Susan asks Denver.

"Yep."

Tired feet, little sleep, tired mind, but her pockets are quickly filling with cash, and she isn't lonely anymore.

The conversation turns to the subject of Chris. "Susan, I heard saw him grab his plates today. He practically pushed you aside".

"I know". Her head hangs low. "I don't know what to do. Saying something only makes it worse".

"It used to be me". Liz slides a little closer to her friend and nods to the others. "He was so rude to me from the start. Then, he kind of snapped. Through his tray in front of everyone- back of the house. Everyone was mad, and well, I think the peer pressure got to him, because he came and apologized. Like a Tolkat charity project, everyone started treating me really nice. You know, doing special favors, taking orders out for me if I got behind. It sucked. I mean, it does suck. I know what it's like".

"Oh my, what a miserable person he is. I wonder what his life was like. You know, before he came here". Rebecca shares, tilted her chai from side to side.

"Karma". Susan replies. "I'm not worried about him. He can act that way. It's on him. I'm not letting it influence how I feel about my day".

The girls agree.

As they near the last sip of Chai, they each take the final swig, then peer into the aesthetics of the mugs. Each woman is looking for an image etched out of nutmeg remains at the bottom of the cup. This is their ritual, marking the end of yet another chai session. Contemplating what each nutmeg design reveals or predicts about their day, or week, or adventure, or life.

As Liz squints, and tilts her cup to the right slightly; she announces, "I can see the silhouette of a raven with wings stretched out in flight!"

"Mine is a star," chimes Denver.

"Oh, yep, uh huh. Mine, right here, is definitely a plate of reindeer sausage with a short stack and a ramekin of lingon berry butter. I stare at those plates all day long. I see them in my sleep!" Susan pushes the cup towards Liz.

She's found her balance between the running and rushing, dollar counting, food serving, moody coworkers, to the hippies chilling and doing absolutely nothing, until all the afternoon disappears like the drink in their cup. Sitting by the window in the Blue Bear coffee shop, watching people pass by, listening; to the clump, clump, clump of feet shuffling down the boardwalk that runs outside the long strip of gift shops. She just sits, savoring every minute of her time in this place that takes Liz so far away from where she was.

Midnight Sun

Sunday, June 16th 2002

It must be getting close to eleven pm. It's a work day tomorrow, but Liz is trying to make the evening last a little longer, because she doesn't want morning to come. Her feet are still sore, and her whole body got worked hard today; waiting tables. She's sitting at the employee bar. She finds herself visiting the bar on a regular basis lately. She enjoys the Alaskan ambience, it's alluring and rustic. There are two neon beer signs, racks of pint glasses, shot glasses, and wine glasses, all framing a back drop with a few liquor bottles and beer bottles on display. There are high slanted windows on each side, but in true bar form, the place is usually dark. The cave-like mood is nice, now that it's June, and the midnight sun blazes, screwing with everyone's biology.

The midnight sun is notorious for keeping people up, keeping people energized and impulsive. The sunlight is one of the reasons she's not quite ready to retire to her bed for the evening. On one side of her sits Susan. On her other; a guy a few years older than her with wild curly hair, tall and thin, with dark eyes.

Beer in Alaska is expensive; there are very few drink specials, especially in the middle of nowhere Denali. By her fourth beer, she's thirty dollars in for the evening, which is twenty five percent of her earnings that day. She's been spending a lot of time out, but makes a solid effort to keep a tight budget. It's so easy for seasonal workers to come up, and spend everything they earn on entertainment, going home broke, but having had the time of their lives. Liz is trying to achieve both, but the priority is making sure she's going home with a nice chunk of income to invest in her next diversion.

Agitated with the wish for sleep, she reasons she just needs a bigger night cap to help her get a little slumber before the early, so early morning shift. The guy sitting next to her had introduced himself to Liz a bit earlier in the evening, but she's been more preoccupied by her conversation with Susan to really notice him. His name is Ryan.

Susan is in the midst of a story; "Liz, you need to come to Bellingham, it is paradise. I have so many friends that you would love, and there are so many galleries! It's so much better than Alaska, and-"

Liz interrupts the .amusing story. "Drew can I have another Amber Ale?"

Drew looks up, and gives her his sexy nod. She sighs. Susan takes the last swig of her beer. "I'm going to bed Liz; I can't stay up any longer. I hope you don't mind."

Liz gives her a hug, and stands up in a fond farewell, watching Susan make her way to the exit. "See you in the morning Mehora!"

"Buenos Noches Mehora." She calls back.

She now finds herself solo, a lone wolf, waiting for sleep and another beer to come her way. She realizes this is the first time she's been alone in a bar since the first night she felt brave, when the Alaskan boy took her to the park. She hasn't seen the boy. She hasn't been to the park. This depresses her.

With a flash of his great smile, and a wink, Drew brings her a fresh amber ale. "This beer is on me."

Liz analyzes the gift: either he appreciates her business, or she's looking hot, or he can see how bad she needs to go to sleep. All of the options work.

"Thank you Drew." She does her best to sound sweet and attractive.

She settles into her bar stool, staring into the bubbles swimming their way up to the surface of her drink.

Ryan shifts his body so that he's facing her. "Liz, where did you say you're from?"

He catches her eyes; they have a quick sly moment before she answers, "I didn't." She leans in a little closer to feel the heat from the spark of conversation. "Stockton, California."

Before, she wasn't very interested in chatting with him, because although he was cute and she really likes his hair, he seemed too mellow. Yet, she noticed he did hangout for a while next to her this evening. She feels bad she hadn't really noticed before.

His eyes brighten, "I spent time in California, while I was hiking the Pacific Crest Trail."

It's true, Liz doesn't care for hippie guys so much; however she does hold a torch for mountain men, nature lovers. Maybe it's the fifth beer, or that the sun is finally starting to back off, and clouds are rolling in, but all of the sudden this guy sitting next to her seems extremely interesting. Not only that, but he's equally interested in Liz. Up until this point in her ventures, she hadn't really met any guys who were specifically interested in her, other than the flirty ways of her coworkers.

"I'm a neighbor of California. I'm from Oregon. I work over at the Teklanika Cabin Outfit. You would like the Tek crew Liz, they're really cool and always doing fun things." He chats away, while he stares into her eyes. Under normal circumstances this stare would probably make her nervous, but the compliment from the free beer, and the tipsy way it makes her feel masks any insecurities she might harbor.

"I can't believe you did the entire PCT by yourself, Ryan. Tell me about the experience. Tell me why you decided to do it?"

He takes a sip of his drink. "Well Liz I decided to hike the trail after finishing my degree in hydrology."

She sits happily listening to his accounts of the miles and months he had spent on the trail.

"Liz, why did you come to Alaska?"

As many times as she's asked this question, she always struggles to find a clear and precise answer.

"I came here to experience Denali." She responds, blinking her sleepy eyes.

"I spend a lot of time in the park. I'm a shuttle driver, our outfit has a special permit to drive the park road to transport guests. It affords me lots of opportunity."

"I need to go back to the park."

"I can take you sometime."

Liz bats her eyes. She likes everything he says. She lets him do most of the talking, while she slowly nurses her final drink, intending to linger a bit.

He explains his experience on the PCT. "The secret and greatest challenge is in the preparation. I had to pack many boxes and mail them to multiple locations."

Her beer is gone, and so is her best effort to stay awake.

The dinner shift is starting to trickle into the bar. She rarely sees them in their element. They've finished their shift, have pockets of money, and are yelling, singing, and dancing. They're all so sexy, hip, and fun. If they are out, Liz is definitely up past her bedtime. She must have been truly tired, because she's losing interest in her conversation with Ryan, and is now completely focused on going to bed.

"Well Ryan, I would love to stay and visit longer, but I have to be up in four hours for a super long work day."

He tips his glass up, downing the rest of his drink, stands up with Liz and asks; "Can I walk you home?"

This makes her blush, and her heart beats a little faster. At first she doesn't know what to say. She's really kind of surprised by his offer, and finds it extremely tempting.

"Sure, only I'm just up the stairs . . .but if you want to walk me up a stair case, I would love the company."

The two acquaintances make their way out the side door of the bar. He doesn't have far to go, since her employee housing is just outside and up the stairs. They walk and visit, keeping their voices low, so as not to disturb anyone who may be sleeping. They reach her door, confronted with the awkward moment. She steadies her tired and tipsy self, before opening her door. She turns to face him. Unsure of how to say goodnight.

He opens his arms to offer a hug, she accepts and lets her head rest against his chest a second longer than she should. She pulls back, "Thanks for walking me home!"

With this, she closes her door, and this Ryan character is gone. She kind of regrets not running her small hands through his gorgeous curly hair. She's so depressed that in four hours, she'll be on her way to work, possibly with a hangover. "Goodnight, Liz".

Monday, June 17th, 2002

The hello kitty alarm clock clinks away, and morning sun assaults the restful shadows of her room. She lifts her aching, tired body from bed, and submits to the mornings work. She's not sure, but suspects she's still a little drunk from last night's beer.

The ability to be here is a privilege; and it comes with a high price. Liz pays this price each day, and it costs her and taxes her in more ways than she can measure. It's good she's here, existing among this variation of human function. This revolving door of old people and fried halibut with chips.

Her hangover is faint, and will be gone with a little hydration and caffeine. Her eyes are dry and kind of hurt, they're angry at her because they need more sleep. Her eyes are denied.

Susan greets Liz, and immediately asks, "What happened with the cute guy last night?"

Liz starts to blush, kind of embarrassed; wondering how she suspects something."

"Seriously?" Liz starts to laugh, the way she did back in high school. "That guy. I don't know. Is he why you left me? Oh my God! I had no clue."

"Well, I did. He had been trying to find a way to cut in to our conversation a couple times last night. I was starting to feel bad for the guy. He's cute."

"Nothing happened. Honestly, I didn't realize. I mean, I knew a little. I think I'm just sort of closed off right now. There's so much, you know? I want to meet someone, any other time I'd be all about that Ryan. I guess I'm just working some things out. She gives Susan a defeated look. "Maybe it's been too long. I forgot how to talk to guys."

Susan nods somberly. "I respect that. I think we came here for similar reasons. Are you ready for our trip?"

They both have the next two days off.

"The hostel's booked?"

"Yes, the shuttle tickets are reserved. We'll be in Anchorage by three. We need to get away from the Tundra Lodge.". Susan's job is stressful, and a lot of their coworkers are rude and demanding of her.

Liz hesitates; "Susan, you have to give me your word that we we'll make it back to work in time."

Susan yawns. "Don't stress Liz."

The day moves along at a slow and painful pace. As they stack clean drinking goblets onto the server shelf, the older guy, Doug who looks so comical in his vest and bow tie, with his messy grey hair joins the collected group of servers behind the protective panel, cussing and moaning. Doug always stands with a slouch, his pelvis pushed way out.

"My table is a fucking bunch of assholes!" He rants. Doug always uses colorful language.

The servers peer around the station to see two old ladies with their lips closed tight, angled down in rigid frowns, clutching their cups of iced tea. Jane and Liz look at one another and start laughing uncontrollably. From this moment on, the entire breakfast lunch crew vicariously refer to all the guests as assholes.

It's now common and frequent for them to walk back to the server station and say something like "Mark, you just got seated a four top of assholes." Or, "These assholes are from New York, or, "My asshole only wants egg whites in his omelette."

Thanks to Doug, they finally have an appropriate and playful name to call the guests.

Tuesday, June 18th 2002

The water keeps falling from the sky and rivers are filling up so fast, that she can no longer cross back from the direction of which she came. Unable to cross back to her sleeping place; she has no choice but to walk the river, listening to the deep and steady flow; while water falls down onto her thick coat and runs onto her long face. With the clouds hiding the sun, and making everything so dark, the wetness is starting to make her uncomfortable and hungry. Up ahead are six figures emerging from a low, thick fog. She stops to watch. Four big ones and two little ones. The two little ones make her wonder if it's Mama and the twins in this group. With the thought of Mama and her muscle tearing bite, she backs up to a safe distance, before lifting her nose to smell.

She can see that they are not bear, and she can smell that they are not moose, they are those other ones. She has crossed paths with them before, when she was little with Mama. She remembers, she was not afraid of them, and they did not seem to fear her. She takes her path back alongside the gushing river, and approaches the funny heard. They have long eloquent legs, tall outstretched necks with big antlers that rise up to the sky to let land and air predators know they have weapons. Their long legs transitioned from a walk to a trot, exposing the steady ancient gait these animals possess. They move directly passed her without as much as a glance. The quick moving trot is irresistible and she wants to run after them and chase them, but she is wet and hungry. If they had gone any faster, she wouldn't have been able to control herself. Running and chasing is a bear's delight, and although it is reserved for more important circumstances, it can be so satisfying.

She continues down the river. She smells something. It's overwhelmingly powerful, and she can tell its food. Good food.

She picks up her pace and hurries down the river bed, until she sees several ravens and some mugals, flying and squawking about. It's some sort of bird party, and they have something to eat. She moves in, closer to the food. She's beyond herself with pleasure as she finds a pile of bones, and fur that once belonged to a fox. The birds back off, and she stands above her meal with interest and anticipation. She eats it all, and she doesn't mind a bit that it's been picked over so much. She crunches and grinds the little fox bones into a nice powder, and sometimes she swallows them whole. The ears are deliciously chewy and full of flavor, and the mouth is the most enjoyable. Within two minutes her fox is gone, and so are the ravens. She likes the ravens, much more than the eagles. They are like bird mamas, helping her to find food.

She wonders where they go in the rain.

She wishes she could follow them, and cuddle up and sleep with them like her Mama, but then again, she probably would try to eat them.

Tuesday, June 18th 2002

The weekend finally arrives; Susan and Liz board the bus bound for Anchorage. "Susan, this is going to be so much fun."

"Liz, I just need to get away from these people and the lodge!"

Liz nods, feeling agreeable. She's beyond excited to leave Denali and see a real city. A place she's only heard about, read about, or seen on television. She's so curious, and wants to explore and do as much as possible within the short time they have.

The shuttle ride is so long, and Susan and Liz don't talk much. Instead they gaze out the window, seeing what they can of big, bold, wild, Alaska. Whether she's looking out over the ridges and sweeping vistas in the distance, or the clusters of deep pink fireweed dotting the highway, tangled in pools of green fiddle-head fern. She pulls her journal from her bag and jots down a few words:

"I'm in love with Alaska. For me, it's the greatest state. It's not just a state as in a territory; it is also a state of mind. I'm reminded that we are all only passing through, using this space, and learning and growing because of it. Unpopulated, untamed, and preserved; images of wilderness and elemental challenges. Curiosity, imagination, and hope; fuel a traveler's passion to see and do in this remote and ever transitioning environment."

Anchorage is a whirlwind site seeing trip. The women find a steak joint called Blondie's, gaze out onto the bay, and enjoy a shopping spree in a local thrift store. They've booked a night in a shady hostel, with beds more uncomfortable than in employee housing. They manage a long brisk walk through the city before making their way back to the hostel. "Susan you were right; Anchorage was just what we needed."

The sun drifts to the top middle place in the sky, it's very late, and it reflects a brilliance that causes them to stop walking down the city sidewalk. They turn to gaze out on the big expanse of sapphire blue water. Liz takes Susan's hand, and Susan squeezes hers back. She leans over and puts her head on Susan's shoulder.

That night, Liz takes out her journal and jots a few poetic lines before drifting to sleep, she writes: *"The culture of old traditions and art, fused with an urban metropolis inspire. A back drop of a gorgeous deep inlet, smothered in the abrasive hues of the midnight sun. It was so powerful to leave work, and work life behind, as well as the people that add to my stress. Susan is my gift. She appeared without notice, and coaxed me out of my room, to laugh and play among all those who I traveled so far to meet".*

Friday, June 21rst 2002

Liz can't help notice Susan's vocalizations about how much she hated the Tundra Lodge. She consistently spoke of the corporate generalizations, the way it oppressed, and her thankless job. She seems unhappy, and starts to look tired from trying to make it work. The morning back to work after their trip is a trying one, and it takes everything in Liz to cowgirl up, put on her uncomfortable black waitress shoes, and drag herself once more; out the door. Bound for the Tolkat.

It turns out work isn't only giving Susan a bad time, everyone's energy is low this morning, the front of the house, as well as the back of the house. They are now dredging in the midst of peak season, and the waves of assholes just kept crashing up against their spirits, filling the tables, and wanting the bacon crisp.

Since everyone wakes so early, no one really finds a chance to eat breakfast for the first three or four hours into our work day. Sips of coffee, juice, and soda are what keep their heads above water. Then, when they finally have a few moments; they raid the pantry for whatever looks good. Liz grabs a couple of the mini bagels with peanut butter and strawberry jam, in two motions, they're shoved into the toaster. She sees Jane approaching with the look of a scavenger. Liz steps back, pulls open a cooler door and reaches in. She pulls out a quart of the strawberry yogurt and pushes it in Jane's direction. Jane reaches for the parfait glass, she empties a storage container of granola into the glass, then accepts the yogurt from Liz. "Oatmeal at seven, yogurt at ten."

Liz replies by biting into her peanut butter and jam bagel. "Mmmm, hmmm."

They share a silent moment of nourishment. Chomping and swallowing as much as they can between the pulse of guests. Liz gets two large bites in, then grabs a tray that Susan has set for her, and she's out the two-way kitchen doors. Jane follows, three steps behind.

By the end of the lunch rush, Liz pushed through the doors to try to get Susan to sing a song with her. Susan wasn't in the kitchen. She went back out to the floor. By the end of lunch, Liz still hadn't tracked Susan. Other servers were also annoyed that the expediter is missing. After the breakdown of the lunch shift, she rushed through her own meal, tipping out twenty before counting her day's tips. With very sore feet, she climbed the steps to the wrap around balcony. She counts the doors, until she reaches her friends. She knocks twice.

Susan kicks open the door. She doesn't turn to greet Liz. Liz stands in the doorway, taking in the scene. Suitcase is out, clothes are being jammed in, and Susan is in a rush.

"Babe, I've got some news."

"Wait! I know you had a bad day, but . . ." Liz stops. She knows the pain, the disappointment, and the loneliness. She will not judge or challenge Susan's choice. She knows about the isolation, the cliques, work-pressure.

"Today?" Liz squeaks.

"I'm on the five o'clock train. I'm going home Liz!" She throws a sweater into her suitcase and turns to hug her friend.

Liz freezes. She wants to process what this news means for her.

Susan must have known. "I've already talked to Denver and Rebecca. They are going to watch out for you, for me. They want you to know, they expect Chai afternoons, same as always. I'll never forget holding those sled dog puppies, or our whitewater rafting adventure! We had fun. "

Liz nods. She watches Susan gather all her things together in silence. A simple but loving vigil for her sad wayward friend.

Susan leaves, but not without leaving behind a few words directly from the heart; "Quit Liz, and get away from this unhealthy, corporate, toxic world! Come to Bellingham, I mean it." She hands Liz one of the paintings she had recently finished. With that, she's gone.

Back in her own room, things are the same. They feel the way, it felt before she had met Susan. Her clothes scattered while her roommate's in perfect order. She isn't going anywhere. She's here, in the thick of the season, with so much work ahead. She leans the painting on her headboard, the best means for displaying with the furniture she had to choose from. The painting a gift, inspires her to take out her journal and add to the chapter that coincidentally is dedicated to Susan:

She was my gift, and this painting in my hands is representative of that. The painting has bright oranges, teals, yellows, and pinks, with a girl facing one direction running, and a silhouette of another girl's image in the background facing the opposite direction. It's nice; I like the movement in the painting. It fits perfectly propped up against the wall on my old eighties style hotel headboard. Yes, this makes my room look a little less sterile, and more like home.

She resigns to her own experience here. Her commitment to herself.

Wednesday, June 26th 2002

Her first day off without her partner arrives. Liz is thrilled, because with nothing on the itinerary; she's going for a hike in Denali National Park. With a piece of fruit, and a bag of chips, plus some dark chocolate from the gift shop, she makes her way down the road to the park visitor center. There are shuttles she could use to get a ride down there, but she wants to walk it. There's something singularly inspiring about walking down the Alaskan highway, alone. It feels good.

About a mile and half later she arrives at the visitor center. Nothing gets her senses revved up more than a National Park visitor center. She revels in the buzz and activity. Clutches of people who come from all around the world to gather and experience something special. Nothing compares to the grandeur. She relaxes her focus and takes in the walls of maps, displays full of pamphlets, and the depot; where people are purchasing tour tickets to enter into the park by bus. Unlike many National Parks, Denali puts restrictions on vehicles. So unless you're National Geographic or a ranger, you're probably relying on a shuttle to bring you up close and personal with her majesty. The visitor center is one big vaulted room. Around the edges of the great space are smaller rooms. To her right is a bookstore with books, postcards, and knick knacks. Beside the bookstore are two extra tall double glass doors that open up to a patio where buses are waiting to take visitors into the park. On the other side of the doors, resides the tour desk and a camping supply store. Next to the store is a backcountry permit center. The wall opposite of the tickets has a coffee stand, with espresso drinks and packaged muffins. Then nestled into the far wall is a dark entrance, which invites travelers to sit awhile, and watch a film about Denali National Park.

Liz can't help but notice all the seasonal employees who work in the visitor center. On a bench, she pulls her journal from her bag:

Their appearance and demeanor are so familiar, despite the fact that they're all strangers. We are a breed so unique. It's so remarkable to find one another; attracted and collected in this remote pocket of geography. Young and plentiful, the whole visitor center seems to be run by employees just like those back at the Tundra Lodge. I wonder if Susan would have had a better experience if she worked here?

The Tundra Lodge is hardly in the wilderness. It's located in a little tourist trap a mile outside the park boundary. This trap is sprinkled with hotels, gift shops, tour activities, and dining choices. There's the Vistas up on the hill, the Moose Inn across from the Tundra Lodge, and the small Teklanika Cabin outfit dividing the massive lodging facilities. For dining options, if they don't fancy any of the restaurants on their property; guests can choose from: The Smoking Salmon, or the Crow's Landing, or the Blue Bear Coffee Shop. Denali also supports an impressive strip of gift shops that sell locally crafted souvenirs, alongside the shelves with the moose nightlights, grizzly Christmas ornaments, and Denali tee-shirts.

She writes, *"All of these businesses, including the National Park Visitor Center are functioning because of us, the seasonal traveler, bum, student, hippie, naturalist extraordinaire. Our common denominator is that we are young, free, and in the middle of perhaps one of the planet's most pristine scenic wonders. As we migrate north in a strange sort of wayside homecoming. I know I have arrived. We all have arrived. Standing here in the midst of the busy humming and moving of people, my back pack slung over one shoulder, my head crooked upward; taking in the sights of the open room, I linger for a moment"*

She eagerly hops off the free shuttle bus that takes visitors to one of the first stops in the park: The Savage River stop. She watches a few people unload from the rickety old park bus. They scatter, directing children past the lazy incline of the valley and down to the water. She has no plan beyond this point. The plan is to get here and hike.

She looks around and notices there are no marked trails that are defined like back home in California.

This is definitely not Yosemite.

She looks to the left, then to the right, and deduces she should head north, following the gradual sloping canyon, to see where it goes.

Thanks to the tenacious permafrost, the tundra remains low and close to the ground.

Everything is short, like me. I can see out for miles in every direction.

A slow rising hill lifts up and blocks her view. The land here rolls, and is covered in tiny plants, shrubs, and flowers. If you relax your eyes and gaze out at nothing, the colors seem to run together, the contrast fades and the landscape looks like brush strokes on canvas.

She continues to hike her way up a curve alongside the river. She stops in mid step. Before her, stand four large animals. These creatures are unfamiliar to Liz. Caribou are grazing, and as she bravely steps forward, they raise their heads, lifting up their expressive antlers. They stand, looking at one another. She embraces this encounter and against her good judgment; steps forward as close as she can. She moves in slow motion with stealth, until she's close enough to get a photo worthy of bragging rights. The great beasts sense her strange behavior, and one of the largest caribou raises his head; disrupted from his grazing. He stares Liz down mercilessly. She gets in close, snaps her pictures, enjoys her moment, before sensibility takes control again, and something tells her to back away from the caribou. Before she clears their defensive space; two more caribou raise their heads in irritation. With her head bowed, and an apologetic heart, she rejoins the unconventional trail.

She continues down the trail thinking about caribou, and the Savage River, and where she might be going. This time she has her camera out, ready (in case she runs into any other animals during her hike).

Later, she writes this:" *Who is this girl, hiking down a trail along a glacier fed river, with her muddy jeans, and damp sweatshirt? I feel as though she was hiding within my soul this whole time, and finally she has a chance to get out. To travel and see what she knew we needed to experience. I'm so far away from the old self that kicked around the valley of California, spending her days complacently watching her boyfriend play video games, and getting her exercise on treadmills at the gym. The first two years of my twenties were so comfortable and convenient; I was so lazy, and closed to the chances, risks, and dreams that are available, and ready for the taking. All I know is that I have a lot of making up to do, and I'm not wasting one day here in Denali. Every day will be lived fully and lively*".

The wind blows against her face, through her hair; it has hints of arctic origins. The river moves forward, whirling and tossing itself against rocks. The water has cut so deep into the canyon that the trail quickly narrows into a v. The sun is a little lower, and the shadows shift. This shift makes her uncomfortable. Paranoia creeps in like shadows in her peripheral vision. She heads back to the bus stop with a quick and nervous pace. Back on the bus, back to her room, her day off was everything she had hoped.

She adds, "*Denali, I love that you scare me.*

Even in this place, I suppose I'm odd, as everyone else groups up, choosing more social activities. I'm the recluse, heading out discretely to spend my time touring the park, thankful for the peace, quiet, and reflectiveness of a day without assholes".

Not that Susan's good work was done in vein, because Liz has a date with Denver, Rebecca, and Coral, to drink and mingle at the Trapper's Line. The Trapper's Line is a local bar located eight miles away.

Liz isn't used to preparing to go out. She rummages through her limited wardrobe options. Tonight, will be similar to what she wore during the day, a sweatshirt, a green henley top, and jeans. After a long, steamy shower, she steps out feeling fresh. She runs a comb through her long hair, as it dries, it curls up in subtle waves. She works with intent, applying her makeup with great care. Pouting her lips that wear a fresh coat of an earthy red shade, curling her eyelashes and inspecting her eyeliner.

She cuts through the employee bar. Drew is standing in his usual spot behind the bar. "Hey Liz!" Going out tonite?"

Liz nods, still moving through the bar.

"I'll see you later, then." Drew calls out in approval.

"I hope. Not sure how long I'll hang.!" Out of the bar, Liz rendezvous with the girls. "Hola Mehoras!" She calls out, waving to them in anticipation.

"Hey Love . . . Are you ready to go?" Denver extends her hand out, which Liz accepts with a squeeze. "You look beautiful."

All three lumber up to the road, preparing to be picked up by the free Trappers Line shuttle that's scheduled to come by every other hour. It's close to ten at night, and they will have their choice of a ride back arriving at either midnight, two, or four am. The ride takes at least thirty minutes, since it has a few other stops before it rolls back towards Healy.

The girls are draped in natural toned hippie shirts, sweaters, long skirts, and boots. Their hair is also fixed nice, and they smell really good.

Josh the driver seems happy to see them; "Hey Rebecca why don't you sit up front; next to me."

All three women exchange a sly glance in response to his suggestive invitation. Rebecca graciously accepts the open seat beside the driver. When the women climb aboard, they can't help but study him. Liz wishes she could hear what Rebecca and Josh are talking about, it looks cute and awkward, but the van is too noisy. The shuttle is actually a beat up, well-aged minivan that smells like soup. It couldn't be more comfortable, and it's intriguing how many liquor-challenged people can squeeze into the Alaskan wonder.

Soon, the shuttle fills with passengers. The group of bar goers moves from their ride into the noisy, confusing bar. Liz's eyes grow wide, while she tries to devise a strategy for the evening. But, before her thoughts get too far ahead of her, someone catches her eye. She keeps stopping to pause and watch him a little more. He's been sitting with a girl who works at the gift shop at the Tundra Lodge. Her name is Gemma, and Liz avoids her back at the employee housing, because she seems a little weird. She watches the poorly paired couple. She decides she's going to take her assessment of their conversation as an open invitation to try her luck with him. She feels confident, considering she spent so much time to look good. Liz is eager to try out her good vibes on him. With a clink of her pint, she leaves her chai latte buddies, and moves about the room alone. She's prowling, and it feels good.

"Hi Gemma, how have you been? I never see you out."

Gemma rises from the cozy little table and gives her an exaggerated hug. "Liz, I'm doing great, this is Charles."

She pulls back from the heavy hug from the weird Colorado girl. Liz turns to face the man. He sees her for the first time.

"Here Liz, sit down with us," Gemma pulls out a chair from the table.

"Liz, you have a nice smile." He offers with encouragement. She melts. His Southern accent is rich, and delicacy she isn't accustomed too.

"I'll go grab more beer!" Gemma declares.

"On me, Ms. Gem". Liz pushes a twenty across the table and soon she is on her own with Charles.

He leans in, "I'm from Georgia".

"I'm from California". He responds with little interest in California. Close to two hours pass. Most of the conversation is dominated by Georgia's many attributes, and the many reasons why everyone needs to visit California. Gemma's lost somewhere in the middle, and sits with a sullen and bored expression that makes her look depressing. Gemma stares deep into the refracted light that shows through the liquid in her pint glass. Liz is working hard to get him to hold eye contact with her a bit longer, in between their stories, and jokes. Gemma eventually moves on. Liz deduces this is progress.

Charles has a tall physique and ash blonde hair with dark brown eyes.

"How old are you?" A forward question for Liz.

He gives her a look; like she's guilty of something. "I'm twenty four."

The connection shifts, and she can sense she's struggling. She can see him glance over to the bar with increasing frequency. The signs are negative. All of the sudden, he excuses himself and heads off in the opposite direction of her. She's left sitting at the table, frustrated and wondering.

She moves about the bar, trying to find Rebecca and Denver. It seems they've already taken the shuttle back to Denali.

"What time is it?" Liz asks the guy who works the door.

"You have forty five minutes." He replies over the roar of the crowd.

With Charles and rejection fresh in her mind, she steps up to the bar to order a pity-party beer. Waiting for the bartender, she reviews in her head what she did or said wrong. Her first attempt to meet someone and she fails. Her thoughts are interrupted by the sweet sounding voice of one of her favorite people in Denali.

The voice shouts over the crowd and the music, "I've got her drink too!" Through the mass of people vying for the bartenders service, she sees his sparkling eyes happy to see her. It's Drew and he's hugging five sweaty pints of beer in his arms. "Hey Liz! Whatever you want, just tell Scott."

His genuine affection instantly brings her out of her sad place. A perfect distraction; he's so handsome and nice. She's certain now, and admits to herself that she officially has a crush on Drew. She feels coy, and unsure of how to act around him. Scott the bartender passes Liz her drink, I took the liberty. Alaskan?".

"Thanks Scott." Liz feels proud she knows his name, thanks to Rebecca and Josh introducing her earlier in the evening.

"No problem Santa Cruz." He buzzes away, keeping up with the thirsty seasonal patrons who have bottomless pockets and bottomless appetites for alcohol.

Liz looks down at her sweatshirt and grins.

Liz makes her way over to Drew and relieves his arms of two, of his five pint glasses. "Gotta use those server skills!"

"We're sitting in the back by the band, follow me." They shuffle the glasses like the food industry professionals they are.

Liz follows him, not questioning any instruction he has for her. A table of the night crew is posted up, and looking amazing. They're so gorgeous and exotic compared to Liz and the other daytime people. The girls come from places like New York, and New Orleans. They're warm and welcoming to her, but she's sure she isn't the only one who senses that she's out of place. Unlike the dayshift crowd, they're less uptight, and are more relaxed when it comes to visiting with her. Liz will get no criticism here, since the group is so cool; they've evolved beyond that sort of conduct.

They take their beers from Drew, and all the women flirt with him at once.

"Thank you Drew, you're so sweet." They each say, generously pining over him.

Drew retracts with bashfulness from the attention by the gorgeous girls. Brent is also at the table, Liz passes him one of the pints she's been carrying. He's a funny guy because he isn't a stereotypical ladies man, yet he always has all the attractive girls around him.

"Hey Liz, how's the day shift treating you?"

"Brent, it couldn't be better." She answers with a thick layer of sarcasm.

Brent has coke-bottle eye glasses, pasty skin with freckles, and brown hair cut into a bowl-style. Brent flirts, and his confidence is infectious. While sitting beside him, he rubs her back with one hand, still drinking his beer with the other.

Some of the girls in the dinner shift are the actresses from the dinner theatre. They are truly special. Articulate and cultured, Liz finds herself drowning as she tries her best to keep up appearances with the group. She hopelessly feels her own inferiority, yet they would never let her know it, if they thought the same. The one thing she has going for her, is that she's a day person, who they rarely get to see given their work and night life. She's a novelty, and with that she's more than welcome to join them. After finishing off her second free beer, she can feel the bitter morning ready to cut its way into the night, replacing it with bright sun and the endless flow of tourists.

She decides it's time to seek shelter and sleep. "Well, it's time I go to bed. Have a goodnight dears."

She turns to blow them a kiss, sending a special wave to Drew in recognition for the drink and invite to join them, before going to catch her Denali bound shuttle.

She's one of the first people to climb into the shuttle, so she heads to the back. She's happy to see Josh's friendly face behind the wheel. Next a boy and girl climb on; drunk and sleepy. Two Taiwanese girls who can't control their giggling load up third. Then Liz's jaw drops; Charles climbs onto the shuttle. She had nearly forgotten about him, and his mixed signals. She thinks, "a second chance, fate?" He sees her too, and hesitates. He climbs in; looking forward, pretending not to see her. Her jaw drops in protest to the reality of herself.

Tired and lonely, she watches with interest at the two Taiwanese girls who are giggling and asking Charles questions. He's very flirtatious with them. And the trio burst into laughter several times during the drive. The booze-mobile makes its first stop at the Moose Inn; the girls get out.

Liz is happy to see them go. They tug at Charles shirt and say, "You, come with us." Giggling and seductive. "Come with us."

And with that, he slides out of the shuttle, taking a girl on each arm. She watches them stagger off into the almost darkness of an Alaskan June night.

I guess it's just one of those nights.

Soon the shuttle pulls into the Tundra Lodge parking lot. She throws a few dollars into Josh's tip basket, "Thanks Josh."

Then finds her lonely way back to her room. Somehow, conversations from earlier in the week happen to haunt her as she walks. She thinks of Gabe, and thinking of Gabe, reminds her of an interaction that left her unsatisfied. After the breakfast rush, while everyone set up for lunch, Gabe joins Liz to help her pull creams from her station. His tone is different, less playful. The clouds outside happen to match his mood and Liz can't help but notice.

"Why here?" He's calm but applies pressure to his question.

She tries to be funny, "I needed to run away."

Gabe frowns.

"You mentioned you had a boyfriend. Is that who you ran away from?"

She stops pulling the creamers and steals a view of the vista from the big window in her station. "It's not like that. He just didn't treat me nice. I, umm, I didn't tell him."

"Woah, what? What do you mean you didn't tell him? How did he treat you?"

She picks up a few more creamer dishes and sets them on Gabe's tray. Kendall walks up. It wasn't a private conversation, but both Liz and Gabe stiffen their backs in response to Kendall.

"It's not okay to just leave people. Have you talked to him?"

Liz pulls back, she wanted to open-up to him, but he seems as though he's closing, judging.

"Well, there are a lot of things that are not okay about that relationship. I just needed to get away. I needed to see Alaska."

"So you just left your boyfriend without saying anything?"

She would never be dishonest with Gabe. "Yes, I did." It was the only way, or I might have stayed with him. He would have tried to keep me there."

He looked at her in a way that Liz had never seen in him before, like he sees something deep inside, and with Kendall watching both of them, the whole interaction felt confusing.

Friday, June 28th 2002

The following day Liz feels restored and ready to dig her heels in. She's all set to earn some serious cash. Jane and Lauren are spending more time with her lately. Liz believes this is because their relationship is on the rocks. They both look like they could've stepped right out of a North Face catalog. Liz envies the way Lauren and Jane look so detailed and clean.

The whole crew is becoming a close family. A family that has to get up before dawn, and work, then work some more, to have meals together, laugh together, and cry together. Liz feels completely grateful for them.

Many early mornings the group finds themselves unsettled by the sight of dark, slow moving figures milling about the grounds like zombies. Another thing they've been schooled on from working at the Tundra Lodge is that elderly people often suffer from insomnia; which results in them walking around at all hours of the night. These night lurking old people are often stooped over or limping, resembling a zombie. Liz fears she'll never get used to turning a corner, caught by surprise by one of the slow moving figures, creeping through the empty twilight.

In her journal, she writes: *Who knew that the Tundra Lodge would transport me to some ethereal post-apocalyptic landscape, during the strangest hours, when the midnight sun tries to fade from the sky?*

This is also why the restaurant opens at four thirty in the morning. The old people have been up for two or more hours already, and are lined up out the door at four thirty, starving, and ready to eat some breakfast. The strangeness, just keeps growing stranger, and Liz's life feels more like a David lynch film than reality some days, with all the twists and abnormal characters.

Music

Monday, July 1rst 2002

Joe, he's over a year younger than Liz, and won't turn twenty one until the final week of the season. He works in the cafeteria, his job is to keep track of what employees come through to eat. He's cute, and is always hanging out with the hip crowd around property. Everyone knows him, and he's very popular. Like Susan, he's from Seattle, but dresses like a mountaineer and less like a hippie or grunge rocker. He sports a clean short shaven haircut, shaved face, and true blue eyes that he flashes at the ladies all through the day.

Liz is sitting with Robyn the Tolkat hostess, happily chatting and drinking herbal tea in the employee café.

"Robyn your scarf is so brilliant; I can't believe you crocheted that!"

She holds it out for Liz to see the tiny imperfections "It's the first crochet project I've ever done." She shakes her head, half proud, half embarrassed.

Liz really likes Robyn, she's a bit younger, but ended up coming to work at the Tundra Lodge because her sister had been working in a main branch of the company for a few years.

Halfway through their cups of tea; Joe joins them. He and Robyn sort of have a thing.

"Robyn have you been rafting on the river yet?" He asks, hopelessly trying to entrap her.

Joe is definitely interested in her. So is Kyle, who Liz invites to sit down with them. He takes the girls cups, and refreshes their hot water. Liz loves his gesture, and turns her complete attention to him. She's really fond of Kyle. He's a complete nerd, wearing horned rimmed glasses, and argyle sweaters. She feels content, enjoying a night with the under twenty-one group. She feels a little abstract being the only member of the group, who's of drinking age, but it also makes her feel wise. She's humored by the way the two guys fuss over Robyn, who she isn't sure . . . realizes the attraction. Kyle is passive, and Joe is much more aggressive. From what Liz can observe; she infers Robyn will decide to pursue Joe back, but it really isn't that fascinating to think too hard about. Time passes, and one of the cooks joins them.

"Hey Joe, that was a crazy night last Wednesday." The cook congratulates Joe.

Joe nods.

"Moses how was your day off?" Liz asks with great interest, glad to have another "over twenty one" join the group. She was starting to feel like a fourth wheel, sitting there watching the boys fawn over Robyn.

"It was so great, we went white water rafting, and grilled on the island in the middle of the Nenana." He answers with enthusiasm.

Liz tries to imagine the cool chef party out in the middle of the white water of the river, grilling and looking like a beer commercial.

"Hey, let's all go up to my room and you can help me finish my bottle of Patron." Moses suggests. Then he leans over the table, and repeats himself in a robot voice, "Pa-tron."

Joe stands up "Let's Go." He says, looking over his shoulder at Robyn.

"Yes please. It's time for a drink. I can't stop thinking about how I have to be back at work waiting tables in less than eight hours." Liz adds, standing up next to Joe.

Robyn and Kyle gave each other a private glance, before deciding to call it a night. Liz is a little disappointed to see Robyn go. But, thinking proactively she's moving on to the second phase of her quiet evening. The three friends; Joe, Moses, and Liz are now sitting on the floor of Moses's room, tilting a bottle to their lips. She's entertained enough; just to watch their facial expressions as they hand off the bottle, taking big fast swigs of tequila. She loves the funny faces they make, followed by cheers and grunts of tolerance. After twenty minutes, another chef shows up. Liz finds herself a little buzzed, and surrounded by men.

"Hey Moses lets go. There's a party at the Moose Bar tonight. Are you in?" The new chef queries.

The chef nods at Liz. The hours are escaping her now, but she thinks she has to be up in about six hours to start work. The tequila causes a judgment lapse, and the prospect of partying with the chefs sounds like too much fun. Not wanting to over-think the choice, Liz finds herself walking through the forest, down a hill, up a hill, trailing behind several chefs who are on their way to the Moose Bar.

The bar's crowded, and Joe realizes he shouldn't be there since he isn't twenty one. Liz realizes she's exhausted, and needs to go to bed. She wants to summon the motivation to dive into the bar and socialize with the random crowd, but work looms deep in her soul, and she can't tolerate a long day of old people that follows a sleepless night.

Joe turns to her. "I'm going back."

She answers, "me too."

Without skipping a beat, they're back outside of the bar, heading in the direction the two had just come from.

When Joe and Liz step into the secluded shade of the trees she feels the energy between them shift. They aren't talking, only breathing heavy and hiking, with deep, slow tequila breathes. It's as if the bottom sort of dropped out from under them, and a weird uncomfortable quiet pushes in. All evening they were with a group, and she realizes that she and Joe hadn't really talked to one another at all. She wonders why she can't talk to him.

Then all at once, with one step towards the other; they grab and reach, and kiss. It's like this was expected, and they knew it would happen, because they were both lonely, and wanting to feel close, against someone, alone, private in the trees, in the concealed woods. Hands moving across one another, holding, touching, and pulling. First outside of their clothes, then under their clothes.

It doesn't last long. He stops and whispers, "let's go somewhere."

"Okay."

Stunned at the unexpected change in her night, she's unable to comprehend that this change is happening with Joe. Liz feels easily agreeable. She wants to have fun, feel something, and get lost in it.

She follows his lead. They make their way down one hill, and up to an area where a campfire ring is grouped, settled in a clearing. There are wooden benches arranged and inviting. It's a good place to stop and kiss.

"Joe," she sighs into his ear, while she kisses it. Joe moans a word she can't understand, his hands run up, and underneath her sweatshirt.

He slips his hands back out of the warmth from under Liz's shirt. "Let's go."

Once again they work their way back to their property, trying to touch and be close as they traverse up the next hill, through long bending shadows. She doesn't want to go back to the employee housing, where eyes and rumors would penetrate this exchange of lust. Besides, they both have roommates back at their dorm rooms. There's a mutual want not to be seen with the other. This is something different.

There's no one around, he stops. Joe leads her past a clearing of trees, over to an old rustic building. He pushes her up against the side of the wall. He presses himself up against her and kisses her neck. The contrast between the cold night air, and their body heat magnifies their senses. This is it, she can have and take whatever she wants now. She kisses back, and touches him, but she's distracted. What is this building? He starts putting his hands closer down to her waist, while simultaneously springing open a latch on the building. . . .

Oh, it's an old, real Alaskan outhouse!

She pushes his hands away from her waist

"I have to go to bed." She whispers softly in his ear.

Joe drops his hands in frustration.

"Goodnight Joe, thanks for the walk back."

Liz walks the rest of the way alone. She doesn't look back, but departs with a smile, because Joe can kiss very, very well.

Sunday, July 2nd 2002

Work is unrelenting, and all her long nights are catching up to her.

"Your eyes are so red Liz," Robyn tells her. Then others.

"Oh, it must be the tequila." She groans, and lifts her hand to her aching head.

Robyn runs to the gift shop and brings Liz back some Visene.

"Robyn I need to stop partying so much." She mutters, taking the eye drops.

"Come out with Kyle and I, tonight." She replies.

"What are you guys doing tonight?"

She pats Liz on the head. "Not drinking."

"That sounds perfect Robyn. Thank you for the drops, you must be a saint! Saint Robyn of the Tundra, Patron Saint of the Hopelessly Hung-over!" Liz proclaims, as she holds up her eye drops, pretending its holy water.

That night they negotiate a board game of RISK with the Mormon bussers, Robyn, and Kyle (who apparently is an avid RISK player). Plus, Amanda the Sous Chef agreed to sit in for a couple rounds, planning to lose sooner than later. Robyn and Liz have never played, and it turns out to be really, seriously fun. Not only is RISK fun, but it happens to be addictive, and for six nights in a row the newly formed group establishes a standing date to play after work, and into the late evening. No drinking, just RISK. To make the game special they would find different meeting places to play; which includes: up the hill at the Alpine Vista Lodge, across the street at the Blue Bear coffee shop, and the employee recreation room.

Young Robyn knew exactly what Liz needed. Her spirit felt lighter, having kept company with those who are more ambitious than many of the hippie-traveler types that congregate on this land. Yes, it's true, she may be closer to the hippie, partygoer, but it's good to know she can breach the surface and join in the ranks of those who have fun without drugs, booze, and sex.

The only risky behavior taking place here was in fact the game of RISK. She would often form alliances with Robyn, and they would try to overtake the boys night after night.

"Robyn we need a good intimidating name for our alliance."

Robyn laughs. "What is the most evil, dominant name?"

. . The friends are quiet momentarily, imagining pure evil and badness.

"I know!" She looks at Liz, ready for it . . . "Team Hitler!" She tosses her hair back and grabs one of the black game pieces. She puts it under her nose to make a little mustache, and yells "Team Hitler!"

Liz grabs one too, and they do their best to strike fear in the hearts of their opponents.

Friday, July 7th 2002

She'd see Joe once in a while in the cafeteria, he would make it a habit to drop his eyes, or look off at something more important across the room. That's where they both are now, in the cafeteria, and the tension is thick. She has to admit it feels a little devastating. The disappointment of his intentions have become undeniable. Even though he seems shady; she's interested in him. Liz is sitting at a table with Chris and his girlfriend Amber who bartends at nights in the Tolkat. Liz really likes Amber. She has spikey black hair, and is a good match for uptight Chris. She's still unsure about the root of her friendship with Chris. His behavior, while forgiven continues to leave a slow-healing wound. No one wants to be verbally assaulted at their place of work. Especially, when their place of work is also their home.

"Amber you have to see Liz in action. She's so funny at the restaurant. Hey Liz, sing one of your Proper Storage songs!" Chris, leans against Liz, coaxing her for a song.

Liz blushes, unsure if she should sing on the spot.

Amber bails her out. Amber gets up from her seat and scoots close to Liz. In a sweet and big sisterly type of way, says; "You should avoid Joe, he's dirty."

Liz freezes, her eyes grow big and reveal more than she would like. She looks over at Chris, feeling caught and unprepared for an answer. He just nods at her, confirming Amber's warning. Her first distressing thought is that he has lots of unprotected sex; but he looks so young and clean. Her second disturbing thought is: *How do they know I have or had something going on with him?* She wants to slide away from Amber, and hide from the knowing glares from both of them. Then she scans the entire cafeteria.

If they know . . . who else knows?

They look at her with a serious expression, and then change the subject as if it were never mentioned. Amber and Chris are good together, and are being so nice about whatever they might be thinking and believing about Liz. They're protective of her. So she decides to take it for the value that it holds, and not to really think too hard on the subject. As far as she's concerned; she dodged a bullet.

Liz is leaning up against the counter, tucked behind the server station out of view; when Gabe walks up to her. He flashes her one of her favorite Gabe smiles, and she can't help but drop her eyes in fear she might get caught staring at him. He's looking at her, unconcerned and secure. She tries to fix her posture, and act casual.

"Hey Liz, do you want to go backpacking with me next week?"

This was the first time he's ever invited Liz to do anything with him outside of work. She figures it would be with Kendall, which she imagines to be completely awkward for her.

"Ummm, hmmm. I don't know? Who's going?" Liz looks doubtful.

He looks encouraged, "Just me, and a couple guys."

She contemplates the invite, "*Hmmm, mystery guys. Is Gabe trying to set me up with a friend? I want so badly to say yes, but I don't trust myself on a backpacking trip so close to him. We can be so close and familiar at work. I'm not sure how that same closeness will translate outside of our professional boundaries*".

She thinks of Kendall and replies, "I would love too, but it sounds like a guy's trip. I would ruin the fun."

He looks at her intently for a second, which drives Liz crazy because she can't figure what it is he's figuring about her.

"Okay Liz, let me know if you change your mind."

She wants to change her mind.

An hour later, she finds Gabe near the time cards and coat rack. "Gabe? Why would you invite me, if it's all guys?" She can't take the suspense.

"Because, you're my friend Liz, and I thought you would have fun."

She breaks, "Okay, I'll go." Her voice waivers with her answer, which causes Gabe to raise his eyebrow.

He laughs, and walks back to the dining room to drop off the check to a guest down by a big window table.

As soon as her shift is over, Liz makes a dash for her room to write in her journal: *"There must be a reason why Kendall wouldn't go. Again Gabe is so nice, he really just wants to hang out. I'm afraid I'll be tempted to flirt with him, and I'll be rejected. I've noticed my choices have been more selective, and my judgment surprises me. Perhaps it's because I'm on my own here in Denali, and that self-preservation is critical to make it through the next twelve weeks. If I'm a good person, who makes wise choices, I would not go camping with Gabe. I'm a bad person, who makes dumb choices, and is going camping with Gabe. I'll make better choices next week, after my camping trip".*

Wednesday, July 11th 2002

Before she knows it, she finds herself all hussied-up, back at the Trapper's Line for a marathon night. She wants to meet someone she can have a romance with so bad at this point, but her track record is proving to be a series of misfortunate events.

Liz has her hair pinned up in two buns on the side of her head, a tight blue long-sleeved shirt, and a great push-up bra. She has the softest pink lip gloss, and jet black eyeliner. Tonight at the Trapper's Line a band from Anchorage is playing. She's sitting at a table close to the front with Denver and Rebecca, and Amy who lives in the room connected to Liz's room via their bathroom. Amy's from New Mexico and has impeccable taste in music.

"Cheers Ladies, to a good night!"

Amy leans in, holding her drink tightly like a total lush, "Oh girls, every night is a good night in Healy." She winks at her dates for the night.

Their foursome is a force to reckon with, they have one agenda: fun. Denver and Rebecca are now dancing together, while Liz remains at the table with Amy. The songs are slower, and more soulful tonight, which pushes Liz deeper into her apathy and loneliness.

She's comfortable backed into a corner of the table. Taking inventory of potential dates who mix and mingle around the massive bar. She's not finding anyone who stirs any reaction within her. She stays, her back against the wall, facing the band as they play beefy sets. She's getting drunk.

Even though the dating pool turns out to be a disappointment, Liz finds solace in the fact that the band is really good. During a break, the band grabs themselves drinks, then sell a few of their cd's. Including a cd to Liz.

She hands the Anchorage musicians her cash and tells them, "I really like your music, you're very talented."

The whole band now have their attention focused on her. She does her best to stick her chest out and bat her eyes, tilting her head ever so slightly. Most of them are rocking fitted jeans, and plaid shirts with western style pockets. They have a pen ready to sign her newly purchased album.

"What's your name?" The guitar player-singer asks her. He notices her flirtatious stature, and looks flattered. He looks down at the table, smiling with amusement.

"I'm Liz."

"So Liz where are you from?" The drummer chimes in.

"I'm from California."

She gives him a sharp smile, then turns back to the guitar-singer and smiles once more for him.

He looks away sort of embarrassed, then raises his eyes again, more composed. "My name is James."

He's passes the cd back to another band member. They each sign a name over their picture.

"Thanks for coming all the way out to Healy to play for us."

"You're welcome." The handsome guitarist responds.

They head back to the stage for another set. Liz watches them walk away. All night she's been watching these guys, and finds it surprising that it isn't until she spoke with them, that she realizes how enticing and cute they are. It's almost midnight. Liz has a choice to make, she can catch a shuttle, or stay for two more hours. The band lifts their instruments to begin; the guitar player points to Liz and says; "This one is for Liz from California!" He gives her a true wink.

The guys in the band echo back, "Yeah Liz."

Oh, she slinks down in her chair, unbelieving they just did that. Yes, that's all he needed to do. She was preparing to go home with her cd in a few minutes, but after that sweet gesture she's stuck in her chair listening to those melodic songs for another hour. Now a little drunker, and grinning the silliest expression at James.

He definitely notices during the set, because when the next break arrives, he comes over to sit with her.

"Hi. Tell me about where you live."

"Here, I'm in Denali, well not Denali, you know . . . the tourist trap area before Denali National Park. Oh wait, you mean where I'm from in my life. Umm, California. Stockton. I'm from Stockton, California." Her nervousness is transparent. He likes it. Finally, a decent evening casts out the stagnant emotions. She fondly watches him rejoin his band to play another set.

His drummer signals to him to return to the stage by waving a fresh beer at him. He gives Liz a nod. "Can you hang out a bit? About an hour more?" Then, returns to his guitar and pint.

Something is going on between them, and it's so playful, and understated. Yet, she must seem so shamelessly interested. When a girl looks across a crowded room at a boy the way she is tonight, it's easy to tell, that she's infatuated. Still a stranger, they haven't even really spoke, just a few words, and a heavy, intense connection that has to be maintained from a distance across a room.

By this time, her table of hippie girls have been replaced by a table of the night shift crew, including Drew, Brent, and the hot girls.

Brent whispers in her ear; "Yeah, Liz and the guitar player!" Teasing and laughing.

The night owls immediately notice her silly doe-eyed stares, and are quite encouraging. They decide her crush is sweet, and are entertained as they drink beside her. Drew enjoys watching Liz in action.

James makes his way over to her, and sits down again, they smile without any words. She has only one thing she needs to say to him.

"When are you finished? Do you want to hang out?"

He instructs her to hold on, leaves to have a drink with his band, then comes back to tell her, "I can finish after four more songs." He hands her a fresh drink, and leaves her to enjoy his performance

Liz nods her head, and squares her shoulders provocatively.

It's now a quarter to three in the morning. After the band's set, her friends along with the majority of the bar leave to go drink at a bonfire down by the river. She stays, vulnerable and alone at the table. The bartender flips on the bright lights, and many of the patrons scatter, and retreat to unknown locations. Her guitar player slides his guitar back into its case, winds up the cords, the whole time with his back turned to Liz. He's going slowly, like he might be shy. He stands up straight, turns around, and goes to her. It's late, but there are still thirty or so people drinking, and having fun at the Trapper's Line.

"What do you want to do?" He asks her with hesitation. He has short brown hair, a nice smile, and broad shoulders. She gives him a displeased look.

"I want to hang out, but I have to catch the shuttle in forty five minutes to get back to Denali."

He's quiet for a second. In a firm tone he tells her, "I can take you home when you're ready to go, so we can hang out. I understand if you have to go though."

"No. I want to stay. I mean, not stay here at this table. I've been here all night. But, you know. I want to visit with you if you're not tired."

Her love struck grin spreads across her joyful face. Despite that it's three, and she's had several drinks, she's revived by the prospect of this wildly talented man standing in front of her. Following this exchange is a bit of awkwardness. She now has to follow through on all those heavy sultry looks she's been giving him when he was playing on stage.

"Let's go outside. I need to get out of this smoky room." He whispers, his voice is strained from the long night of singing.

As they walk out the side door into the cool air, he asks, "What do you want to do?"

They find themselves in a court yard of sorts, surrounded by an L shape of run down motel rooms. The court yard is covered in dew drenched grass, but in the middle is a bench built for two. Liz points to the bench. "Let's sit."

James and Liz make their way over to the bench. He has his guitar in hand, and she wraps her arm into his free arm. He's warm. She scrunches in, surprised at how easy it is too hold on to him.

Anxious for affection, she resorts to mindless chatter. She tells James about the music scene in California.

He tells her, "Los Angeles was a disappointment, I didn't care for California."

So she tries a different subject.

"I play the guitar. I have since the age of twelve." She offers, eyeing his guitar case. She feels pressure, and hopes he doesn't have any obvious expectations. She worries he might not be interested in getting to know her. He looks nervous too, unsure of what to do with the confusing girl who's wrapping herself onto his arm.

He leans back, to take in her expression, looking humored "Will you play me something?"

"Yes."

He opens the case, then sets his baby in her lap. She runs her little fingers across the smooth hard top and over the inlay, she wraps her hand around the neck, cupping the finish gently. It feels good to get her hands on a guitar after all these months without playing. She strums a few chords and softly raises her voice, trying to harmonize as she sings the made up song about the Alaskan highway. It's a short lived moment, and he politely watches and listens. She's under the impression that her song isn't that impressive. So she stops. She passes his guitar back. A bit humbled.

"Play me something?" Even though he's been playing all night, Liz is greedy and wants to be sung to, a serenade just for her, in this courtyard of wet grass, bugs, and early morning song birds.

"What do you want me to play?"

It didn't take long for her to know exactly what she wants him to play. She smiles and asks, "Do you know any Chris Isaak songs?"

He stops for a minute, thinking, then he hugs his guitar close, and begins to play for her. When he starts to sing, every bit of Liz reacts. He strums the slow surreal chords, as the spectrum of his discerning voice hits the notes, as hypnotizing as Isaak himself. She could stay there forever, as long as he just keeps playing.

Her whole self sort of slumps over, and slides in closer to him involuntarily, as if the music is so sweet she can't get close enough to the source.

"Can you teach me that song?"

He laughs, and gives her the chords, breaking them down one step at a time. She stares hard, determined to memorize this. Some of the chords are bar chords which combined with the drunkenness, leaves her struggling, and eventually disinterested. Their impromptu date is quickly turning into a music lesson. Time is escaping them, and signs of morning are approaching. She worries that he'll decide she just wanted to lure him out hear for music. But, maybe she did. For now, everything is in the moment, and just spending time with him is satisfying. This place, here with James and their music is pure and genuine. It's easy for them to be together, not forced, but very natural. She's happy to discover he isn't just some showy guy in a band, but a real person, with a great personality.

Nothing else in the whole world is existing for her right now, everything fades. She's not thinking about work, or catching the shuttle to get back to her room, or where her friends are at, or California, or her ex, or anything else. He sings the song, one last time. His voice slows, and softens, she leans in close, to hear the gentle, intimate song that was so quiet and sweet, and only in range for her. James made everything go away with their Alaskan morning, the rhythm of his song, and the way he looks at Liz, a little shy, but fronting that her heavy stare isn't making him nervous. She moves close for warmth.

If she had her journal, she would write, "*Once again, I find myself in a scenario that I never would have dreamed. Tangled up in music in Healy Alaska, with a true Alaskan man, forgetting it all, because I'm captured in this event. A smudge across the time line of my life. This moment transcends through me and my history, it's stored somewhere deeper in my spirit. A break in my experience, broken by a new experience. Music is so powerful. I'd forgotten how deprived I've been of my own guitar, how deprived I've been of a connection to someone. Boundaries are first pressed, then pushed, with the cool night air, the grain of the guitar's neck, the warmth of his body, and the hypnotic way his voice hits notes that match the tone of the evening, I am glad*".

"How old are you James?"

He stops the song, and looks with care. "I'm twenty two."

Liz takes a breath, she had found her match. She doesn't want to play guitar anymore, or drink beer, or sit in the questionable motel courtyard. They embrace and stay still in the cool empty space. They both sort of surrender to the exhaustion of the long day and night that had come before, and fall into one another.

He releases, "I need to put my guitar away, the condensation from the grass isn't good. Come with me?"

"Yes".

Unfortunately the situation evades them when they make their way through a motel hallway, which is comprised of a collection of jointed portable trailer like structures. All the way to the end of the hall, until they reach his room. He opens the door and leads her in. One of the guys in the band is curled up, half asleep in the opposite bed of James.

There they are; all three; feeling pretty uncomfortable. James looks at Liz, still holding her hand. He puts his mouth to her ear, and holds the back of her head with his palm, "It's getting really late; maybe it would be a good time to drive you home."

This is the truth. It will take him close to an hour to drive all the way back to Denali, and turn around to go back to the Trapper's Line motel. He drops off his guitar, and the spontaneous couple make their way back outside to his old Chevy Blazer. During the walk, Liz clings to him, running her hand up and down his arm. It's been so long since she's been able to just touch someone. During the drive back to Denali, their hands extend across the car, holding, and petting. Their rendezvous seemed to peak, and then plummet rapidly. They talk more, encouraged to tell the other as much as they could think to share. Both wondering what sort of future is ahead for the prospect of both of them together.

She asks him, "Would you ever try playing music in California? Will you be visiting Denali again this summer?"

His answers are, "I don't know."

Liz waits to here if he has any suggestions for her, he never provides them. He's somewhere in his own thoughts, possibly more practical than her own.

As the midnight sun shines light on their union, it seems more complex.

He pulls into the Tundra Lodge, and parks. They sit, negotiating their way around the gear shift, embracing, kissing, and thinking.

"Thanks for taking me back James." She leans in to kiss his cheek. "I like you way too much." She reveals an honest and sad face.

He looks at her, unafraid to try. "Liz, I like you too." He asks her, "Can I see you tonight?"

The question holds any chance they might have. It's all either one have to give. Even his smell makes her want to curl up against him, and forget herself. "Really? Yes. Around six?"

"I can make that work, we have a few sets to play at the line tomorrow, but I don't have to check-in until nine."

"That's our employee bar. Meet me there?"

"Okay. See you tonight, Liz."

With one last hug, she slides out of his Chevy. She turns to leave, looking forward to reuniting with her bed. She wants him to watch her walk away, so that she doesn't have to watch him drive out of her life.

It's now a quarter to six in the morning, and Liz has all day to sleep. Pulling the thick curtains shut tight, off with the lights, still in her clothes and makeup from the long night; she slips into a long, unsettled sleep. Even though her body is so tired, her mind seems to be as active as ever, and the night's events play out in her head, leaving Liz unsatisfied and annoyed because she likes James, but she's well aware of the reality of her poor track record for romance around Denali. The same banner waves in her mind, "He won't show. He's not going to see you tonight. You will have nothing but disappointment. He didn't really like you." She pulls the blanket around her tight, hiding her eyes in her pillow, wanting to block out the sadness. She's overcome by heartache from wanting to be with him.

Thursday, July 12th 2002

It's now three in the afternoon, the combination from sleeping all day, too much booze, and the disappointment that it probably would be a heartache with her romance from the night before leaves Liz in a fog of depression. Last night's encounter was so unusually perfect. A perfection she feels unworthy of.

She picks up her journal from under the bed, she takes her pen from the headboard shelf, *"I'm afraid of rejection. I can't take the chance that I'll go to meet him and he doesn't show. He won't show. I have to protect myself. There's no way I can handle that kind of rejection right now. The safest thing is to stay here. Hide. Protect myself. He won't show. He isn't coming. I know it."*

Six comes and goes, and part of her wants to go meet him, part of her reasons he would stand her up, and the other part of her says to stay and rest, because it's all pointless.

By seven thirty, she goes down to the employee cafeteria. The minute she walks in, Drew calls out from behind the bar; "Liz! James the cool guitar player was here looking for you. He hung out for an hour hoping you'd be around."

Drew nods in approval "He's really cool Liz, way to go!"

She's stuck in mid-step. She freezes. Eyes wide, staring at Drew. "He was here?"

Drew squints his eyes, surprised at how dense Liz's reaction is. "Looking for you."

She blushes. "He is really cool. Drew I have no excuse for ditching him . . . I suck."

He tilts his head in concern, he sees the sadness within her. "It will be okay Liz, if he really likes you, I'm sure you'll see him again."

"Was he mad I didn't show?"

"No."

Liz turns, and leaves the bar to walk back to her room. Interrupted, retreats, processing her huge mistake. Realizing what she had and lost, because she couldn't trust. In passing, Denver stops her.

"Hey girl, what's wrong?"

"I screwed-up bad. I missed the guitar player. He came to see me."

"Woah, what? He did? That's so awesome."

"No, I didn't go to meet him. He waited for me. I flaked. But, now I want to see him. I have to go try. I'll, take a risk and tell him how I feel! This means I have to go to the Trapper's Line tonight. I don't want to go to Healy. The first shuttle leaves at ten, and leaves the bar at midnight; which means I won't get back until twelve thirty, which means I'll get three and a half hours of sleep if I'm lucky, before starting a long day of waiting tables".

"Do it."

"Yeah?"

"Hell yeah!"

"Hell yeah!" Liz agrees. "You've been a big help, Denver."

"I didn't really say much, but thank you. I'd come with, but I have a night planned with Paul."

"No big. I've got this." She reasons, trying to convince herself more than Denver.

She goes, and when she gets there the energy between them is nonexistent or even negative existent. Walking into the open room where he's playing, he looks over and nods at her without a smile. At their break, she goes to him, but he's busy, back turned, talking to his band. Obviously she's the recipient of the cold shoulder, and the message is loud and clear. She waits around anyways, hoping for a chance to apologize. He's not giving her one. As a last desperate effort; she grabs one of the fliers from the bands table, she takes a pen from the bar and scribbles this message: "To what could have been, but was never meant to be – Liz". She hands it to him. He accepts, putting the terrible sentiment in his pocket. "With that, Liz is out the door. She can hear his voice melodic and haunting over the speaker behind her back. She steps out, and when the door slams, his voice disappears. The sensation of misery crashes up against her, regretful for the awkward attempt.

Boarding the Denali bound shuttle, she begins the reflective journey back to her employee bed where she belongs. Ready to be thrown into the jaws of the Tolkat to be worked over hard, and see the friendly faces of her coworkers; her improvisational family away from home.

"You didn't stay very long Liz." Josh, the shuttle driver says, as he pulls up in front of the Lodge.

"I have work bright and early, thanks again Josh, hope your night's a good one." She tosses a couple dollars into his tip basket, before climbing out of the van.

Josh watches her from the shuttle. The only girl he's dropping off, walking heavy and stiff beneath the midnight sun. Once she makes it back to her room, the defeat she'd been working through all day, is a certain reality. The tears fall freely. Her roommate stirs quietly in the opposite bed. Shame, doubt, regret, loss, all of the feelings she deserves. Her journal is still wrapped up in the blanket as she climbs in. She picks up the pen from the headboard and writes in the total darkness, "*Oh, it hurts, I want him back. I'm so truly lonely. I'm sorry. Maybe the effort was pointless, but I like James and I believe he's worth it. Goodnight James. Goodbye.*"

Encounters

Friday, July 13th 2002

Despite all the long nights, and her steady diet of amber ale and margaritas Liz hasn't missed any work. She goes straight to the pantry, having missed dinner the night before, she needed sustenance. She pulls out the yogurt, and starts filling a coffee mug full of it, she pours on a generous amount of granola. She starts to devour the parfait, her back turned to her coworkers. Lauren grabs a spoon, and digs into Liz's mug. Together, they hunch over the yogurt, working like a couple of wolves to choke down the food before moving onto to something else. The gesture, without words, gave Liz a sense of peace. Nothing cures loneliness like sharing a mug of yogurt and granola.

Lauren waves to Monty in the kitchen, "Bacon!"

Monty nods. He starts plating a heap of strips to pass through the window.

"You're a vegetarian."

"You're not. Here. Eat." She disappears into walk-in number two. When she reappears, she has a plate with a slice of cheesecake from last night's dinner service. She sets the desert next to the bacon. "It's going to be a day. How were your days off? It's been intense here."

Liz scoops a bite of cheesecake. "Peak season?"

"Only for like sixty more days."

The cheesecake disappears.

"Fat City," Lauren informs. It's a noun and an adjective all in one.

Everyone adopts the "Fat City" mentality. Confined to the restaurant, looking forlorn out the big glass windows; out into the wide open spaces, and sweeping valleys hugged by proud mountain ridges: they eat. All they can do to cope with the fact that they are in here, and not out there, is to feed. When they can't drink, they turn to their other addiction, food.

Jane explains to Liz, "We're like crack heads, working in a crack factory. We can have all the food we want, anything is fair game if we ask our chef nice enough". Together, Jane and Lauren have been introducing "Fat City". Near ten, everyone is starving again. "It's time for second breakfast. Crab anyone? Liz wants crab!"

By the end of the shift, Liz hobbles up the stairs to her room to nurse her aching feet. They hurt so bad, they're practically numb. Her blisters swell and harden. She enters her room and lays on the floor with her mangled feet, legs pointing up against a wall to redirect blood flow, and restore normal nerve function. She feels okay about the pain because she has never seen so much money in her life. Everyone is working from four thirty to two thirty or three o clock each day. She's so pleased with her income ability, and smart budgeting. Months pass, and Liz can see her bank account swell, resembling her sore and tired feet.

Whenever she accumulates six to seven hundred dollars in cash, she likes to slowly walk her tired feet down to the post office which is close to two miles away. The post office is down the road that leads into Denali. She takes her cash and purchases money orders. She can mail the little checks back home to herself in California.

On this particular afternoon, the postal clerk informs her, "You have a general delivery letter, hold on I'll grab it for you."

"Me? I do?"

The postal clerk extends a long white envelope with scribbles on it. She can see the name on the cover. "Oh wow, that is for me!"

It's from Susan. Liz smiles before placing the letter in her worn grey backpack. Down the rickety ramp of the post office, and on to continue down the road, in route to the visitor center.

The whole disappointing way the night with the guitar player played-out, has Liz feeling aware of her autonomy here. She feels lonely, and Susan's letter shows up at the most appropriate time.

Tonight, my plan is to head to the bar, order a pint and read my letter.

And she does.

Monday, July 15th, 2002

If it's a particularly stressful week, Liz will order herself crab eggs benedict. She's mid-bite into her crab when she notices Lauren laughing at her. "Liz, is this the third day in a row your having crab for breakfast?"

Liz nods, and swallows, then pushes the plate of food towards Lauren to help her eat it.

"Liz, you are the Mayor of Fat City." She announces in delight.

Liz just stares blankly at her blond friend. "As Mayor,. . . Lauren, I promise to fulfill your grandest expectations.

Lauren nods. "Don't disappoint Liz."

As not to be greedy and usually short on time, when one of the servers orders a massive culinary indulgence, like; wild blueberry pancakes drowning in a homemade blueberry compote, they usually summon over one or two others to help devour the goodness. Tucked around the corner, just out of sight, from all the tourists dining by their windows, you might find a small circle of servers crowded-in, stooping over something; working intently. Like vultures, they passionately stab their forks, ravenously shoveling in the food in between orders coming up on the line.

Tuesday, July 16th 2002

Another Denali evening, she sits at the bar watching the ice melt in her amaretto sour. She can't help but feel anxious. The summer is going by too quickly. Although she believes she's making progress, and is more than satisfied with her social community, work, and time spent in nature, she's still reminded of how very lonely she is.

She has her journal with her, and writes as she sits and sips at the bar, *"I'm growing tired of having to always watch out for myself. I would love to just resign and allow someone else to take the wheel, protecting me, guiding me, so I can rest for a while. It can be exhausting to be a twenty two year old single girl, alone, in the interior of Alaska".*

Drew comes over to her careful not to interrupt her writing. He leans over the bar and shares: "I was so drunk last night, I can't remember what happened". He shakes his head, seeking a little sympathy.

She notices how red his eyes are, and notes the hungover state he's struggling through. She can't help it; he's so cute and in pain, she replies: "What? You don't remember making out with me last night?"

He straightens his back, his eyes open full, surprised. His debates with himself if she's joking or telling the truth. She's usually so reserved around him, never crossing any informal lines. Liz enjoys his reaction. He realizes she's teasing him. He laughs because she actually had him going for second. He moves to the other end of the bar, cheeks a little more red than before he shared with her.

Across the bar is the cafeteria side of their employee stomping ground. Her eyes relax, she takes in the atmosphere before indulging in her journal. In walks Gabe with a big backpack on. He has a sleeping bag attached to his pack, he looks rugged and so different in contrast to the usual bow tie and apron she sees him in. What raises her from her bar stool and over to him isn't the sight of Gabe, but what's coming in the door behind him.

Three small boys around the age of eight, single-file are standing behind Gabe. So many months since she's seen children. She has to go say, hello. "Gabe! Who are your friends?" She grins with delight, admiring the miniature adventurers.

"Hey, Liz these are the guys I was telling you about." Gabe greets her with a serious expression. He looks down with pride at his group of backpackers.

Liz is confused. "Nope. You didn't tell me about any kids."

"Don't tell me you forgot, we're here looking for you, Liz. The overnight backpacking trip." He stares into her eyes, and she averts her own before she might catch a connection with him.

"These are the guys? Why didn't you tell me they were kids? This is so great! I have lots of experience working with kids, lifeguard, camp counselor. I definitely want to help out with your trip. But, I thought this wasn't for a couple days?"

"I know, I'm sorry, things got mixed up and we're going tonight. Jane agreed to cover your shift tomorrow, if you still want to come with us last minute. I could use your help." He turns to his troop. "Ready guys? Like I said."

"Please?" They ask together, looking animated and sad.

Completely caught off guard, she stares into the little faces of the three excited children. Liz decides she's going to let Gabe and his mini-Gabe's whisk her away. "I just need to go get my pack and sleeping bag, change my shoes, and grab my jacket."

"For sure! We'll be here, camp counselor." Gabe grabs four cups of water and a dozen apples from the café. . He sits down with his troop.

In less than fifteen minutes, she reappears at the entrance of the cafeteria, her backpack heavy with her sleeping bag, extra layers, and a bag of chocolate for sharing. Her heart pounds, nervous to be doing something outside of work with Gabe, wondering why Kendall is nowhere to be found, but focusing on the kids, and the good way their innocent nature settles her flighty spirit.

"That was fast. Thanks again for coming. Did I tell you we're sleeping at the top of Sugar Loaf Mountain?"

"You mentioned that at work. I've been up their once, it's a pretty steep hike." Liz shifts her weight, and feels the sensation of her pack resting on her hips. If the boys need me to help carry some of their gear, I have room in my pack. So, I know it's not actually dark, but this is like a night hike!"

"Yes ma'am, I've got my bear spray just in case. Ready?"

The three little boys, leap from their chairs, and scramble to line up at the door, revved and charged for the hike. The leader of the boys steps close to Liz. He stares her down. "So, your name is Liz? You're going camping with us?"

Her eyes sparkle, she really missed seeing children. What a gift Gabe has managed to bring her. How did he know? They remind her of her little brother back in

California. She adjusts her wool beanie, tucking her hair back behind her ears before pulling it down snug. "Yes, I'm Liz. What's your name?"

"My name is Jacob. I was worried we wouldn't find you."

She sits down on a stool, so she can look at him at his level. "I was worried I wouldn't find you, too." They smile. Jacob slides closer to her.

. Overcome by an unexplainable feeling, this adventure makes her feel like crying with joy and it hasn't even started, yet.

Another little boy with golden hair as fine as spider's web steps over to her. "Hi Liz, my name is Gentry." He giggles, then runs to hide behind Gabe. Liz giggles too.

The third boy extends his hand to shake hers. She holds onto the little hand for a genuine gesture, she wants him to know what an honor it is for her to meet him. "I'm Bryce, did you bring anything for us?"

"I might have something for you."

"What is it?"

"You'll have to wait and see, come on Bryce, we have a mountain to climb!"

The little boy put his hand out, and Liz holds onto it.

Gabe's surprised to see Liz lead the eclectic group out the door and over to the highway where she organizes them to prepare to cross the road. He's never seen this side of her. She really responds to kids, and Gabe suspects, this is the first time he's actually seen Liz one hundred percent happy. A curious discovery, but he's now bringing up the tail end of their group, and still trying to process this different side of his friend.

The entire way to the summit; the little boys are all a buzz about sharing stories, and telling jokes. They kept the conversation so action packed, that Liz and Gabe haven't exchanged one word with the other. The kids did a great job monopolizing the conversation, and within two hours the group was high above the lodge, and the Nenana, and the Parks Highway. Even though Liz doesn't speak to Gabe, that doesn't mean she isn't thinking about him. She can't bury the question; she needs to know why he invited her. She wants to know where Kendall is, and why Kendall isn't here now.

Jacob, who's more comfortable speaking to adults, vocalizes his own questions on the subject matter. "Are you Gabe's girlfriend?"

Liz is still in the lead, and John is three kids behind her. She's glad he can't see the guilty expression that's curled the corners of her smile. She's also glad he's in hearing-range of Jacob's question, deciding he might contemplate the innocent observation.

"Nope, we're just friends, and we work together."

"Friends?" Jacob sounds doubtful. "You don't like him?"

Liz starts to laugh. In her happiness, she chooses to be brave. "I like him." She answers plainly, and loud enough that he can hear.

"Then you should be his girlfriend." Jacob assesses.

Jacob is now Liz's favorite Alaskan hiking partner.

"I don't think his girlfriend would like that very much."

"Oh, he has a girlfriend, but you're his friend?"

"Uh, huh."

"Is she going to fight you?"

Liz is stumped. She can't answer because she's laughing too much.

Jacob turns his head back to Gabe. "Gabe, is your girlfriend going to beat up Liz?"

Liz and Kendall are good friends. They don't fight. Liz doesn't have to fight anyone to be my friend." Gabe explains.

Jacob turns to Liz. "You're pretty."

"Thanks." She wonders why young boys know exactly how to talk to women, but grown men can't seem to communicate at all.

Now that they've all agreed on the perfect camping spot, Gabe busies himself with setting up all the boy's sleeping bags. He reaches into his pack and pulls out a Dura flame log. He catches Liz's astonished reaction, and holds it up for her to see with pride. "Only five pounds, and burns for three hours. Not too much kindling and wood up here." He explains.

The boys scatter to the perimeter of their mountaintop overlook, searching for rocks to build a ring.

Liz steals a moment to jot a few lines in her journal, her steady companion, *"A grueling hike under the midnight sun, kids, Gabe, and now a campfire. This is turning out to be an extremely good night. Just a few hours ago I would have never imagined I'd be at the top of this mountain, getting to enjoy a Dura flame log overlooking the hotels far below. We're all full of so many twists and turns, it's hard to tell if we're going or staying around here. However, Gabe is going. He has three weeks left, and then he's leaving to make it back home to begin his college semester. I'm going to miss him so much; maybe that's why he invited me to go camping with him. I quickly learn that the thing with seasonal work is that it can be so elusive, and no matter how much you try to hold it, it slips away from you. Those who become so special and meaningful to you are here one minute, and then gone forever the next.*

All you can hope to do is remember them, and if you're lucky, you were open enough to be affected by them, changed a little bit, to improve just from knowing them. Even if it was a joke, and ten years later you remember the joke they told you, and it still makes you laugh. That's them; they are with you in this small way".

She puts her journal away, shoving it all the way to the bottom of her pack. She watches him assemble the campfire ring with the little boys. He lets the kids light the store bought log. This vision of him makes her heart thump. She watches with a fierce longing to remember him like this; to try to capture the mental image in her mind. The fire is ignited, and she goes to join her group of guys.

"Look at me, surrounded by the most adventurous men in all of Denali! Did you guys have dinner?"

"We had pizza before we found you. We also had some apples from the cafeteria." Gabe explains. "You?"

"Ummm, yes."

He shakes his head, "What did you have?"

"A super big lunch close to four at work." Liz squirms. She's embarrassed she's not taking better care of herself. Basic things like eating and sleeping. She switches subjects, "Perfect, then these guys are ready for some desert. Who's going to tell the first scary story?" She goes to her pack and pulls out the jumbo bag of Hershey kisses. She strolls over to the circle of boys, placing a heaping handful in each child's lap. The sleeping bags are laid out, and she places hers on the opposite side of Gabes's, so the little ones are sandwiched in between them. When she gets to Gabe, she holds the bag open for him, so he can reach in and take his own. Now that everyone has their spot, sitting on top of their sleeping bag, vocals of stories, jokes, and songs stir the soft breeze, and gently dissipates into the night. The boys make the perfect chorus, to the signature, "Proper Storage" song, complete with hand motions. Liz begins to laugh, "I keep waiting for it to get dark to signal for bedtime. That's not happening at all! Time in July, in Denali, on top of a mountain seems to have very little meaning".

All of the sudden, by ten thirty, every boy seems to instantly pass out. Liz stands up silently, and goes to each child, fondly tucking them in tight, making sure they'd be protected from the elements during their night's slumber. She pulls the sleeping bag up over Gentry, trying to cover his soft blonde hair. He's the last child to be tucked in, and now she finds herself facing Gabe, who's been studying her display of maternal care. "You're really great with kids. I didn't know that about you. This trip would have been really difficult, if it weren't for your help." He whispers low, not wanting to disturb young dreams.

She stops and lingers above the children. Inspired by her good work. He's sitting on top of his bag; legs folded beneath him. She feels the awkward tension, and prepares for the inner battle that's about to play out in her soul. This is her chance, it won't come again. She can come clean, take a risk, and try to tell him that she likes him. She can do the right thing, and be a good person, and respect that he's simply a co-worker and friend. A friend who has a girlfriend. A girlfriend who is her friend.

"Hey, do you have any more chocolate?" He whispers, arching his eyebrow mischievously.

A little annoyed that his mind is on candy, while hers is experiencing the tyranny of ethics and lust. She tiptoes over to her pack, retrieves the bag of chocolate, and brings it back to Gabe. She holds out the bag for him to take, her expression cryptic and hindered.

"Sit down." He pats to the spot beside him on his sleeping bag.

The Duraflame cracks with a pop that jolts her nerves.

She hesitates, then dives for the place he gestures too. It will never be night, only twilight, and the sun plays tricks with her mind. When indoors, it's much easier to fall asleep because one can close the blinds, and make it very dark. But, outside, falling asleep can be a challenge. She's encouraged to see that Gabe doesn't look tired either. Together they sit on his sleeping bag, watching the crackling flame start to burn down to nothing. Gabe unwraps a chocolate and hands it to Liz. He unwraps another for himself.

"Who are these kids, Gabe? Where did you find them?"

He swallows his chocolate and answers, "It's a program through the Mormon Church, you know, to take local kids out to do fun things."

"Oh." Liz answers, staring into the glowing orange, waiting for the tiny sparks. "Local kids."

"I can't believe this is the first time we're hanging out Liz. My summers almost over, it's weird."

"I know. I've been wanting to hang out with you for so long."

"Why didn't you?"

"Well, you're always busy with Kendall. Nothing worse than a third wheel." She pauses to breathe. She hates that her comment sounds so cliché. "Why isn't Kendall here?"

"We've been backpacking a couple times now, and she wants a break from the outdoors, but I can't get enough. You know, especially now that I'll be here for just a little while longer. Who knows when I'll get to visit again."

"What? But I've seen her outside of our housing, gutting fish and stuff. She's tough, she really doesn't like sleeping under the stars?"

"She does. She just needs a break I think. We spend all our time together." He hangs on his last answer, thinking on it.

Liz nods, this is more information than he's given her all summer. She's feeling a little more secure now that some of her questions have been answered. It's strange now, the anticipation they both harbored, for what they imagined hanging out together to be like, creates an impeding pressure. A pressure for something fun to happen. Only, neither of them feel fun. At work, it came easily. Gabe isn't flirting now, and Liz is completely reserved. Her knee was pressing against the outside of his thigh, and they both are aware of the contact.

He shifts himself to face her, placing a little distance in between. "So, what do you think?"

It's a fair question, but she's unsure what he means. She thinks a lot, but also thinks it would be unfair to unload all her thoughts onto him, especially the thoughts that are about him.

"I think I'll miss you, Gabe." A safe answer. "Tonight was really fun. Thanks for inviting me."

"You're the only one I pictured doing this with."

Liz pauses, hanging on his statement. She can't figure out what he means. So she does what seems formal, and studies the skyline. There are so many colors in the sky; blues and purples, whites of clouds, and greys from mist across the valley. The view is endless from their vantage point.

"Gabe, can I say something to you?"

"Sure."

She's growing frustrated because he seems clueless to the obvious. How can he miss her feelings without any regard for her? She sucks in a breath before she shares. "I don't understand why you like me? I mean as a friend, but what is it that you like? I mean, you're so good. You don't drink, you give a percentage of your tips to your church every day, and you're moral. I'm the opposite of you. I go out and party all night, meeting random men, and I'm lazy at work. I guess, what I'm trying to ask you is: What is it that makes you want to be my friend?"

"Well, you might do those things Liz, but the girl I'm with tonight; the girl right now is sweet, caring, and considerate. She's funny, and playful, and I like spending time with her. She's not drinking right now, and she's not with a random guy, or cutting corners at a stupid job. If you do those things, that's okay. But I like you for the attributes I see in you, which are noble and admirable, you should be proud of them." He looks out at the sky too. "I just like you. I really do. Don't you think your worthy of people liking you for yourself?"

She isn't sure how to answer his answer.

"Kendall likes you a lot too, she considers you a good friend."

The mention of Kendall complicates her jumbled thoughts. Gabe opens his arm and wraps it around Liz. She leans in, resting her head against his shoulder. "You don't have to worry so much Liz. It's okay to relax and enjoy yourself once in a while."

"I, I, ummm."

He laughs, "Yes."

She laughs to, at his silly answer. Then has to say it. "I, sometimes think you like me, ummm, like you're interested in me."

"Oh,"

Her mind races, "Oh? How is that an answer? I just confessed, and that's his response? My head aches, and I'm dehydrated. I hope to God, I'm not going to develop another migraine. I want to take it back. Why did I say it? There was no need to ruin a fantastic night with a great friend".

"Well, I'm going to go now." She slips away from his muscular arm, and stands up, turning to find her way around the boys to her own sleeping bag.

"Wait." He whispers.

She stops, he reaches out and pulls on her hand. She kneels down beside him. "You don't have to leave. I'm a grown man, I can handle it. What if I told you . . . you're right?"

"Oh."

He hasn't let go of her hand. "Liz, if it were another time, and another place, and I didn't have a girlfriend."

She smiles, looking down at the rocks in the dirt. "I don't believe you, but you're nice. Goodnight Gabe." She jumps back up, and retreats to hide in her sleeping bag, a little regretful, but also relieved to have tried. She wants to make a fast exit, escape the disappointment of the night. She sleeps. The heavy kind, the tired void that often accompanies depression.

In the earliest part of the morning Liz feels someone brushing her cheek softly with their hand. Then a whisper in her ear. "Do you want to go watch the sunrise with me?"

His voice tugs her violently out of her dream-like state. This time, now coherent, she blinks, questioning if Gabe is actually there, stroking her face, and whispering to her about sunrises. She fully opens her eyes and sees him coming into focus. She sits up, shedding the top half of her sleeping bag. She reaches under her pillow, pulls out her beanie, and puts it on her head. She grasps the reality of where she is, seeing the small sleeping boys, Gabe's empty sleeping bag, and the fire ring constructed by small hands. Her eyes grow wide and she looks at Gabe, unsure of what he's doing.

"Come on." He whispers again. "I've been getting up every hour, for bear patrol, to protect us. Actually, I haven't slept. Never planned too. Brought a book though."

She wiggles out of her warm bag and shivers in the cold air. She slept in her jeans and sweatshirt, but the coldness of the crisp Alaskan morning cuts like a knife. She reaches for her shoes but they've been placed with the items away from the sleeping area.

He raises his arm to stop her.

"Forget the shoes, we're going over there." He points to a rocky ledge a few paces from where everyone sleeps.

She looks at all the rocks and cool permafrost on the ground, then back at her shoes.

"I'll carry you." He whispers casually, like it's something they do all the time. He puts one arm under the back of her knees, and the other around her back, he lifts her up in the air, and she squeals in reaction to the strange sensation. All the sudden, she's up in the air against him, feeling her weight being held, lifted. He starts walking, the ground is uneven and slants, she's fearful he'll trip and they'll fall. He doesn't. Soon they're at the end of the big rocky ledge. The one they warned the little boys to stay away from. He sets her down, and her eyes are wide, adrenaline from his advances now course through her body. She feels jittery.

"I thought we should see this together."

She doesn't answer.

Even though he's set her down, Gabe still has his arm around her shoulders. They look out at the sunrise, which is fake, since it never actually set last night. It just goes back and forth, high and low in the sky. Still, it is beautiful. It's always beautiful in Denali.

"I wanted to do this for you Liz. To let you know you're special to me. I was worried you didn't think you're special to me."

His arm moves down her own, until his hand reaches hers. He entwines his fingers around hers. He pulls her closer. She's trying to wake herself up. This isn't real. She figures she's misreading his signals again. He takes his other hand, and wraps his palm and fingers around the back of her head, bringing it close to his chest. He kisses her forehead. She's not looking at the sunrise, she's smelling him. She squeezes his hand back, it's the only safe thing she trusts she can do.

"You didn't think I asked you to come over to sit on my sleeping bag last night for kisses, did you?"

She has a moment of confusion, then remembers the Hershey kisses.

"I would have kissed you last night. I wanted to kiss you. But, when you started talking about all that stuff, I really started to feel bad. But, you know what. I think we should kiss."

"Okay." Liz is in disbelief, and filled with panic.

"Come here." He tips her head up, and they kiss. She takes her hands, and places them on either side of his face, feeling his skin, then pushing them through his hair that she's always fantasized about doing countless times at work. On top of the mountain, above the false sunrise, they embrace, and it's more powerful that either had anticipated.

Thoughts jam up in her head. *"He was going to kiss me last night and I screwed it up! He's my friend. This is weird. He loves Kendall. Kendall loves him. Kendall is my friend. Kendall. I can't. I won't. He doesn't belong to me. I'm not worthy of him. I'm not his match."*

She lets him go, and turns her back. He doesn't move or say anything.

"If it were last night . . . if it were another time, and another place. If you didn't have a girlfriend. I'm sorry."

"If it were last night?" He whispers, letting his own fingers trail against her as she steps away.

Liz walks on her own, barefooted over the cold frigid earth. Small stones digging into her tender feet, step after step, she goes to find her boots. Back to her sleeping bag and puts on her socks. It's nice to be swept away, carried through this place, but it feels good to walk on her own too, and right now, that's what Liz feels she needs the most. To walk on her own.

He stays, staring at his sunrise, which always changes, but never sets in July. They go back to their usual friendship which also changes, but never sets.

The boys, Gabe, and a recently matured Liz, hike back down to the Tolkat where Kendall serves them breakfast

Thursday July 18th, 2002

Liz is sitting on the cafeteria side of the employee bar. She's sitting alone, nursing a margarita as she writes a few notes on a postcard to send to her parents. Some of the Tolkat line cooks who are known for their wild nightlife, enter. They have Joe, and the new girl. Liz notices she's very skilled at twirling her red hair to coax all the boys to attend to her. They greet Liz, filling up her empty table.

"Hello, Liz." Moses is still in his chef pants, a blue hoodie, and a baseball cap. He slides into the spot beside her. "What are you drinking doll?"

"In fond memory of your bottle of tequila the other night Moses, I'm drinking a margarita." She answers brazenly.

"Can I taste it?"

She pushes the glass over to him. He lifts the drink to his mouth for a generous taste. "Too sweet." He pushes it back across the table to her.

Liz shrugs her shoulder, twisting her cocktail straw around the rim.

The chefs grab some drinks, and keep her company while she sips her icy beverage. A few others join the table. Joe arrives. Moses is talking about a keg party happening at one of the other properties. "Liz, are you coming with us to the party at the Teklanika outfit?"

She looks over at Joe, and he's pretending not to see her.

Thoughts form in her mind, *"Joe is officially a complete jerk. I'm starting to feel sensitive, and his disinterest in me is hurting my self-esteem."*

"Yes, my sweetpeas, I'm down to go!" She answers with confidence, turning just enough to detect if Joe is watching. In hopes to demonstrate, Joe that he has no effect on her.

Everyone at the table gets stands simultaneously, heading outside to cross the property in the direction of the party. Ironically enough, the group walks through the same forest that she and Joe had crossed so many weeks before. It's dark in the forest, despite the midnight sun.

The gorgeous redhead who hosts the dinner shift at the Tolkat has a new direction for the group, "Oh wait, can we make a pit-stop? I want to use the restroom before we get there. You know what it's like . . . awkward to ask at someone else's place."

They're all a little buzzed, and the prospect of a bathroom sounds like a good idea to everyone. A sharp right takes them straight to the pizza restaurant at the edge of the forest.

As Liz steps inside her eyes adjust to the light, and her nostrils pull-in warm scents of melted mozzarella and sourdough. There's a comforting hum about the bar as customers visit and clink their pint glasses together. The group separates. Mingling as they pass through; saying hello to the cocktail servers, using the bathrooms, and yes, buying more alcohol from the bar. When Liz comes back from her trip to the bathroom, she doesn't see Joe, the redhead, or the cooks.

She thinks, *"Now I'm hurt, and my self-esteem just takes another fierce blow. They actually just left me?"*

Not wanting to hang out by herself at the pizza place, she turns to leave from the same door she had entered through to go back to her employee housing, visualizing herself alone and pathetic. The walk back will be hard, difficult to deny the predicament those jerks have put her in, walking through the twilight of the woods alone. She's interrupted by a voice that has pushed itself through the murmur of the busy pub.

"Hi Liz."

Liz stops, wondering if she actually heard her name, or if it was the fatigue of the night and the rhythm of conversation playing tricks on her ears. The voice doesn't repeat the greeting, so she turns around feeling quite vulnerable. Her eyes get big, and a smile finds its way back to her face. "Ryan. Hi. I haven't seen you in so long."

They both just stand there, staring and grinning at each other for a minute. He looks sort of bashful, and his brilliant curly brown hair looks even better than she had remembered. After a momentary pause, he continues, "We're throwing a keg party over at the Tek cabins, would you like to come?"

"Yes, of course I want to come." She answers and shoots him the most sincere smile she can summon.

"I'm really glad to see you again, Ryan." She says, with genuine fondness.

He laughs "I knew we'd cross paths eventually. I'm happy it's tonight." He pulls a red beanie out of his back pocket and places it on top of his head, pulling it down to cover his curls. "Okay, then, let's go!"

Strange, that he's randomly at the pizza pub, because when they leave, there are no others with them. Liz is beyond happy for the twist in the night's plot, *"I've learned that when I fall, I can trust in the universe to pick me back up again, just when I think I'm out of chances. If I know how to look for it, feel it, and hold it, this whole world is willing and able to care for me, providing me with everything I need. Here I am learning this lesson in this place, where I am reduced to a small employee room, sparse with old eighties hotel furniture, a duffle bag of clothes and a pair of cheap black waitress shoes. I have no vision for my future. Yet, I find enlightenment in the sway of a moment.*

Still, I must admit, that I suspect these coincidences, these bending branches of charity are more complicated and somehow related to this place, Denali.

I didn't just pursue her. She called to me, and I answered the call, as natural and with such strong urgency as the migrating birds that flock here seeking summer resting grounds.

Together, Ryan and Liz step up onto the big deck that's adorned with tiki torches. There are forty or so people quietly milling around, laughing, talking and drinking. "Have you been to our property before?" He asks.

"No, I really like it." She answers, distracted by the need to assimilate.

"It's one of the few locally owned companies in the area." He explains with pride.

Lead by her date, she's escorted right past Joe and his posse, whom she notices are lacking keg cups.

Ryan walks her over to the keg, "I'll be right back Liz." He disappears into the house and reappears with two red cups. He pours her drink, then his, and together they make their way over to a railing, looking out over a shaded clearing in the woods.

"Mmm," . . . Liz tilts her cup of beer up to her mouth in an exaggerated, I hope you're watching me Joe, sort of way. She doesn't look his way again.

She's with Ryan, the cute nice guy who left such a warm and sweet impression on her all those weeks ago. She imagines having a romance with this naturalist, mountain man-type. Someone who will lead her off into the wilderness and openness, spending time gazing at the stars in the sky, or examining the leaves on the ground. He's tall, strong, lean, with deep soulful eyes, and curly wild hair, draped in flannel and fleece, with corduroy pants that were washed this morning but immediately have been saturated in four different kinds of dirt. She wants to have a good night with him, and she's interested in him. She thinks about his story, about all the months hiking alone on the PCT.

"How have you been Liz?" He leads into their conversation as if they're old friends catching up. "I've been hoping I'd run into you."

She blushes. "I've thought about you too Ryan, it's weird, I haven't seen you in so long."

He nods, "The Tek Company keeps me pretty busy, and I'm driving their private shuttle into the park a lot."

Liz transfers her weight to her other leg, and readjusts her lean on the railing. "I've been working a lot too." The topic of work begins to tug at her sense of responsibility and as much as she knows she should remain, all she really feels she needs is to go home and sleep before the long shift in the morning. After all the ups and downs, her evening begins to fall flat, similar to the taste of her beer. She's preoccupied, tired, and a little drunk. Her mind keeps thinking about the summer, and about work. She thinks about her friends ditching her tonight. She has another drink, and then breaks the news to Ryan; "I have to go home, because of work in the morning."

He graciously takes her cup and sets it inside of his, then holds out his arm. "Can I walk you back?"

She's momentarily struck with the realization that she just called her employee housing room; home. It is, she lives there, and on some level she's bonded with the place. After all, it's hers to hide in, nurse hangovers in. She tucks her arm inside his, preparing for the long walk back to her room.

The walk is slow, neither is in a rush. Instead, they are using the time and the steps to think and interact. They talk about hiking in Denali. She wishes Ryan would take her for a hike in the park, but she remains quiet, and chooses not to suggest it. Whenever she's with him, she feels an attraction, and they seem to have chemistry, yet he fails to persuade her to pursue him.

They arrive at her housing. It begins to rain ever so faintly. It's ironic the way the world looks at this specific moment; things couldn't appear more romantic. Two people huddled together, while a cool rain begins to fall down around them. A mist hangs low and softens the edges of the buildings. The rain clouds create a fluid grey that makes her want to move in close, and get warm. They go up the steps, and she unlocks her door. She turns to look at him standing there on her balcony, he's wide open. He raises his arms to offer her a hug goodnight; she steps forward and falls into his hug. They stay there for a minute, to feel each other, and for warmth. It reminds her of the two of them so many weeks ago, she was so different then.

"Thanks for the walk back Ryan."

He releases her from the lucid embrace. "I'll see you very soon Liz."

She steps inside and watches him make his way down the stairs back to his home. She imagines him walking back all alone through the woods.

"Goodnight Ryan."

Saturday, July 20th 2002

At work the next morning, the best distraction is in the form of an invitation. Lauren and Jane are planning a road trip, "Liz you're coming with us since you're a core member of the Fat City Crew" Lauren informs her.

"Lauren, I don't have those days off."

Jane grins with pride. "The Mayor doesn't have to worry, I've already talked John and Kendall into picking up our stray shifts, which is okay with them because they can just work a bunch of days straight until they leave for school."

The fourth in their Fat City road trip is Amelia the pantry chef, who's the same age as Liz, and so funny. Jane is good at planning, and all Liz has to do is hop aboard for the journey. Jane's worked out her days off, she's borrowing their Pakistani host's car for the weekend, and she knows exactly where they're going. She's even devised an itinerary.

Fat City Crew is not the only crew leaving for this event, half the staff are making the great pilgrimage South for the Girdwood Festival. It's a free event with camping, music, and food. Jane's been collaborating with Drew the bartender, and a whole group of Tundra Lodge employees have designated a unified campsite, complete with tent arrangements. Liz can't be more thrilled. A weekend with just the girls, and fun hardy seasonal girls at that. Today is feeling much lighter, and her troubles are far from her mind.

She spends the morning skipping back and forth between the dining room and the kitchen, taking orders, bringing orders, greeting assholes, and smiling at them like they're her own grandparents.

She starts to think about them; the assholes. *"They make me sad. I watch them bustle about the landscape, so fragile and tired. They move themselves across the property often with canes, or reaching for rails to steady themselves. They are slaves to their medications, and bodily functions. After visiting with table full after table full, it is common to learn that these assholes are in the midst of their dream vacation. They waited their entire lives to come and experience Alaska.*

The lodge I work for exploits this dream, and takes full advantage of loading the assholes up on trains, boats, and tour busses, racking up extensive charges on their credit cards. I wonder what the experience was like for them. Did they actually see Alaska, the way they had dreamed, or did they buy some cheap knock off version, adapted to suit oldness, that simply projects a stereotypical Alaskan ideal? Was it meaningful for them? Did it change them, to come and realize this dream?

I guess the Alaska of the twenty year olds perception, is just different from the Alaska of the seventy year olds interpretation, which seems to be filled with dinner theatre, and gift shops. I will not wait until I am an asshole to go out and live in this world, I won't make the mistakes of those who surround me here in the Tolkat!"

Behind the server station Lauren confronts Liz with an incomprehensible look across her face; "Did you sleep with Joe?"

"Huh?" Liz is confused. Completely caught unprepared. Lauren studies the guilty look that spreads across Liz's horrified face. She discovers her secret, isn't a secret at all.

If Lauren heard she had slept with Joe, then she concludes many others have too. "Lauren, where did you hear that?"

She looks uncomfortable having to tell her, so Liz helps her out, "It doesn't matter, it's a lie."

Lauren arches an eyebrow giving her coworker a coy smile. She's a natural beauty and her bright blonde hair is always coming undone from her ponytail and falling in her face. In this moment, she's giving Liz a look that is impossible to ignore, beautiful and troublesome.

Liz thinks hard, *"I know I hadn't mentioned him to anyone; there's nothing to tell. I don't get it. First he looks embarrassed and pretends not to know me, and now I find out he's been telling people we slept together. What happened? When did this car get so derailed?"*

She tries her best to correct Lauren. "He's, he's a liar! I don't get why he would say that about me?"

She's embarrassed and annoyed that rumors are drifting around the property about her sex life. Her very private and nonexistent sex life! She can feel her face turn red. She's busted, and at the same time she can't figure out Joe's motive. Lauren looks delighted and entertained as she watches Liz process the information.

It's sort of precarious of her, based on her amused expression, but it's also helpful and friendship-based to let Liz know. She's appreciative of Lauren. If she hadn't of said anything, who knows how many folks around their property were walking around with this information. Liz flashes back momentarily to the night when Amber and Chris warned her that Joe was dirty. That advice is starting to make more sense now. Not that anyone really cares, the only reason it interests Lauren is because she sees Liz every day, and her love life has always been sort of a mysterious topic.

Unlike Jane and Lauren, Liz didn't have a boyfriend, and unlike Gabe and Kendall, Liz isn't a couple, or married like Mark and Sarah. She has somewhat of an advantage here, in this boozed-up, sexed-up, seasonal town.

After work, Liz stops off at the Tundra Lodge coffee shop where Denver and Rebecca are working. She loves the coffee shop. It's usually just her two dear friends manning the place, and during the afternoon when she gets off work, it's usually empty.

"Rebecca can I have a latte, and an almond pastry?"

Rebecca begins steaming the milk, she raises her voice over the whistle of the steam. "I have good news Liz!"

Denver pulls up a chair next to Liz. "We have a ride to Girdwood for the festival!"

Rebecca saunters around the counter and takes a seat, pushing the latte and pastry in front of Liz, "For the Mayor". Rebecca is smaller than Denver and Liz, and quite thin. Her long brown hair runs all the way down her back. She reminds Liz of a woodland fairy. "I'm so happy; we're going to have such a good time!"

She takes a big bite of the pastry, its sticky and flakey, and pairs heavenly with the foamy drink. Denver grabs a chocolate milk out of the back. They sit in the empty café, watching people roam around outside. These women are so good at doing nothing. Liz falls under the enchanting spell of food and drink.

In addition to their two nights in Girdwood, Jane's good negotiating skills paired with Kendall and Gabe's ability to work ten days straight, earned Fat City a third night off. No one, during the season as a group from the same department ever gets three days off. Jane did, and she negotiated those days for all of them. Jane was a dynamo packaged in a petite frame. Her curly hair is always fixed the same way each day, and she almost always wears the same signature red polar fleece outside of work.

Thanks to Jane, Liz finds herself engaging in more healthy activities, away from the reckless party crowd. Away from this make-shift tourist town's more notorious bars. Instead of treading water, and trying to keep up with a lifestyle of partying all night, and working all day, like so many do in this area, she finds the discipline to pull back a bit. She credits this discipline to Jane's guidance. The way so many employees are dropping out, as each week passes, seeing less and less of the same familiar faces, burning out, quitting, or fired. Instead of falling prey to this vicious habit, Liz's coworkers namely Jane and Lauren have somehow scooped her up and pushed her back a little bit. Reminding Liz to slow it down, pace herself, and that there's room for fun, mild activities that still involve a decent night's rest. It seems she had these girls figured all wrong, and they aren't completely snobby, just more organized and focused on enjoying the Denali experience in a different way.

Not that they don't party, it's just they don't party as much as Liz does. The difference between Liz and them, is that they have lives to go back home to, where they have boyfriends waiting, and college, and a plan all mapped out. As for Liz, her plan was to get away from the life she was living. While the thought of returning to it, often scares her.

The other night, she wrote in her journal, *"I'm afraid I'll have to confront the boyfriend, or in a moment of weakness, get back together with him. I'm afraid I'll get some shitty job at the mall selling clothes, or just living at my parents' house being a bum. I'm afraid I'll lose touch with adventuresome Liz, who thinks little of consequence, and takes risks only to discover the strange and lovely way life can be. Yes, I don't want this to end, but luckily I still have time here, and I suspect that when the time comes and the season ends, I may be ready to return. I miss my California".*

She heads out of the coffee shop, bidding the girls farewell, "Thanks again for the food, you make the best latte's in all of Denali!"

"See you later Liz, come by Denver's room later!"

Liz is on her way to their housing building. Sitting in between their building and the employee cafeteria is one strategically angled picnic table. Around the table are a handful of her coworkers, and above them on the balcony are a few more of her friends.

Jane waves. "Liz come sit with us!"

"Let me change out of my uniform!" She yells, and starts to climb the steps up to the second floor.

Today the midnight sun is blazing afire, and everyone appears to be paying tribute; by congregating outside. She runs upstairs to take off her stiff collared shirt, vest, and bow tie. She throws on a black tank top, and black cardigan. She pops back out, to go down to meet her friends, ignoring the fact that she smells like the lunch shift. She turns a corner and runs straight into Joe.

Lauren, Jane, Gabe, Kendall, and Marvin are watching from below, with grave interest. There are a couple other people inside the employee lounge located directly behind Liz who also seem to be watching. She looks at him, and can feel her face grow hot.

He did the worse thing possible: He did a stop, pivot and turn; to go the other way without acknowledging her, or saying hello. This action sets her off, and she doesn't care who's watching or listening. The past few weeks have been irritating, the way he so rudely avoids her, and then the rumors. So with the bold gesture of turning around; just to get away from her . . . he crosses another line.

"Joe!" She yells, even though he's only a few steps away from her. He stops and turns around to look at her; he smiles faintly. This is the first time they've made eye contact since their night together. He's making his best effort to act very casual, like he hadn't noticed her.

Liz commits to be firm; "Hey, why did you tell my friends and coworkers we had sex?"

No answer. As her face turns red, his face drains of all color.

She raises her voice louder, deeper, and very stern. She can sense the eyes of others upon them. "I thought you were my friend, but you go and tell my friends that you had sex with me. Why would you do that? I thought we were cool!" Her voice is sharp and cracks. "This is not cool, these people are my coworkers. I see them every day, and you're spreading rumors about me? What if I went around telling rumors about you? You didn't think they would tell me?" As the words come out, it feels good and honest. She feels sort of righteous.

His face is unable to hide his discomfort, and he looks hurt, embarrassed, and without any explanation.

"I can't even look at you! That really hurt's Joe!" She turns away, hopping down the steps and over to the picnic table.

The group at the picnic table gives Joe an unsettling glance, and then turns their backs to him, greeting Liz with supportive smiles. Gabe comes over and puts his hands on her shoulders; rubbing them for a second. She must look pretty tense for him to do that. No one discusses what they just witnessed, and she's glad they drop the subject cold, sort of like the way she wants to drop Joe.

Pressure

Wednesday, July, 24th 2002

It's five in the morning, and Fat City is meeting up at the Tolkat to poach some breakfast food, and maybe some lunch food, too. Amelia walks up and high-fives the girls.

"Morning Ladies." Jane greets them. "It's going to be a long ride to Girdwood, and we're only stopping for beer and gas."

All four women travel light, and each simply joyful to be included, and invited, and to be driving in a car and not walking with her feet or catching a shuttle. She's happy to put miles between herself and work for a few days. It's time to see Alaska.

Lauren looks back at Amelia and Liz; "I brought Cat Stevens." she beams, radiating her artistic vibes.

Cat Stevens wouldn't have been Liz's first choice, but is nice for the trip. For once her body is at rest, and she slinks back, letting the little Toyota seat hold her. She turns her head out the window and tries not to blink, as she does her best too literally see as much as she can. The absence of conversation is comforting; it's a thing of value when four people can spend time together peacefully, and in tune with one another without having to talk.

They were doing what those like themselves do best, travel. Girls who find their way someplace between the Brooks Range and the Alaska Range seem to have an affinity for it. The women seem to share this. The Cat Stevens tape is now going on its third way round, and Liz is amazed that it's the first time in her twenty two years of life, she's ever actually listened to a full Cat Stevens' album. Lauren must be trying to fit twenty two years worth, right now, on their drive through Alaska. She's amused that Lauren looks completely into it, even though she's been jamming to the same tape for the last two hours. She bops her head along singing the lines "If you want to be . . . !"

Liz has to break the cycle; "Jane! Are there any other tapes in the car? Any?"

"Yup. I saw a big case of them in the trunk. They might all be Pakistani music though. When we stop, I promise you can look through them." Jane assures. "One more hour; then we reach our stop."

Liz pulls her journal from her bag to write, *"I focus my mind out the window, trying to memorize the frilled tendrils of fiddlehead fern tucked away in the shadows from Sitka spruce. The fireweed grows tall, and outlines the highway in a long ribbon of magenta. I heard somewhere that you can measure the summer with the fireweed. As their hot pink petals reach and bloom all the way to the top of their stocks, summer has peaked, and then slowly they drop the petals, until all are gone, and summer has too. I'm glad to see the flowers looking healthy and vital".*

They cruise pass Talkeetna, and Walmikes. They're almost to Wasilla before pulling into a fully operational gas station. The women rush in; trying not to show how bad they need to pee, grabbing candy, and browsing the liquor section.

Jane reminds them, "The plan is to hit a super store as soon as we pull into Anchorage. It's just down that road from here."

Liz digs into the trunk. She finds a cassette holder with close to ten cassettes, many that she can't recognize. That doesn't matter because she sees one she does recognize. This is the only tape she needs. Wrapping her eager fingers around it, she holds it in a way that looks like she's just caught a tree frog; cupping it carefully in her excited hands. Liz has in her possession a cassette of the original New Kids on The Block album "Hanging Tough". She's practically jumping up and down with excitement. Immediately she has plans for her music discovery; the audio system in the Tolkat plays cassettes. She can't wait to play some jams during breakfast for the oldies.

It's amazing what a good road trip can do for a girl, they haven't even really done anything yet, and she's feeling her best. She's being playful, and pushy with her friends, and they're pleased, since they rely on Liz for her weirdo antics

The super store is expansive, and holds within its walls an American dream. They haven't been in a big super store in months. This store has everything you can think of; including gold pans, running shoes, groceries, furniture, diamond rings, and art supplies. The objective is to find food for camping two nights in Girdwood, sort of. They can buy food, and probably will at the festival. Beer is important, and this store has an entire wall; over thirty different varieties. They each grab a twelve pack of the best available which in their opinion: is Alaskan.

Something in the kids section catches her eye. It's a pink parasol, with ruffled edges and a thick pink plastic handle. She wants it. She's not sure why, but the bubble gum shade of pink calls to her. The hard plastic is so tactile. She gets in line with a package of yogurt, some crackers, some candy, a case of beer, and one pink parasol. Her travel companions are still busy shopping and hoping she won't demand they listen to The New Kids on The Block. She does.

"It's "New Kids" all the way to Girdwood. Talk about sing along music! Now I'm the Lauren in the car".

They're now driving down the Seward highway, and she's never seen anything remotely close to the way this landscape expresses. Towering above them are the dramatic Chugach Mountains, while to the right: is a vast stretch of water that kisses empty beaches which rise up into other great mountains. For someone who's never seen this sort of geology in her short lived life, the images burn into her soul, because one is driving right down the middle of a love hymn offered up from the earth to the great creator. This is beauty and poetry, and soul, all stretched out, and elevated.

Liz writes, *"If I was in some sort of accident, and my mind was locked away in a coma within my body, I imagine I would go somewhere deep in my own head, moving and traveling, and seeing spaces that defy reason. I imagine this coma world would look a lot like the views beholden to those who travel the Seward highway, of course that's because I haven't seen Whittier yet".*

With all the traveling and stops complete, the women finally pull into Girdwood close to noon. The village reflects its roots as they drive past cabins that resemble ski chalets and little pizza places scattered about. They aren't exactly sure where they're going precisely, but are happy to join a small convoy of cars that appear to be headed towards the festival.

Amelia and Liz step out of the backseat together. She's looking over at Liz laughing, relieved to be free of the New Kids music. Amelia has a great laugh, she's the largest member of their foursome, really tall, and her voice is nice and deep. Like Lauren, she parts her hair right down the middle, but has long straight, almost black hair.

Liz looks at Jane "Let's go shopping."

Jane is their manager for the trip. She checks her watch. "Okay, we can grab some lunch and walk around for two hours, then we should find our camp."

They walk through the crowd, divided in two's. Jane and Liz are together, and Amelia and Lauren. The talls and the shorts.

There's a bluegrass band performing, salmon quesadillas for buying, and arts and crafts all over the place. It's a good thing Liz is a server and has plenty of cash at hand, virtually all the time. She carefully scans each craft booth to uncover the best souvenir to mark the occasion. Something that will remind her how far she's come, and what she's experienced thus far. There are handmade clothes, home dyed hats and fabrics, crystals, and drums. Everything is crafted and local, and it's interesting how certain pieces speak to specific people. She knows this, because as they walk by a booth, a piece calls to her. It's a vendor who has pottery, and clay figures. Among her subjects, Liz finds a small clay whistle that's shaped and painted into a snowflake attached on a simple black cord to wear around one's neck. It reminds her of snowboarding back home in California, one of her favorite activities. It also reminds her of her secret wish to see snow in Alaska. "How much for the snowflake flute?"

The long haired hippie woman with the crooked back waves her hand over all the whistles on the table. "All of these are twenty five each."

She pays her twenty five dollars for the treasure, and decides her shopping is complete. This is all she wants. Even though she hasn't experienced any snow during her travels in Alaska, she's at a ski resort and will have to use that fact, to validate a snowflake as a memorable symbol of her journey.

Jane is trying on a backless wrap-shirt..

"Jane that is hot!"

Jane turns and strikes a quick pose for Liz. "I'm not sure it's me."

"That top looks amazing on you, I'll be mad if you don't get it. I wish I had the figure to pull that off. It's good. Really."

Jane does one more rotation in the full length mirror leaned up against a pine tree "I'm going to get it."

Liz realizes her style is distinctly different from Jane, Lauren, and Amelia. Among her group, she's depressed to notice she's the only one who doesn't own a high-end polar fleece, or a heavy wool sweater. All she has are cotton based synthetic sweaters, jeans, and her snowboard jacket.

As the women regroup back at the car, they continue to cruise around a big looped tour of Girdwood. Jane finds the road they're searching for. Slowly they crawl past clusters of cars pulled over to the side in camping groups, they look hard, trying to find their people; The Denali group. Soon, they spot them. Drew has Brent's beastly VW van, and with him are a couple of the cooks, a few girls from the night crew, and Denver and Rebecca. It's a good group.

Fat City pulls off to the side of the road and parks behind the van. After climbing out, Jane hands off their tents. One tent belongs to Jane, and the other she borrowed from John and Kendall for Liz and Amelia. Liz is beginning to feel spoiled, thanks to the way Jane's taken care of every detail for her.

Jane confesses to Liz, "I'm having a hard time enjoying our trip because I feel guilty that I'm not going to visit my boyfriend who's working at the Seward Lodge. It's about an hour down the road."

Liz can see on her face; she's really doing some soul searching. Liz gives her an empathetic look, and nods.

Jane's face switches, she looks much lighter and grins "I could go see him tonight and come back in the morning. But, I don't want too.

"Stick with us, Jane." Liz looks in the direction of the festival.

It's not uncommon for Jane to have mixed feelings about her relationship, and she seems to have a lot on her mind now that we are all closer to the end than the beginning of our time in Alaska. Liz pauses for a second, so slight and undetected, she feels compelled to check-in with herself, thinking about how to be a better friend and wonders if she could try to help Jane figure it all out. This is difficult, because she's so used to seeing her friend as so capable and independent. In her mind, she is reminded of all the times she speaks to Jane, sharing her thoughts and opinions; Jane truly focuses and listens. She'll bring up something Liz has shared earlier, which can feel significant since Jane had remembered it all this time. Liz shrugs off the pause, inconclusive. Together they walk out to the meadow, choosing good tent spots.

"You should definitely stay with us tonight Jane, it's all about Girdwood." Liz gives her a wink. All she can think is to reassure.

Tents are erected, makeup is reapplied, and jackets are on. It's time to convoy down to the local Girdwood bar for drinks. Every single member of the crowd is living up to Denali's wild reputation. The group is eager and ready to get crazy and drunk. It's a celebration, a holiday just to be in Girdwood. The local bar is more than Liz anticipates, and upon entering the doors, her incorrigible and savage group spreads out; disappearing into a sea of people. It's so crowded, and a different type of crowd as well. These are not just seasonal workers, but locals, and travelers, and others all churned up and dissolved into some other diversion.

She needs a drink for this, but as she turns to the bar; her heart sinks. The bar is a long horseshoe, with half a dozen bartenders and a couple of bar backs fluttering around, automated like machines. Above them hangs a complex menu of drink specialties. Ordering the drink will require a commitment.

Finally; "A Cadillac margarita, and a tequila popper, please."

The room has a DJ, but the crowd is so noisy, the music is pointless. Liz grabs her drinks and works her way along the wall until she makes her way out into the backyard of the establishment. She finds her friends, amazed that somehow they had all acquired drinks before her. The backyard is enclosed with a fence, and is nothing more than a big lot of dirt and sand, with a large bonfire. She looks out and sees Jensen the guy who works with Josh the shuttle driver at the Trapper's Line. Jensen is often the doorman, checking Liz's id and enforcing the rules. She's buzzed, and really celebrating the fact that she's found someone she knows. It's late, and she can't find her group that she's arrived with. So she does what she can, and clings on to Jensen. He's happy to oblige. The night fades, but after all of it, she finds herself arm in arm with Jensen walking down the Girdwood road with four others in their group; heading back to camp.

Liz has no idea where camp is, but trusts they are going to get there, and continues to follow the leader. Drew is with them, and is walking a few steps ahead with one of the dinner shift servers.

This is when he says the line; "I'm so drunk, I can't remember what happened."

"Oh, What? You don't remember making out with me?" She calls out, loud and boisterous. Liz is drunk, but can't resist a repeat of her joke.

At that, Drew stops.

He releases the arm of the server. He spins around to look at Liz. His expression is undiscernible as he stands in the middle of the gravel road. Liz and Jensen stop too. Liz takes a step backward, unsure of how he's reacting, since he's not laughing like the first time she told him her joke. He walks over to her aggressively, puts his arm around her hips, a hand around her head, and then tilts her way back. He gives Liz the most sweep-her-off-her-feet kiss, earth stopping sort of passion, then tilts her back up, let's her go, and rejoins his position in the front of the group. She steps away; struck in a daze. Blinking.

She looks over at Jensen, the one whom she's been hanging on all night. He gently smiles, but looks sensitive. Liz resumes her place beside him with a shrug of her shoulders.

As she walks back; she's still thinking about the kiss, right there in the middle of the road in the dark, in front of all their friends. She wonders if he even knows she has a crush on him. Is this a mutual fondness?

Liz piles into the tent with Amelia and the stray she seemed to have picked up; known as Jensen. She totally picked up the poor guy, led him back to her tent and then passes out cuddling up to Amelia to stay warm while he slept against the edge of the tent, happy to be included but unsure he understands the function of this particular Denali group.

Thursday, July 25ᵗʰ 2002

Liz wakes up. Jensen is on his way out of the tent; "Thanks for the fun night. I'll see you later at the festival."

Feeling a little awkward. Happy Amelia is beside her, she replies, "Jensen, thanks for keeping me company last night, I'll see you later."

Immediately Amelia makes her feel better as she teases, "So you had a good night with Jensen, you two make a cute couple."

Liz shrugs her shoulders and prepares to chase the hangover away with a little more sleep. "It's all in the past, until I meet him again today and see what happens. Oh Amelia, I had a lot of poppers last night, and am feeling subhuman this morning."

"Suck it up Liz, we still have another night!"

After they try their best to refresh without showers, apply new makeup, and clean clothes, they're ready to go to the festival. Liz follows the coffee shop girls along a trail that winds through thick trees. She's completely preoccupied with the foliage in Girdwood. She feels like she needs to touch the curious tendrils of every fern she passes. They feel almost tropical. This is not the way she stereotyped Alaska, and she's intrigued by this new, non-interior ecosystem. She could stop and sit with the bark and the fern all morning if she weren't being herded forward by her group.

Round two of shopping. Liz enjoys watching the different trinkets selected by different friends. She's on the lookout for gifts to send home to her family. Nothing catches her eye, but the day is young.

"Come on Liz, we're all getting our faces painted!" Denver points to a table under a canopy of a large spruce.

"Oh, I love it. Haven't had my face painted since summer camp!"

"Well, welcome to Camp Girdwood. I'm doing vines!" Rebecca announces, cutting in front of Denver and Liz.

"Hmmm, I think I'll do the same. I'll pick a different color, though." Liz scans the options on the tag board, deciding the vines are most suited for their day of music under the trees. Liz is last to get her face painted. She loves the slick tickle of the brush as it traces the outer frame of her face before wrapping a bit below her eye.

"All done". The face painter says, dropping her brush into her water. Liz opens her eyes and picks-up the hand mirror. Her eyes widen, admiring the gorgeous green vine with blue flowers and sparkles winding and complimenting the hazel of her eyes. She sees something else, a transformation beyond the paint on the surface. She's vibrant here in this forest, it compliments her. She sets down the mirror as quickly as she picked it up. Thanks the face painter, and joins her friends at the tennis court that had been converted into a skate park.

Liz has her hair in two simple braids. She's wearing a fitted long sleeved shirt that has a screen printed Japanese design. She's wearing baggy jeans that float around her hips. Not high fashion, but the best she could do with a limited wardrobe, and months living in the middle of nowhere, which is actually somewhere. Somewhere better than anywhere she's been before.

The three friends rejoin Fat City who have been sipping green tea by the main stage. The women are content to rest and people-watch, enjoying the different bands that grace the stage. Liz is ready to decide on food option. There are so many. Alone, she turns a corner finds herself standing opposite of Jensen, a wide open space between them. She stops and holds her hand up in a wave. He waves back, then turns to walk in a different direction. She's surprised he won't come over to say hi to her, and she doesn't want to be the one to go to him. This activity reminds her of Joe, and it's more than annoying, it screws with her self-esteem.

She's grateful for some time alone to walk and think. It's a relief to be in a place where no one knows her. Everyplace she goes in Denali, she has friends. She takes the long way around the perimeter, people watching, and contemplating. It feels safe to think about Gabe and what happened. She hasn't allowed herself too. It's too tender, and she feels fragile and has so much to do before she can indulge in a spell of depression. Strange, she feels okay with what happened. Sad, but okay. By the time she reaches the beer garden, which is fenced off to the left of the stage, crowds have collected. She watches a sultry set from a jam band, followed by a new band who plays bluegrass. Liz decides, she may as well grab a drink. With beer in hand, she stands near a post holding the beer garden fence. Something or someone catches her eye just below one of the tallest trees across from the stage. Two very attractive backpackers with very large packs on their backs are watching the band. They look familiar, she's seen them somewhere before. The packs persuade her to say, hello. The two men watch her approach. She tries to look friendly.

"Hi, I'm Liz."

"Hi Liz, I'm Aaron, and this is Joseph."

"I notice you have your packs, do you have a campsite figured out for tonight? We have a campground not far from here." She's straight to the point.

She's staring at Aaron, interested. "You look so familiar."

"We came from Healy. We work at the Ptarmigan Inn." Aaron explains. "We hitchhiked all the way down this morning."

Liz's energy engages with the connection, she can feel her eyes sparkle, and not just from the glitter from her face paint. "That's amazing, my friends and I are from the Tundra Lodge in Denali!"

Joseph and Aaron look at one another and communicate something without speaking or revealing in front of the friendly girl. "Yes, a campsite for tonight with the Tundra crew sounds awesome."

"Good choice." Liz replies.

"Liz, can we buy you a beer?"

"Yes. Please."

Joseph goes to the bar to purchase three drafts infused with lingon berries. Leaving Aaron and Liz to continue with formalities.

"Hitchhiking? When do you have to return to work? What if you can't get a ride back?"

Aaron smiles and lifts his posture. "It was easy enough catching a ride here. I'm not worried about getting back. We have to go back tomorrow. You?"

Liz lifts her posture, "We are going to Homer tomorrow, then to Kenai. Kind of a girl's trip."

"That sounds awesome."

Joseph places a cold cup of beer in her hand. The three say, sipping for two more songs.

"Want to go?" Liz has a feeling there is probably something entertaining happening back at camp.

The men respond by slipping their backpacks over their shoulders. "Lead the way, firefly."

It's a thirty minute walk through a few intersecting trails back to camp. They pass the vendors, the face-painter, and the skate park. Now the evening is finally starting to feel more interesting. Her self-esteem is once again lifted, as she walks into camp with the two hot guys in tow. The girls in the group look over, jaws dropping, wondering who the handsome backpackers are. Apparently she has some sort of Girdwood skill, since there are no shortages of men in Liz's world over the last twenty four hours.

"Oh, Lord another night in Girdwood. I am not sure my liver can survive this!" Liz calls to Amelia. Introductions are sweet. Everyone's happy to watch our camp population grow. The granted immediate acceptance as one of their own, having come from the hotel across from the Trapper's Line. They belong with this camp. The men go to set-up their tent.

An hour later, Liz emerges from her tent with her last pair of fresh jeans and her pale green snowboard jacket, a beanie pulled down over her ears. She pauses to admire the sight of the new tent that belongs to Aaron and Joseph, nestled in the mix of their busy tent city. It's just past seven in the evening.

Drew and the cooks are setting up a keg, right outside of the van; their treat for the Denali crew.

Drew calls Liz over. She goes to him. It's the first time they've spoke since the embrace the night before. Thrilled to be the object of his interest, her heart beats a little faster.

"Liz," he says: "Do a keg stand."

"A what?" She isn't even sure what it is, but after watching a few of the girls and guys get flipped upside down with the nozzle to their mouths, she will soon learn.

"Nope, I'll fall. I'm too heavy."

"I've got you. Come over here." He flashes a killer-smile. She submits.

"One, two, three!" Her world's just been flipped upside-down and she now has cold fast beer rushing up her throat. Then once again; feet to the ground and cheers from the crowd. Right side-up, feeling like a champion, she's now standing across from the backpackers. They look intrigued.

"Good job, Liz. Who's next?" Drew continues to host his crew.

"Them!" She points at her guests. They oblige, each taking a turn getting flipped up-side-down. Hours pass, and the night is nothing but friends old and new, laughter, bubbles and foam, and a gentle breeze blowing over from the coast. Liz realizes, that Girdwood has more of a twilight, and less daylight than Denali. This helps her festive mood. Soon, the party is standing in the road making wolf howls, stumbling about and discussing a game plan to hit up the bar with the bonfire one more time.

Trying to play hostess, she stands beside Joseph and Aaron. Joseph breaks down how the two friends ended up in Denali. "Yeah, I know, we started kind of late. There was a conflict with school. We grabbed our Ptarmagin job's on the fly." He gives Aaron an odd look.

Aaron, adds, "Everyone's so chill and nice around here. We need to catch up, lots to see and do. If you know of fun things to do, let us know. We want to see as much as we can."

"Have you been to the park?"

"Aaron and Joseph instantly light up, "The park is amazing!" They both nod, feeling the buzz of alcohol and the warmth of new friendship.

Everyone begins to organize a trip back to the bar from the night before. Half of the group elects to go, the other is ready to pass out. Joseph declines, "We have to make it back to the Ptarmigan tomorrow. I need to rest, or it will be a day. Thanks again for the invite. This was so fun."

"I'll go with you, Liz." Aaron looks inspired by his new friends.

Joseph gives him a quiet look, "Goodnight!" He turns to go to their tent.

Liz and Aaron share a mutual energy. She can see that he's caught by the same romantic ideals, wanting to experience all that's available before it's gone. They stare at one another, the way those who are buzzed and less inhibited can do in the partial darkness beneath a dense canopy of trees. "Fat City, let's do this!"

One by one, each girl resigns their interest in the bar. "One night there is enough for me, Jane shares. Here, take the keys, but buckle-up, only one drink, and straight back when you're ready." Liz nods in compliance, remembering the three instructions. "Aaron, make sure she only has one drink at the bar. Remember, there is plenty here at camp, once she's done driving. If you end up drinking more, just leave the car and walk back. Okay?"

She's given the keys to the Toyota, and they're now convoying down the empty dirt road to the bar. Three cars full of Tundra employees begin a slow roll down the dirt road. Liz and Aaron are the last car.

"Where are you from Aaron?"

Aaron answers steadily, "From Berkeley."

Liz gasps in delight, "Aaron, you are the first Californian I've met this summer!"

Aaron explains. "I'm from Berkeley, but my parents sent me to North Carolina, because I was getting into trouble back home."

"I grew up just a couple of hours away from Berkeley in Stockton. Funny that we meet so far from our origins!"

"I know what you mean. That's what I love about it here. It has a way of bringing people together."

The analog clock on the dashboard shows close to ten. They pull into the parking lot of the bar, but neither of them bother to unbuckle their seat belt. The bar is loud and more crowded than the night before. Liz spots Jensen enter into a side door. After the lovely time with just their group at the campsite, the bar seems overstimulating. Suddenly, Liz doesn't feel loud and social, not now that she has this new person in her life, this passenger. "Are you going back to Berkeley soon?"

"I really don't think so. It's a little complicated. I'm in the middle of school, it's my main focus for now."

"Oh." Liz feels low, she wishes she had a focus, something complicated that keeps her, defines what she might do with her life. She feels inferior beside him.

They stay in the car and continue to talk. He shares with her his story, and she listens carefully trying to take mental notes. She can't help but find herself inspired by the unpredictability of life. How is it she's driving a random car through an Alaskan ski town, with a handsome backpacker who's a Californian, just like her? Before they even exit the car, the Denali crew are climbing back into Brent's van, and the convoy reverses direction; going back to camp. Everyone is eager to partake in another keg round with their smaller more intimate group. "Sorry Aaron! I kept you from the bar. It's really fun, we could stay and go check out the bonfire. Or we could follow the group back to camp. Your choice."

"Don't apologize. I like talking with you. I'm really glad to meet you."

Liz is quiet. She likes his sweet reply.

After following her buzzed convoy back to the safety of camp, she watches Aaron climb out of the car. He has a small build, light brown hair that had once been cut well, but is in the process of growing out. Liz notices his amazing stature. He's been so respectful and genuine, sending Liz all the right signals, and from the beginning of the evening they've coddled a gradual attraction. The direct way in which she went to him earlier today was too natural, the way he wanted to come with her, follow her to the camp, to the bar, anywhere she asked him too. He's the one, clearly, after all these months of feeling lonely. Liz is sure she's found someone. The musician had too much invested into his career and schedule, Gabe had Kendall, but, Aaron, he's wide open, here and back home in California.

An hour escapes the Denali Group, everyone is laughing and joking, and singing made-up songs. They're also watching Liz. She's been standing off to the side of the bonfire with Aaron. He puts his arm around her to keep her warm while they celebrate the night away. One by one, sometimes two by two, friends abandon the keg and wander back to crash in their designated tents. Liz catches Drew admiring them, curious. Aaron and Liz are the last two remaining. She trails her hands across his chest, tracing the definition of his muscular form with her fingers, wrapped up in his arms. He holds her. They stand there in the darkness, her cheek pressed against his chest. Lost in the strange evening, caught unprepared for the possibility of romance. Entangled in the Alaskan twilight.

He whispers gently, "What do you want to do?"

They're quiet in a sweet drunken bubble; all she wants is him like this.

She scans their surroundings and weighs her options. "We can go sit in the car. It's a little warmer."

Once in the car, they continue to whisper. She asks him little things, wanting to leap the hurdles of formalities. Hoping it would get them further along, closer. "What are you studying in school?"

"That's what my parents keep asking me. I'm not sure. Right now, I've been taking some anatomy courses, math. What I want to do, I haven't decided. You?"

"I want to teach. I still have so much school"

"How much longer will you be in North Carolina? How often do you go home to Berkley?"

He doesn't answer. Instead he reaches out and slides the beanie off of Liz's head. Liz puts her hand up to smooth her hair. He puts his hand on the middle of her thigh. She looks down, watching his hand rest there. The sun starts to rise, and they can feel their time together fleeting. She's leaving in a few hours to do some more road tripping with the girls, but she doesn't want to let go of him.

Aaron leans in, and with a kiss, whispers, "Let's take a walk."

"Yes." She responds half smiling, half falling.

The lust struck travelers walk past the tents in the meadow, over to the trees at the edge of a clearing. He leads her, taking her trusting hand. They're still in the moment, and there's nothing more, it's only Aaron, and it's only Liz. Now that they're hidden by trees, they find themselves less polite and more honest. The touching and grabbing are intense and deliberate. This attraction that began so many hours ago at the festival has grown concentrated and pressurized. Time closes in, and whatever they have is cut short. The sun rises, birds are singing, bugs are buzzing, and over by the tents people are waking. Before they walk back over to the camp, they stand facing the other; like they have most of the night. He has both her hands in his, and is looking into her eyes. She can't tell what he's thinking.

"Are you ready to go back?" He whispers, looking over at the group of tents.

"Yes." She replies.

Friday, July 26ᵗʰ 2002

All the girls are up, and Liz removes her backpack and sleeping bag from the tent. Amelia starts to break it down. Jane is ready to go. Liz is glad to be moving on, because what just happened was too much on her mind.

Holding her backpack over one shoulder, she walks over to Aaron's tent. He and Liz stand outside of it, looking at each other. He pulls her into a safe embrace.

"Come and find me when you get back to Denali." He commands with reassurance.

They're both still in their bubble, adoring one another. He has both her hands in his, and is looking down at her short self. They hug again.

Once in the car, Fat City gives Liz the look, "Liz you had fun last night!" Amelia states, with encouragement. Her three friends simply laugh and agree that Aaron seems really nice.

"I really, really like Aaron." Liz announces.

Four members of Fat City pull out and slowly drive down the faded dirt road. She spots a bubble gum pink parasol tangled in some bushes.

Her plan is to sleep in the car, all the way to Homer. Unfortunately Liz is too happy to sleep. She just sits in her seat, reliving last night in her head.

The Toyota pulls into a gas station. "I need caffeine. Oh, I'm not well, too much alcohol and no sleep." Liz grabs her stomach, which feels like a science experiment gone wrong. She thinks about her diet from yesterday. Fried food, coffee, and beer.

Everyone forages in the store, and Liz finds a cold bottled coffee. The jolt of caffeine surges through her body, which these days is starting to feel more like a machine. A crazy, wired machine that runs on alcohol and doesn't require sleep.

"I'm so glad it will be girl time for the rest of the trip."

Amelia laughs, "Too many boys over the last couple days Liz?"

She nods in her direction, smiling with embarrassment.

Jane turns to Liz. "I talked to my boyfriend!" She's looking like her usual-self again. "He's going to meet up with us in Homer for lunch."

"That's going to be fun, I'm so glad you're going to get to see him. I can't wait to meet this boyfriend of yours." She answers.

According to Jane's itinerary, the foursome will tour Homer, before driving to another Tundra Lodge near a coastal river.

"I can't wait to hit the shower at the lodge." says Lauren.

"Perfect, a little rest and relaxation on the river. It feels like a different world, getting away from the Tundra Lodge." Liz answers in between sips of her coffee.

The women are getting along better than could have been assumed, laughing, joking, and gossiping about work. "To the first official Fat City field trip." Lauren exclaims, holding up her green tea in a toast.

"To Fat City!" They all chime back.

Amelia hands Liz her travel pillow, "Here you go. You need it more than I do". Amelia's great; she's so easy to be with, smart and funny. The women needed a chef in their crowd to balance out the servers who can be kind of narcissistic. "You would be surprised how intense culinary school can be, one time we had to ring a bunny rabbit's neck, butcher it, and prepare a gourmet dish out of it." She describes passionately. "Our teacher wanted us to understand that meat is a life, and to treat it with respect, and to never burn it." She continues.

"Woah. You killed a bunny? I don't know if I could do that." Liz comments with interest and amazement.

"You could do it, Liz. You'd be surprised at what you could do. It wasn't so bad. But, yeah, it was bad."

Lauren, a vegetarian is quiet, and seems to have something far away on her mind. While Jane is still plagued with guilt about arrangements or drama with her boyfriend. Today in Homer they plan to have a seafood meal, right on the spit.

"Come on Amelia, Liz, we're going to the Salty Dog!" Calls Lauren, keeping up behind Jane.

"Lunch is on me girls." Jane's boyfriend announces.

"The only thing Fat City loves more than food, is free food." Lauren explains to Orin, Jane's boyfriend.

"Fat City?"

"Actually, Liz is the Mayor." Jane informs.

So, you both are working as servers in Alaska for the summer, but Orin, you are working down here, and Jane, you took a job in Denali?"

"Yes." Jane smiles, "It just kind of worked out that way. Orin's returning for a second season at the restaurant he's at. I really wanted to see Denali. We thought we'd see more of each other, but we all know how busy we've all been."

After lunch they stroll down to the water's edge for picture taking. The white clouds roll and sweep in the wind, and the mountains off in the distance seem to frame the whole landscape. Orin, Jane's boyfriend from back in Oregon is wonderful; he's a hit with all the women. He's so tall, and articulate. Liz is glad Jane has a chance to get to see him on the trip. Even if only for a few hours. Amelia, Lauren, and Liz kick their tired feet into the course pebbles and sand. Jane and Orin make time for a long walk along the water. The wind presses into the sapphire waters, a roar of foam beats down onto the shore, seagulls have a lively conversation above their heads while the tide brings in waves as relentless as Liz's thoughts of her new love interest.

By four everyone is settled back in the car, looking forward to exploring the River Lodge. Jane follows a highway that's so remote and scenic, they may have only passed three other cars in two hours' time. Liz keeps shutting her eyes tight and opening them, trying to correct her vision because she is seeing the river in Technicolor. She's never seen a turquoise river before, it practically glows. She feels like they're driving deep into an animated land, and the only thing reminding her that she's still in populated areas; are the little cabins, and café's tucked alongside the road, spread apart for miles. Soon they're winding up a long hill that wraps around a mountainside. They pop out at the driveway of the River Lodge. Jane is navigating this like she has GPS in her head.

Hot, long showers in an Alaskan-themed room. Dinner with generous tips for their server, flourless chocolate cake to take back to the room, a hot tub session, a crackling fire, and no makeup. No one has drinks tonight, and they go to bed early.

Liz drifts to sleep, feeling included, and not so lonely anymore.

Saturday, July 27th 2002

Morning comes, everyone sleeps a little more. Lauren stretches in bed. "I don't want today to be here, I don't want to go back"! It's the sad song, they all share.

Liz answers while yawning, "I know exactly what you mean; soon we'll be back; waiting on assholes".

With one last look at the grandeur of the Kenai ecology. It's a straight shot back to Denali.

They drive all day, and their conversations are less upbeat and more focused on preparations for work tomorrow. Many hours later they pull into the Tundra Lodge, grabbing their humble belongings and trekking back up to their rooms. It's almost August now, and Goodbyes are fast approaching to some of their crew. Liz is extremely glad that Jane, Lauren, and Amelia are staying for the end.

"See you in the morning." They wave goodnight to one another, and the burly women of Fat City enjoy a second good night's sleep.

Sunday, July 28th 2002

Her journal reads, "*Sleep, I didn't realize how vital and pleasurable it is; until I became reacquainted with it.*

In the morning Liz has a proposal pitched her way that surprises her, but she finds to be very agreeable.

Jane explains, "My roommate is going back to school, and I'm worried that I'll get one of the new people moved into my room. So I'm going to move in a roommate before human resources gives me one I may not like." Jane continues, "Liz I know you aren't thrilled with your roommate, it might be fun if we lived together."

"What? You want me? I'm a strong candidate for a potential roommate?"

"Well, yeah, Liz. You're my friend."

Without thinking it over; "Sure, just tell me when to move my things."

Liz can tell by Jane's smile, that it's going to be a good choice. It will be different having a roommate who's a friend, and a coworker. The roommate she has now is practically invisible, they never see each other. She works evenings at the pizza pub, and she never goes out at night.

Liz imagines waking up together in the morning, lumbering across the property to work. Jane is detail oriented but definitely not uptight. She's easy to talk to, and Liz likes the way she listens and gives feedback. Sometimes Liz can annoy Jane, but it must not be too much, if she wants Liz for a roommate. Based on her performance over the past week; she can contest that Jane's a good leader, and she's in need of guidance. She's only a few years older than Liz, but she's one of those old souls who takes in information and processes it so clearly.

Tragic

Thursday, August 1rst 2002

She's hungry all the time, and without Mama, she's constantly searching for the best ways to get food. Getting food is difficult some days, and she knows she's not doing a good job, because she feels so tired. She tries to feed herself, all the way into the early morning light. She walks very far, and has not found a territory in which to pick food from. Occasionally she finds herself acquiring food in other bear territories. She carefully tries to remember not to do this, and on several occasions she's been attacked. The wounds heal, but the hunger continues, and nothing seems to satisfy it. The aching, and desire to survive pushes her forward, on into the next range after drifting range. Roots are her main source these days, but yesterday she spent the entire afternoon trying to catch ground squirrels. An activity you aren't likely to catch an older grizzly involved with.

The sky is no longer dark, and light floods over the peaks and valleys, washing into her defiant spirit. She carries on. Nightfall has arrived and she's come to a peculiar river bed. It's completely flat, with a smooth, well-formed indentation. There is no water on this river, but the gravel and moisture are present. She follows the strange path for many hours, and it passes directly through several territories, but she sees no bear. She finds a few ptarmigan, they flutter about, and skip away before she can catch them. It takes so much energy and concentration to hunt these small creatures. She finds she has more satisfaction with bugs and roots.

Now up high on a bluff, after walking the odd river, she can look out and down, where she spots another bear. This bear is big and blonde, and she wants to pass undetected. One foot after the other, she slowly progresses, with nothing particular in mind. As night falls away, and the early morning earth exhales and releases its frozen tension, she tires. She stumbles off the river bed, and finds a soft patch of grass to curl up in. She closes her eyes, waiting for sleep to come. She will dream of Mama, and the den, and the long winter sleeps.

Tuesday, August 2nd, 2002

Something happened between Jane and Lauren, something Liz missed. They kind of went separate directions. Maybe Jane got tired of Lauren's mischievous sense of humor, or the fact that Lauren has been spending a lot of time with Tom, who works for the flight tour company. Its possible Jane is starting to feel like a third wheel. Whatever it is, it's hardly noticeable, and the two friends are still close, spending plenty of time together. Liz can see how it could grow old, passing an entire season with only a couple exclusive friends the entire time.

Speaking of new people, this evening she's heading to the Ptarmigan Inn to find Aaron, and she's bringing Celeste the new cocktail server at the pizza pub, as well as Denver. From what she understands, Aaron should be working at the bar tonight, and if he's not working; she's sure he'll be somewhere around Healy. Liz needs the girls with her for courage. It's only been a few days, but the wait's been agony.

As people begin to leave, the lodge introduces new people to fill in some of the gaps; Celeste definitely can fill in a gap, as well as a t-shirt. The food and beverage manager designed new uniforms for the two cocktail girls at the pizza place. Tight black jeans, and a tiny white shirt, that exposes their naval. Both the girls look amazing in the costume, but it's weird to see a work uniform so sexed-up on Tundra property. Celeste is from New York, exposing Liz to both personality and fashion style she can't find back home in California.

"Thanks so much for coming with me tonight, Celeste." Liz says, loaded with sincerity.

"No worries Liz, I'm looking forward to it." She answers. "I want to meet this hot guy of yours!"

"I hope that if I show up with some girls, I'll seem less needy, and not appear as desperate as I actually feel. I want to see Aaron so badly!"

"He likes you. Don't fret." Celeste leans against Liz's shoulder.

After work, she spends an hour getting ready. She showers, carefully applies her makeup, fixes her hair in two un-kept buns just below her ears. She puts on her best white lace push-up bra. She covers the bra up with a simple grey sweatshirt, slips on her favorite jeans that hang on her hips perfectly. Finally, she decides she's ready. She works hard to look like she didn't work at all on her appearance.

"Liz, what's up?" The girls call out to her from the lawn below.

"Two seconds!" She shouts. She takes a big breath, looking at herself in the mirror. There's so much pressure to get this right. She's not sure why she feels like she's trying to recruit him. He did invite her. He told her to find him.

"Hi Loves, I'm so nervous".

Denver gives her a hug and says, "You look really pretty, and he'd be a fool not to like you. Come on, you're the Mayor!"

When they reach Healy, its half past six. They make their way to the infamous Ptarmigan Inn.

Liz recalls Lauren's warning earlier that day at work, "It's a bad place, it's haunted."

With a brave face, she walks in, passing through the big double doors into a dim entry way. She can feel the obscure energy. The place is empty, around the turn of a corner the women proceed down a long hall to the bar. She's glad the bar is bright, and the sun shines in through the windows.

There he is, working behind the bar; just like he said he'd be. He's arranging a group of wine glasses. He looks up at Liz, and waves with a perfect smile. He isn't surprised to see her today. In fact, he's been waiting for her. Liz likes the way his attention goes to her first, and only after she exchanges a greeting; does he say hello to Denver and Celeste. This is a positive sign; he's warm, and happy to see her. Liz and her friends order drinks, and check out the bar.

"Aaron I heard the Ptarmigan is haunted."

Aaron confirms, "Once the window curtains that hang in the dining room opened slowly on their own." He continues, "The dishwashers saw a man in the dining room, when no one was there."

The girls are fascinated to sit in a haunted Alaskan motel.

"Well Liz, my shift is just about over." He pulls a twenty out of the bars till and hands it to Liz. "Why don't you and your friends go across the street for a drink while I close the cash register and change my work uniform. You know my roommate Joseph, who you met in Girdwood; he and I will come over and join you."

She bashfully agrees. Liz and her friends leave the enigma of a hotel, and cross the street over to the Trapper's Line. Denver and Celeste are great help, confirming his interest in Liz. Celeste is bubbly, "Liz, Oh my God! What a great guy, I know he likes you."

Denver adds, "You have nothing to worry about Liz".

She doesn't have to wait long for her Carolina backpackers to walk into the Trapper's Line. It's only eight, and their favorite bar has a different feel to it so early in the evening. When Aaron walks up, Denver and Celeste thank Aaron for the drinks, but ask, "Do you mind if we head back to Denali, we're tired?"

She gets a big bear hug from her friends. Liz feels a big heap of gratitude for them as she watches them skip out the slanted door of the bar.

"That sucks that your friends have to go so early." Aaron comments.

"They're really great aren't they?"

The two men and Liz sit at a table divulging in small talk. Discussing nothing in particular. The energy is starting to feel different. Aaron's friend who is so nice, with tan skin, dimples and gorgeous eyes tells her about his school back in North Carolina, how the two men met, and how they ended up at a place as random as the Ptarmigan Inn in Healy, Alaska. She listens with care; wanting to know everything, as much as she can. Within the hour, more people start flowing into the bar. He's fond of Aaron, and seems to be selling Liz on his friend.

Aaron brushes his hand across her hand, "We should go somewhere and talk Liz, let's go back to my room." His touch sends a charge through the nerve endings in her hand and up her arm. His room is exactly where she wants to go. She follows his lead out the doors of the bar, once again, back across the street. They walk up three flights of stairs until they reach his floor. Her heart beats fast, maybe from climbing all the stairs, or maybe because she's feeling so nervous to finally get to be alone with Aaron. Lauren's words resonate as she moves deeper into the labyrinth of stairwells and halls. The carpet and walls are dark reds and greens in color, and the long hall reaches on forever; looking like a vortex from a carnival fun house.

They arrive at his room. He unlocks the door. They enter and kiss. He moves an arm's length away from her. Something's wrong; she's not sure what it is.

Aaron takes a deep breath and says, "I have to tell you something."

Liz can see, something is going be problematic. She feels a slight hint of a headache, a throbbing behind her eyes.

He takes a step toward her. He's looking serious, firm, and right into her eyes. "I like you a lot, and what happened the other night was great, but I have a girlfriend, she lives with me in North Carolina. I love her, she's really cool and she's flying out here to stay with us next week."

There's nothing he can say to fix this, her dream is crushed. The turn of events sting. It feels like she's been punched in the stomach. He sees her disappointment, and she can see he's dealing with guilt, and genuinely feeling bad about hurting her. She nods her head in an understanding submission.

Then, she doesn't care. She doesn't care about him, or his girlfriend, or any of that. Right now, she cares about herself. In a rolling whimper, she replies, "I know you have a girlfriend, but right now I'm really disappointed and I want you to hold me for a while. Can you just hold me, this one last time, the way you did in Girdwood, and then I'll go, and won't come back."

She can tell by his expression, this is not what he wants to hear. It was probably difficult for him to assert his position. She tries to knock it back down.

He tries again, "But I want us to be friends, we can still hang out."

She won't let him see her cry, but she knows her eyes are revealing more than she can hide. "I don't think I can be your friend. I want to be more than your friend".

"I can't," He whispers. He reluctantly opens his arms, and she goes to him. They lie down on his little twin-sized employee bed.

She takes her sweatshirt off, and tries to look seductive for him in her lace bra. She whispers; "Don't you like me?"

"I do", he whispers. "But I can't do that to my girlfriend."

She lays her head back down on his chest; he strokes his hand up and down her back, lingering past the clasps of her bra every now and then. Not much time passes, when they get a knock on the door. It's his friend, probably prearranged in case she was a psycho and he needed a wingman. She supposes it's sort of true, because she really doesn't want to leave, but she has no business being there. At this point, she's not even sure she's welcome there.

Liz puts her sweatshirt back on and his friend enters the room.

Aaron backs into the wall, then says, "I'll be right back." He disappears out the door.

Awkward has just been elevated to a whole new level as she stands there in the room with Joseph, who's giving her the most awful, apathetic look. He's warm and friendly and she needs someone to share her heartache with, since he knows the story, she figures she can tell him how sad she is.

"Joseph, I guess you know. It sucks. I'm an idiot. I thought he liked me." She looks into his eyes for some sort of sign of redemption.

This is when she gets apology number two. Now, not only did she have to hear the super disappointing apology from her man, she gets to relive the experience with the friend. "He thinks you're really cool, and he does like you, but he feels really bad. He can't do that to his girlfriend".

There's really nothing to say. All she can do is leave these men in peace and accept her defeat. She's squinting hard, to keep the tears at bay. She turns and grabs the door handle, swinging it open, and scrambles out of the room without saying goodbye. So there she goes, one foot after the other, out into the creepy long hall, sad, rejected, and more alone than ever.

She finds a bathroom on his floor and she goes inside to hide and pee, and to wipe the tears away. She thinks, "Not just Aaron, but every time I try to get close to someone I just fail tragically. It's all been building up, and I had manipulated myself into believing this guy and I had some magical ridiculous romance. It was all in my head".

Now alone, so abstract, in this very sideways sort of hotel, feeling even more misplaced, and not belonging. The bathrooms have orange and red walls. The stall doors are yellow. Inside of the stalls are actual built-in ashtrays. She wipes a tear, *"What is this place?"*

She finds herself staring at the ashtray with wonder, tears washing over her hot cheeks, when all of the sudden the bathroom faintly fills with the smell of fresh cigarette smoke. No one else is in the bathroom. With that, she bolts out of room, down the hall, down the stairs, and straight out the front door. Lauren had told her that supposedly the Ptarmigan was the world's largest stackable trailer motel, and that it was creepy because it could move. She's certain it's haunted. She's grateful for Lauren's sharing, and her words carry Liz right out the door, momentarily distracting her from her wayward departure.

"Liz!" a voice calls out.

She turns, its Aaron. He's out front smoking a cigarette. He throws it down, steps on it, and gives her a confusing, wanting look. She reluctantly walks over to him.

"Are you leaving?"

"I have to catch the shuttle back to Denali."

"I'm sorry Liz." He offers. Shaking his head, pardoning her, the way a doctor looks at a terminal patient.

She hates the way he looks at her when he says it, like he was really sorry for her.

She shakes her head in resentment, trying to smile. She takes a breath and tells him cheerfully, "I'm okay."

Truthfully she feels sick. The emotion is poison; she can feel it in her head and gut. The butterflies in her stomach that she had earlier are now dead. She considers taking a chance to give him another hug goodbye, but opts not too. Instead, she steps back, turning around to go across the street.

At least she got to experience the haunted hotel, it's a fair consolation, she decides. Liz catches the ten o'clock shuttle back to Denali. When she reaches her room, she washes her face, before putting her head on her pillow to cry. She cries half the night; silent breathless sobs, wallowing in hot regretful tears. She doesn't want to get out of bed in the morning. A headache pulses, and she prays it won't fester into a migraine. It's not just him, it's all of it together, the whole season. So much rejection and disappointment. Loneliness. Working so hard, trying to put her heart out there, only to be hurt. She's worn out. Work has been long and constant, parties take the best of her and give nothing in return. She's worked so hard at being the lone adventurer, going out with one group one night, and then another the next, moving about, not committing anywhere, as to fool people into thinking she's confident and interesting.

She takes her journal, she needs to get her thoughts out of her head and onto the paper, "*The truth is that the breakfast-lunch crew was right about me in the beginning; I fall short, and am not quite good enough. How could anyone like me? I really don't like myself? Why did I have to take my sweatshirt off, why am I always so desperately pursuing things that aren't intended for me? Once again, I'm alone sharing an evening with my good friend's "shame", and "humiliation". I am of bad character, and there's nothing to do about that; other than change myself.*

So, tomorrow is a new day and I won't try so hard to force things to happen. I'm going to spend more time with the mild and mannered, and more time in the park. I have to remember what actually called me here. If I look within the park, I know I can find what I need. Even if I just take the time to sit there, watching and listening, and feeling the way the seasons pass. Perhaps this activity, these desperate wishes are simply a season within me, and it is now passing. I can transcend into an autumn of absolution. Just be in this place and stop trying to make things happen. I've had enough of the bars, the liquor, and the heartache. I'm ready to treat myself with more respect".

She closes the journal, and decides with this action, she will close her heart to romance.

Saturday, August 3rd 2002

In the morning, at work Lauren and the others innocently ask, "How was your big date with Aaron?"

Then they see the way her face scrunches up, her eyes drop to the floor. All of her coworkers; it seems, were hoping she had met someone too. They're sad for Liz. These coworkers really do care about her, more than she had credited them for.

Gabe pulls her in for a hug. "Don't worry Liz, he doesn't deserve you."

She imagines her role in the crew is similar to the goofy, stubborn kid sister. Everyone's protective of her feelings, and knows just how to bring her out of her depression. Lauren tells her the latest gossip of who's sleeping with who. Marvin brings her ice cream with Irish cream drizzled on top, and Gabe sings her some "Proper Storage".

Jane is the best, because she has direction for Liz. Her instructions are: "Pack your things tonight, and after work tomorrow, I will help you move into my room."

With that, her lonely nights are officially in the past.

Wednesday, August 8th 2002

The next page in her journal reads, "*My evenings are filled with a newfound companion, someone who really understands, who lives the life right beside me. I work, she works, I eat, she eats, I sleep, and she sleeps, and so on*".

Living with Jane is grand. Liz was a little wounded, stray dog. Jane picked her up, took her home, and is now nursing her back to health. They laugh about everything. If their feet hurt, they hurt together, and they laugh all the time, because it's so utterly hopeless. They laugh about Fat City and traveling. Jane tells her about some of the other national parks she's worked in. She shows her which shoes are best for working in restaurants, and she tells her about the hundred dollar tooth brush she plans to buy with her tips. Jane is more fascinating than Liz had imagined.

A little guidance was in order, and Liz is happy to have an ally, in this harsh Alaskan existence. She now avoids the bars, and has opposite days off from Jane.

During this time; Liz goes to the park. As tired as her feet are, and as sore as her back feels from raising and lifting the giant trays piled with heavy china up and over her tiny frame, she still gets off work and spends her late afternoons in the park.

With a time constraint she has limited choices of trails she can fit in after her double shift. She hikes them all at least twice. There's the trail to Horse Shoe Lake that meanders down through the dense taiga. There's the trail to the lodge that connects to the visitor center; which twists and turns, and she never sees another soul, no matter how often she frequents it. There's the Savage River trail, and a few mountain trails which ascend up, revealing a landscape that gives a bird's-eye view; full of tree tops and more twists and passages of the Nenana River and the Teklanika. Mt. Healy is a favorite, Liz refers to this trail as the Alaskan stair master.

She loves the hidden trail that goes from the visitor center to the Tundra Lodge, it holds so many intricate features. It takes her an hour and a half, of what should only take half an hour because she has to stop and look so many times. If she finds an aspen grove that quakes for her, she's compelled to stop and listen to it. Listening, until she understands what it means. Sometimes it's a mushroom or spore that has her crouched down, close to the tapestry of foliage covering the ground. Once she balanced her camera on a rock, setting the auto timer, to snap a self-portrait of herself standing on her trail. She wants to capture her quiet, independent adventures. They're hers alone. She could hike with someone, but she needs to hike with no one. Among the trees there is total acceptance. So gentle and strong.

The dirt is full of tiny leaves, and little pieces of bark, layers of earth that bury deep secrets, which will remain, until someone comes digging them up.

She loves to attend the visitor center presentations, and often will walk through the sled dog kennels, listening to the rangers tell stories of how the dogs work in the arctic winter climate of Denali. With less drinking, and more hiking, she's feeling stronger, and her clothes are looking really good on her reconciled body.

Change

Monday, August 13th 2002

Claire the Tolkat manager calls a meeting. The entire crew gathers together, eager

to learn what Claire has to offer them. Liz sits down at the long table with a big

halibut sandwich, Lauren gives Liz, her signature mischievous look and proclaims,

"This is a sandwich worthy of the Mayor."

Liz gives her a wink and bites into the fish.

Claire begins, "The meeting will address two things. The first is that it's Gabe,

Kendall, and Adam's last days. The second matter is, I want to know if our current

staff is willing to work six days a week instead of five. If you would like to work six

days for the extra income and overtime, I can arrange that. If not, I'll be hiring two

new servers." Claire casts a heavy look over her hard working breakfast lunch crew.

"No, to Gabe leaving. Yes, to six days a week." Liz replies.

Now that it's August, and Liz isn't out all night, she would love to spend more

time making money. A sixth day will add a nice bonus to her already impressive

savings. The more time she spends alone in the park, hiking and finding solitude, the

more she's reminded of going back home, and when she thinks of going back home,

she gets nervous because she lacks a formal plan. The concept of earning more

money means more opportunities, so this is where she decides to focus. More

money means less anxiety about going home. Jane is as empowered to make money

too, and it's nice to share a goal with someone. Of course, five days a week has

proved to push everyone to their working limits. Getting up at four in the morning and finishing sometime close to three, has them working over a ten hour day, multiplied by six days a week, will require a solid commitment.

Saying goodbye to Gabe is anticlimactic.

She gives him a quick hug, whispering in his ear "I'll be lost without you, do you have to go?" She pushes him away and throws up a Proper Storage hand sign. She goes to give Kendall and their busser a quick hug, and the three walk out the doors of the Tolkat for the last time, not knowing if and when they will ever return.

Just before the doors to the restaurant shut, Gabe turns around and yells, "You're the best Liz, Kendall and I are going to come visit you in California."

She shouts back. "Tahoe!"

These are the first goodbyes Liz has to settle, and she can't deny that it hurt. The experience of letting go of someone or something, reminds her of how impermanent and temporary her own life in Denali is.

That afternoon at the visitor center, she reads the park bulletin board. A flyer catches her eye. It's a help wanted sign; to work in the visitor center bookstore. Now that college is starting for many, they're shorthanded. She takes the flyer home with her, and presents it to Jane.

"What do you think? Many of the international kids are working two jobs, so we know it's possible." Liz tells her, shifting back and forth with excitement; like a little kid who has to pee.

"Should we get a second job?"

"I'm not sure Liz, but I'll think about it."

"Well my Jane, I love it there and I'm going to do it!"

Wednesday, August 15th 2002

Liz can't talk Jane into working the second job, but she does convince Kyle, one of her under age RISK playing buddies.

They both dress nice after work, grab the park shuttle down to the visitor center, and walk up to the counter. "Hi, we're interested in applying for the help-wanted positions."

A woman extends her hand. "My name is Brandy and I'm the manager of the bookstore. If you have experience working a cash register, I can hire you both right now."

At the counter, Liz gives Brandy a summary of her background. Kyle does the same.

"I want to tell you a little more about the bookstore, and myself. I'm a year round resident in Healy. Do you know Healy?"

Liz nods.

"The bookstore is part of non-profit that focuses on natural history of Alaska. You will find anything that has to do with Denali and Alaska, here. We can pay ten dollars an hour, and you can make your schedule work with your first job."

Liz is thrilled to meet a woman who's a year-round resident in the interior of Alaska.

"Follow me."

She takes Liz and Kyle outside of the visitor center to a trailer sitting in the parking lot .Inside of the trailer she disappears into a sectioned off room, reappearing with something in her hands. "Here are your uniforms, and if it's okay with you . . . I'll put you down on the schedule to work now." She hands them both a hiring packet, "Take these with you and bring them back complete tomorrow with your identification".

"Want to work a little this afternoon, get to know our materials? It's important you're familiar, so you can educate the public."

Liz opts to work there four days a week, immediately following first job.

In the trailer she assigns them their first duties. "Liz you can take these prints out of the boxes, roll them in a tube, and secure them with a rubber band."

Then she turns to Kyle, while scanning the trailer and tapping her head. "Kyle I am going to have you price our new book shipment."

As they dive into their humdrum tasks, she gives both Tundra Lodge converts a pleased look, before she exits the trailer. This is odd, Liz is stunned to walk in, ask to work, and within the hour: she's working. What an ideal second job. She's peacefully pulling out poster prints from flat boxes, rolling them up and wrapping rubber bands around them. Every time she pulls a poster, she steals a few seconds to admire the image. All the posters contain images of the park.

On her second day she gets familiar with the walls of books, which all meet one of two criteria; they must be about Denali or Alaska.

She catches the final shuttle back to her property from the visitor center. Her feet feel heavy, and all she can think of is her bed. She crash lands into the covers, stripping her shirt, and socks off from under her blanket.

"Hi Jane, she calls, muffled in her pillow.

"Liz. You might rethink the second job. I admire that you want to work, but that's a long day. Look at you!"

"Jane, I love it. It's so different than the restaurant. It's a lot less money, but I just like being in the park. I've already learned so much about Alaska and Denali. I'll be okay. Two more shifts, then I'll have some nights off."

Jane kicks her own feet onto her bed, preparing to flick off the side table light, "And, you're closing?"

Liz turns, raising her head out of her pillow, "Yeah, they needed a closer. It's so surreal. I'm going to be the last person in the center most nights! Our deposit box is up in this little room above the theatre. That's where I balance the drawer."

"And you catch the shuttle?"

"I was the only one tonight."

"Where's Kyle?"

"So, we're splitting the job. He closes the nights opposite of me."

"We'll talk more in the morning." Jane grumbles, "Second job."

Thursday, August 23rd 2002

First job, first breakfast, second job, second breakfast, everything is in excess, and Liz's cup hath over filled. Jane proves to be her saving grace; picking up her slack. "Jane, you washed my uniform? And, my bed is made!"

"Both uniforms, there's your pressed and folded bookstore shirt on the table"

Liz jumps on her bed, where Jane has a tray waiting, filled with various choices from the cafeteria's employee dinner. "That's the kindest thing. How do I even say thank you?" She scoops a bit of pasta salad into her mouth.

Jane watches Liz eat for a moment, contemplating their new routines. "

"Liz you look so tired, how about I go downstairs and bring us both up some tea?"

Liz nods in compliance with Jane's suggestion. "I'll take tea."

Jane leaves, reappearing on point, with the timing of a seasoned server. She chose a simple Lipton tea, she added cream to both cups. The curls of steam tickle Liz's chin. She puts her face into her cup to take in more smell and steam before taking a sip.

Jane waits for Liz to take a drink before she shares her thoughts, "Liz you look terrible, it's no secret that you're burnt out." She half laughs, half warns.

"I know, it's hard to explain. I just need to try this. Try something different. Working is a comfort right now. It's steady and reliable. It distracts me from other things."

By her third sip, she confides in Jane, I haven't thought about Aaron at all, or anyone else in that way. That dream died, and it was silly anyways. I'm now a Denali Realist. First job, second job, first lunch, second lunch."

Jane laughs at the wit, but her expression drops quickly. "Sure, second lunch, but then you miss dinner. Liz, you know how when people are depressed, they can be persuaded to harm themselves?" Jane sets down her tea.

Liz takes two more bites of pasta salad. "I do."

"So, I know you're feeling sad about that guy. I know it was sad seeing John and Kendall leave. Working, and missing dinner and things, is it like that? Is working all the time your way of coping?"

Liz moves the tray off of her bed and sets it on the night stand to drop-off in the morning. She tips her cup, and drains the last of her tea before setting it on the tray. "It's related, but not exactly that. The work is about me, not him. I really like working in the visitor center. I like the responsibility of closing. Being there at night, the only one. It feels special and so different from everything on property."

Jane smiles. "Okay."

"Sleep?"

Liz reaches across the wall and flicks out the light.

Friday, August 24th 2002

The crushing and pressing of ice; breaking and pushing wakes her from a light slumber. Unmeasured walking and hunting has brought her to a deeper place, more connected with something that channels her instincts. She knows this place, and why it is, but not because she's been here before, or because Mama has taught it to her. This is something else. Her primal vision is undeniably familiar. This place, it means something to her tribe of lonesome travelers. She arrived last night, and lay down beside a cold, hard, frozen river. As she stares into the cool prisms of blues and whites, and the clear parts which fracture the light, she notices something deeper. It is a light from within the ice. It's beautiful; so she stays. Another day, and another night, and she's only had flowers to sustain her. She moves on, away from the thundering, calving and shifting, of the powerful force.

She makes her way past a wolf den and several of them gather outside, forming a militant and sophisticated line. They watch her, seeming casual, but ready to attack at the slightest inclination. She walks on, head down, stopping every now and then to dig for bugs and roots and to smell the wolves.

This night, with the sun still so high in the sky, they sing. Howling haunting stories that cry out with melancholy and hunger.

She lifts her head, tilting it to the side, adjusting her ear; so it picks up the song. She believes she is part of what they sing of tonight.

She can hear her name in the song. Bears do not know wolf language, but when one's name is being spoken, it is common for one to notice, regardless if they can interpret the rest of the dialogue or not.

As she hears her name, she moves forward, deciding to hunt and find meat. It's time to try harder, and to salvage the rest of the summer, so she can feel better, so she can sleep this winter. Survive, eat, fight, don't die, these are the rules of this existence. She has no choice, but to continue.

Sunday, August 25th 2002

Her days off are very aloof, her approach indifferent. She's become reclusive with them, and usually purchases a ticket to take a bus deep into the park for exploring. Grabbing a bit of food, a hot coffee from the cart in the visitor center lobby, she puts on her headphones, focusing on the lyrics of Ani Difranco who never fails to sing her into perspective. She grabs a window seat. The empty seat next to her to holds her backpack, camera, discman, and lunch.

Today, she's brought her journa ,"I want animals, lots of pictures of animals. Sheep, caribou, moose, wolves, fox, ptarmigan, swan, otter, and beaver, and of course the main attraction other than the mountain, the grizzly bear".

Within the boundaries of the park, at any time, one can get off at a stop to remain wherever they please, at the discretion of the wildlife, for however long they want. Liz considers when and how she plans to catch her ride out, now that she's settled on a destination near the Eileson Center. With only one road, all the busses head back to the visitor center eventually.

Thanks to many hours spent working in the visitor center Liz has a specific criteria for what she's looking for, where to look for it, and its significance.

She writes, *"This place, the land is ancient and pure; it's like a strong concentrated tonic for the soul. If you take too much; it can infect you, and if you don't take enough, you have missed it completely and your efforts were in vein.*

You won't find it on a tour bus. It is critical one gets off the bus and walks away from the road and into the bush. Follow braided rivers; watch the gold sparkles in the ripples play tag with the sun. Find the glacial erratics, then look backwards trying to imagine their journey as they traveled down with ice and mass that have been gone for centuries. Peer into the earth, and see the way the valleys have been pulled and stretched, and breaks in the crust where they have been pushed upward to praise its maker. See the way the tundra contrasts the long expressive clouds above. Give yourself to this place, let it accept you, and take you in. Become part of the landscape here. The strange dance between life and death, as animals kill other animals, kill plants, as weather kills animals, and kills plants, as everything lives, and struggles, and survives, and dies.

The word wild cannot be fully understood until one looks out and sees the wolf pack venturing out from the den, running and hunting, fighting, and living for life. The mountain herself lifting and settling, laying ground for the rest of her range, mother to the rivers that flow from her glaciers, she is majesty, and all beings in this place love her and fear her".

Polychrome is an area that is named after its colors. The minerals and flora and fauna in this specific area are the most expressive and colorful visions Liz has ever observed. Coppers and purples, reds and gold's, browns, and blacks streak across the earth, violently, sweeping up and over, a kaleidoscope of dirt and rock that challenges even the most jaded of hearts to not fall under her spell. Every point along this road will invite new thoughts, vistas, and prayers.

"First I see Denali with my eyes, and then after a while I can see Denali with my heart. This land is a ghost, a soul transformed into a being. Everything here is connected, like some singular organism that functions through tiny parts, vital and distressed. That's what makes it beautiful here, because it is distressed. The extreme temperatures, the inability to sustain, and yet those who are here, live

anyway. My favorite animal in the park is the grizzly, iconic, graceful, and with eyes that seem to know, and what they know is sad."

Life within the park is serene and the perfect place to disconnect from her world. When she comes here, she' not concerned with her own issues and experiences. Instead, she's filled with curiosity and intrigue. Every time she goes into the park, it holds something new for her. She's attracted to it so much, because she's afraid of it. Denali is big and dangerous, and there are infinite ways a person can die in the park.

Monday, August 27th 2002

Everything finally seems to drift in a calm sea of routine, and each day she's stepping into this place; directed with purpose, and more busy than should be physically possible.

Jane worries about Liz, and she's one of the few people who know how demanding first job can be. She watches Liz with interest in between her comings and goings. Now that the midnight sun is receding back to its rightful position in the sky, darkness pushes its way into their world. The dark brings new emotions and sensations. With the darkness comes cold. It's brisk, just slightly, but with her fatigue from work, she's been sensitive to temperatures. For those sparse hours of darkness; the whole place seems to retreat, finding the sleep they've been chasing since June. Maybe, she has managed to escape her depression and loneliness during the day with her busy schedule, but at night, it has a way of finding her.

The dreams are always reminding her that before this summer ends, she needs to make it count. Vivid dreams that drift through her subconscious. She wants her meaningful revelation during this journey. She wants what she's come for, and she believes she's come for reinvention. She came here; so that she doesn't have to go back to the person she was running away from. Like the ice, snow and water that carve new terrain in the pliable frozen earth, Liz wants the stress and transformation, to be moved, so that she may realize a new version of herself.

If the land in the park were always preserved, and stayed the same, if there were no sources of ice and water, and tectonic activity to move it, peeling off layers, to pull and push on it, it would grow sick, toxic, and wouldn't be able to sustain life, it would die. It's the new valley's, and kettle ponds that feed into the tundra, growing shrubs to feed bears, opening up burrows for rabbits who get eaten by fox, who are food for the wolves. It moves away old trees, and opens up the land for the small blueberry bushes, and wild flowers, it allows the willow to branch up and dig strong root systems, where the moose hide.

In the morning, she must look as tired as she feels. Jane confronts her, "It's okay if you want to quit second job."

"This morning Jane, I am going to seriously consider it. I like the visitor center, and it keeps me out of trouble. I've learned so much. All of the quiet evenings in the bookstore. I've browsed through practically every book. I've been learning the names of plant species".

"You're such a nerd! You know I'm jealous."

Jane pauses, looking down at Liz's feet. Liz tries to tuck them under her bed, but I's too awkward and obvious so she shrugs her shoulders, smiles and looks away as her roommate examines what has become hard to ignore. She suspects there's nerve damage from the long serving shifts. The bottom of her feet are white with little red dots where all the blood vessels have broken from repetitive pressure. Liz tucks a leg under her, bringing up her foot to rub. When she tries to rub her left foot she feels it ache. It's squishy and full of fluid. Her ankles aren't much happier.

"It's weird to think about it." Liz mumbles, entranced with the nursing of her feet.

"What?" Jane raises an eyebrow. She's grown to enjoy her roommate's philosophical stupors.

"The tips. How we take them."

Jane leans back, "Yeah."

"It was hard at first. For me. To hold out my hand and take the cash. It's a little awkward. I felt bad it was too generous and they look like it's more than they can afford. I feel bad when it's not enough, and I went the extra mile for them."

"Those assholes."

"No, but, it's not like that anymore. I'm okay with holding out my hand and taking the money from them. It's humble. You know?"

Jane nods.

It's the humility, like the song amazing grace. It's gracious to be accepting."

"That's why we're here."

"You think?"

Jane claps her hands. The lights go out.

"Jane! Oh my God, you bought us a clapper!"

"Just arrived today."

First laughter, then sleep. A goodnight.

Saturday, September 1rst 2002

Liz has the afternoon free, time for Chai Lattes. No, not on property. Across the street at the Blue Bear Coffee Shop. Jane opens the screen door, and the hinges make a wonderful rustic squeal. "Thank you." Liz steps in and to the side to wait for her friend. Denver, Rebecca and Celeste synchronize a way. "It's about time. Late much?" Celeste continues, "I'm ready to order my second scone, but felt it was only right to wait for the Mayor."

Liz nods to Celeste, but her eyes have settled on something else. "Look at the sign Jane!"

Jane looks at the hand written paper, taped to the cash register. It reads: "Fresh baked blueberry scones and muffins now available, also trading coffee and food for fresh picked blueberries".

"Oh jeez, Liz, don't tell me you're going to be a blueberry picker for your third job?"

The girls laugh, imagining their new enterprise; canvasing the backcountry for berries.

"Coffee shop currency. No doubt. I'll start skipping the shuttle and walk my trail, I'll pick as I commute."

After they've each pulled up a chair, and hold a cup, Rebecca catches them up on the village gossip, which includes her main news. "A couple of people around town have come down with Mono".

"Yikes," Jane exclaims. "Who?"

"So far, no one on our property." Rebecca explains, but she drops a name that surprises Liz.

"Do you know Ryan who works at the Teklanika Cabins?"

"I know Ryan, he has mono?" Liz recalls the lovely walk back to her room all those weeks ago. Her eyes refocus, anticipating clarification. But, Rebecca surprises her even more: "No not Ryan, his girlfriend who works at the convenience store has mono."

"His girlfriend?" Liz asks? She smiles for them, "He walked me home once or twice. Do you think he had a girlfriend then?"

She sets her chai on the table, "Wait, don't answer that. I'm willing to bet he did. That's my luck with the Denali dating scene. Nothing happened between us. At least there's that."

Rebecca slides a little closer. "I don't know how long he's been dating her."

Liz is incredibly pleased to be at the Blue Bear, sitting on the couches, squeezing her mug of chai, with the women who've kept her from falling off the edge. The gossip feels catty, but it's vital, and really can help one another from making big mistakes.

Jane stands up first, collecting all five empty mugs to take to the bus bin. "Okay, Fat City night at the Crow's Landing!"

"Is it okay if we go back to room so I can change and fix my hair? We can grab your red polar fleece". She turns to the others, "Meet you up there?"

Fresh makeup, a comb through the hair, and warm layers send Jane and Liz back out to collect Lauren and Tom. The four friends head up the steep bank to the road. They hike all the way to the Crow's Landing. A large group of from the property have already ordered pitchers and pizza. Laughs and hugs, are spread through the room. Fat City is there. The room is warm, everyone is smiling, and collectively there is a love spread about, it's the breakfast lunch crew and their friends.

Denver, Rebecca, and Paul announce they're heading to Healy to continue the good night. Rebecca turns to Jane, "You and Liz need to come with us, it's a good group, and a really great band is supposed to be playing tonight."

Filled with the spirit of friendship and bonding, Liz answers, "Yes, to going to the Trapper's Line!", even though she has to work both her jobs; beginning bright and early tomorrow.

Jane opposes, "Sorry Liz. Sorry girls. I'm going to have to decline tonight. I'm already tired and we have to be at work so early."

And so Jane and Liz continue on, in separate directions.

Jane calls to her, "Have fun tonight Liz! You deserve it."

The Trapper's Line always seems to have the best fun, tangled with the worst trouble. With all the work, she missed having fun, and tonight she intends to enjoy herself. As her group walks into the bar, it's more crowded than usual, dark, and smoky. Bodies are moving about, and the band on stage has a familiar friend playing the bass. It's Josh the regular shuttle driver, who still has the most obvious crush on Rebecca. He's on the tall side, and Rebecca is extra short. She's so small and adorable, and has the longest beachy brown hair, which she tucks under a crocheted cap. Someone else who works at the Trapper's Line also has a crush on Rebecca: Molly, the only female bartender who works at the Trapper's Line. She's been flirting with Rebecca a lot lately. This has been beneficial to Denver and Liz, because Molly usually treats Rebecca and anyone who's with Rebecca to a round of drinks. Rebecca is great at flirting and flattering Molly, but she's decided that things are looking serious with Josh. Denver and Liz are thrilled for Rebecca to finally take the slow moving courtship to the next level.

Then she sees them, over against the wall; sitting at a table. She almost turns around, and walks out the door. She doesn't want to see him. He notices her and gets up; he's walking over. It's Aaron, he looks so cute, and she hates that seeing him can still make her whole body feel weak.

"Liz." He smiles at her.

"Hi," struck without a plan, her instinct smiles back.

"How are you?" When he says this, he gives her a depressing, apologetic look.

The look annoys her. She doesn't want him feeling sorry for her. "I'm doing great, just here with my friends."

"I haven't seen you around at all. I've been hoping to run into you. I'm really glad you're here." Followed by more unfortunate body language.

She tries to look over his shoulder as she replies. "Yep, I've been working a lot, and spending time with my friends at the Tundra Lodge."

He steps forward, and his closeness reminds Liz that her desire for him hasn't faded at all, despite all the distractions and efforts to overwhelm herself in Denali. She can't help but wonder, "What is he doing?"

"I want to introduce you to my girlfriend." And with that, she follows him foolishly over to the table. Failing to find an opportunity to think her choice through.

His friend Joseph and his girlfriend stand up to give Liz warm, welcoming smiles, "Sit down." They say.

She sits, like a dog following commands. Liz is now in full panic mode, and she's disturbed that this girlfriend is even more gorgeous close up, than from across the room. Sitting next to her makes Liz feel like a toad. Two attractive guys, a beautiful Southern belle, and Liz- the toad woman.

"It's really good to meet you Liz, everyone is so nice around Denali." She extends warm conversation her way. "I'm still getting used to the climate, it's a shock having transitioned from a Carolina summer!"

Liz looks over at Aaron, he's grinning at her. It's making her skin tingle in an uncomfortable way. Her breathing gets shallow. She has to get away from this, it's too much. Why would he bring her to the table, to his girlfriend? Liz offers each person a fake smile, and excuses herself; pointing to Rebecca, Denver, and Paul. She's apologizing, but explaining, "I promised to spend time with them tonight."

She desperately makes a beeline for her own people, and works very hard to not look back at the table of beautiful ones, where she obviously does not belong. Denver and Rebecca leave the issue of seeing Aaron alone, as good friends do, and takes Liz's hand to move on, to take back their night together. This comradery turns out to be good medicine, and almost takes the sadness away.

Denver squeezes Liz's hand. ":Hey Mayor, you need more beer. Love you. We all do." Liz nods.

The women stand up and dance to Josh's jam band funk. There are new faces here tonight, and one of them grabs her hand, and starts to swing and twirl Liz around the dance floor.

He takes her hand and doesn't let go of it. They're doing fast dancing, slow dancing, and sexy grinding dancing. She's not questioning why he chose her for a dance partner, but she believes he's her gift from the universe, because she needs to dance. She hopes Aaron is watching her, so he can take that "sorry-for-her" look he gave her, and realize she's doing just fine, and she may not be a hot Southern belle, but she's still attractive, and she's dancing.

Eventually their dancing becomes quite affectionate. He's very grabby, and in control, and the nameless guy now has his arm around her waist. He instructs Liz to go outside with him.

"Sure, why not." She replies. Using him. She knows she's using him, all to prove a point to Aaron. She wonders if he saw her sadness from behind the beer glass. She wonders if he knew she needed someone to use. He's making such a show of their affection. They've become a hot item at the bar tonight, arm and arm, looking like an intriguing couple.

She spots a familiar friend, its Leah from the Moose Inn. She's tall and modelish, but with a sweet and fragile personality.

She runs to Liz, and gives her a big hug. "Liz, I haven't seen you in a whole month!" She gives Liz her news. "Owen, left me. I don't know what to do. I'm ready to go home, Liz."

Liz opens her arms wide to give her another hug, happy to be released from her friendly red-haired date with the goatee. "Leah, (she says with bitterness) you'll have much more fun without that loser."

She sadly whispers in her ear. "I know Liz, but my heart is broken."

The words touch her, and she looks into her friends eyes, recognizing the pain. Her own heart has had its share of broken feelings this summer. Leah is so beautiful, but lacks the most basic level of self-esteem. The two women pause in this exchange, the music and drink are far away now. They are caught in one another's eyes. She sees Liz. Liz can see her too. The weight of heartbreak, loneliness, and loss. Depression. She shivers, before returning to the place they happen to be in.

Following her improvisational date and Leah, they turn and enter a hall into the motel. Soon, Liz is lingering outside of a room, a room they are now, all three entering. There's a group of people from another property. Liz leans against the wall, declining a bong hit. Soon the whole group, Liz accompanying Leah, while her dance partner follows behind, head back to the bar.

His name is Ken and he's really nice, and he's given Liz his full attention since the moment he grabbed her hand to dance. It's nice to be the one being picked up for a change, and she's enjoying his efforts to get to know her. He lives on the other side of Denali, opposite of Healy. Towards Talkeetna.

"I came out to Alaska while traveling across the country with a theatre group." He begins. "This is my second year in Alaska, I have no plans to leave, I love it here, Liz. Right now, my interests are learning to tight rope walk, and fire dance."

She grins, realizing she's in the midst of an artist. A free spirit. Resisting urges to sleep, Liz likes that he's doing most of the talking. She needs this tonight. She feels so grateful for this fun and colorful guy who walks up and grabs her, pulling her out of herself for a few hours. Unfortunately, she's not in a romantic mood, and came out tonight to find a buzz, not a boyfriend. Even though he has great sideburns and deep brown eyes that seem so content to just look at her.

Before the night ends, one last twist in her evening occurs. Sitting at a table with the girls and Ken, her eyes fixate on something beside the bar. It's Molly, the bartender. Her yellow hair and tight white tank top all wrapped up in some guys arms. A tall hippie guy with dreadlocks.

She sits there watching her for a second, and then she feels compelled to walk over to them. She's not sure how drunk must she must be to rationalize this action, but, here she is; standing before them both. Liz taps Molly on the shoulder. Molly turns, looking over and giving Liz a hot lesbian smile.

Then the hippie and the bartender realize Liz is frowning at them. They look at one another then back at Liz. "I thought you liked girls! Why are you kissing him?" Liz is starting to wonder when her buzz evolved into belligerence.

Molly just stares at her, sort of confused, trying to understand what Liz is communicating to her. She moves in a little closer, tucking her hair behind her ear and trying to understand.

Liz wants to make her understand. So she tries again, "Why are you kissing him?" She points and rolls her eyes at him.

Molly and the hippie just stand there, confused. Liz has to make herself clearer. "You should be kissing me."

Molly understands this, and steps forward to put her arms around Liz. She leans in to collect the kiss that Liz is suggesting. Every person standing at the bar is now surprised to be watching their favored bartender grope and kiss one of the seasonal girls. The kiss lasts long enough for everyone to get a good show, and then Liz lets go. Molly lets go. Liz discovers all words have abandoned her. She looks at Molly. She looks at the hippie. She looks at the crowd at the bar. The crowd is looking back.

She turns to Molly and drops her hold of her, she announces with satisfaction, "That's better." Before turning to go back to her table with her friends, who are now laughing hysterically at her.

From this point on, she tries her best to keep a very low profile. She sneaks away, to hide outside. She can't concentrate enough to continue her evening with Ken (who doesn't mention the random kiss at the bar). Liz and her dance partner end their night with an exchange of hugs, and even a kiss or two. She especially likes the way he pets her hair.

When Liz stumbles into her room, doing her best to not disturb Jane, she goes to her tote bag instead of her bed. She rummages until she finds her journal and a lemon Luna Bar. It takes her another minute to locate her pen. She gives her hands a muffled clap. The lights flick on. She giggles. She writes, *"I have to say; it was another smashing good time in Healy, and if I can't find at least one way to embarrass myself in an evening, then I probably didn't go out"*.

She claps her hands.

Monday, September 2nd 2002

She has less than an hour and a half to sleep before work starts, and somehow she's waiting tables. It's simply a matter of forcing her eyes to stay open, and her legs to hold her upright. Just hoping the assholes don't ask any complicated questions. Sometimes they want to know trivia about the park, like how tall Mt. McKinley is, or what the name of the river out the window is. Before, the servers would accommodate these requests with simple flat answers. After some time, the breakfast lunch crew learned that the guests are searching for tour guide answers. Elaborate stories, with privileged information that they can take back home with them, to bring up at dinner parties. So Jane made up some stories to tell them. Stories that are lies that give the servers a cheap thrill. Jane has a great one that she likes to tell her customers. When they ask how tall Denali is, she gives them a great explanation.

"Well," she begins . . . "You used to be able to see the mountain but it is actually shrinking because of global warming."

It's fun to watch them listen to her, without the slightest clue that it's false. She lays it out for them in detail. "Scientists have recorded that it shrinks six centimeters a year."

Liz is so tired it hurts, but she's immensely glad she went out last night. The interesting events that play out in her mind seem really harmless and kind of funny in the light of day. The dirty dancing with the hippie, the angry lesbian kiss, and meeting the actual girlfriend of Aaron, who of course looks even better than she'd imagined. She's okay with it all, because she really doesn't have to go back to the Trapper's Line. She's not worried about what the people there might think of her behavior. With only weeks left, she can just hide at work, blending in, with all the other workers in their black and whites.

Bitter and Sweet

Tuesday, September 3rd 2002

It's the weekend, and Jane is borrowing their host's car again. "Thanks Merhabda, you're the best." She takes his keys, while they stand in the reception area at the Tolkat.

While walking back to the server domain; Liz turns to Jane "What time are we leaving tomorrow?"

It's their one day off. Jane looks up, as if to query the imaginary clock in her mind. "How about ten, then we can get to Anderson around lunch time." In true Fat City spirit, the itinerary will be designed around eating.

She's anxious with anticipation for another epic, Jane organized, adventure. She's even managed to include time for them all to sleep-in. Rest, music, and yummy festival food, and most importantly good company, leaves Liz eagerly awaiting tomorrow.

Wednesday, September 4th 2002

Anderson is sunny, open, and adorned in thickets of willow. The fresh air is putting some skip back into their step. The festival is perfect, with a full parking lot, but not too crowded. The group finds an open picnic table towards the back of the crowd. They chose a spot quite a ways away from the stage and dancing hippies, and closer to the food. Today is more of a Fat City day, than a party day.

This is exactly what Liz wants after the other night in Healy. She has a strong desire to use her day off toning things down, keeping a low profile. After the wild night at the Trapper's Line this week; news spread all over town. Lauren had approached Liz with her "I know something about you smile". She begins by giving Liz a chance to tell her side of the story.

"What happened with you and Molly at the bar the other night?"

"I'm not sure who your sources are, but I'm impressed. You hear everything. Hmm, there's not much to tell. I saw her kissing a guy, and I really liked thinking of her as this cool lesbian bartender. You know, she'd buy our drinks from time to time. I got kind of territorial about her when I saw some guy making out with her. It was some lame hippie guy with dread locks. I don't know. I wanted to intervene." It feels good to explain herself to Lauren. After she purges the long breathed explanation, Lauren laughs hysterically.

She looks at Liz with a grin and says, "Liz, that's her boyfriend."

"Oh, what?"

"Molly isn't a lesbian. She has a boyfriend. They've been a couple for over a year, and she's a little bisexual". Lauren, laughs again and says; "That's so funny, because you two kind of look like one another."

Liz blushes, watching Lauren picture the kiss in her mind, thinking about how they look similar. She looks at Lauren, and asks in a small, worried voice, "Is her boyfriend mad at me?"

Lauren gives her a reassuring look, and replies, "No, he's a friend of Tom's, and he thinks it's really funny."

"Well, at least they're all laughing, and there's no harm done". Liz feels like she's always so socially awkward, and it feels like she's always making people laugh, sometimes on purpose and sometimes not. At least she gets the joke. It's worse to be the joke, and not understand it.

Throughout the day at the festival they bump into people they know from Denali.

She even gets a hug from one of the male bartenders at the Trapper's Line; "Liz it's awesome to see you." She wonders if he saw her public display of affection the other night.

After saying hello, Liz takes a walk further from the stage, following the perimeter outlined with willow. She likes the way the music sounds as it's carried in her direction on the breeze. She considers her role, "*Maybe I have it down to a science, only make appearances ever so often, and when I do; leave them with something interesting to talk about the next day, then lay low, and resurface just when the idea of me is out of mind.*

It's a simple rule, I put love out there, and it's returned to me. Openness without sensitivity is a good position to maintain here in this seasonal world. Looking out at the sea of bluegrass goers, I am reminded of how impermanent we all are. Transients, only passing through, and when this moment is gone, years from now, nothing of us will have remained. There will be no record that I was here, and so were they. That's what makes this time so good, it's superficial, and meant nothing, but to us as we experience it, it feeds into our spirits, and we take away light, and the vision of playful individuals without shoes dancing in the mud in front of a stage. Rhythms of music flow out from the fair grounds and into the willow, over the valley. Alaska, I think I'm starting to get it. It's a state of mind. I can revisit this state of mind, whenever my soul needs to wander".

In the spirit of movement, the Fat City foursome, Amelia, Lauren, Liz, and Jane decide to move on earlier than later, and they head down the highway to an Alaskan style roadside bar for night caps.

It's a quiet ride back to the Tundra Lodge. Liz falls asleep, and when she wakes they're still driving back to Denali. But as she opens her eyes; she's tense with panic. It is fully dark. Completely black; at least this is what her mind's interpreting.

"Oh, God! Jane, its dark! It's night!" She sucks in air and hold's it.

Laughter from the driver seat, "Yes it is."

"Jane how are you driving, how can you see?" The midnight sun is gone, and night has finally found her place back in the Denali sky. It's been dark lately, but not a complete night. Liz is in awe, observing nightfall in its entirety. She keeps blinking her eyes, trying to readjust her vision. She's captivated by how challenging it is to get used to the absence of the sun.

She's confused that night has snuck up on her like this. Confused, that it chose not to gradually make its way back into her life, the same way the sun had appeared. "Lauren, wake up."

"What is it Liz?" She groans.

"Lauren it's night!"

"Liz, you are crazy." Lauren murmurs, then falls back asleep.

For the rest of the ride, she just looks at night. What a gift to be able to see the starry sky as if it was for the first time, new, brilliant, and a little terrifying.

Friday, September 6th 2002

Several days pass, and pass quickly as she works both jobs. Hanging out with Fat City during the in-between times. But, it doesn't take long before Liz agrees to be Denver's date to the Trapper's Line. Now that the end of the season is only weeks away, she wants to fit in more adventure, and have more experiences. Just like working two jobs, she's becoming greedy, and she's out to take whatever she can, before it's all gone. This isn't unusual, and more employees around this seasonal town are out, living and exploring, dancing, and drinking. They can all feel the end is near, and there's nothing any of them can do to slow it down or stop it.

Liz writes in her journal, *"The question is, will it end us, or will we end it?"*

"Denver my dear, you look hot tonight."

"Thank you. I like your shirt Liz."

Liz is very proud of her shirt. She found it at a thrift store in Anchorage with Susan. It was tight, buttoned down, and made of nylon. She suspects it's from the disco era. She tries to put her hair in an exotic bun, and accent her eyes to finish off the look.

Josh isn't driving tonight; it's her cuddle partner Jensen from Girdwood. "Hi Jensen," She greets, working too sound as casual as she can be.

Jensen is happy to see her. He tucks his shaggy brown hair behind his ear. "Liz, it's good to see you, girl." He blushes a little.

Relief, floods through her, he sincerely has no issues with her. Denver and Liz exchange a look, giggle, and climb into the minivan.

She's in a good mood, almost a romantic mood. She slips her arm into Denver's as they ride in the very back of the shuttle. Now that night is back, and the temperature has dropped, and the fall colors have softened the light, everything seems surreal. Like walking among some sweet, familiar dream. She's more comfortable and less nervous in her environment. She feels her own connection to this place. She's managed to channel strength from it. She notices people less, and finds herself more consumed by the way the ground tilts up under her feet, or the way the wind feels like prickly needles when it blows in from the North. As they walk into the Trapper's Line, things are looking even better because the entire bar is overflowing with men. The giggles from Liz and Denver continue.

Denver and Liz have to squeeze in and navigate their way to the bar through a matrix of patrons. She notices someone who stands just a little taller, in the middle of the crowd. He notices her, too. He looks strong and poised. His dark hair is messy and wild, and his eyes give away his thoughts. Her way to the bar has just been sidetracked. She's now making her way towards him. There's something that feels natural about going to him. She doesn't want to question this. With a surge of the crowd, she allows someone behind her to bump her just enough to push her up against him. He had been watching her move through the crowd, but in this moment, their eyes meet. She steps back so they can maximize the silent dialogue happening between them. It's nervous, and intense. She likes this. The nervousness is good. He's accepting her challenge, not backing down. He's curious and moved by her introduction.

She drops her eyes, only to lift them up again, giving him a smile that speaks in a language she's not sure she can explain. She sort of laughs in delight, as she looks at him like she knows him, He does this back to her. Together, they find themselves locked in a kind of attraction that can only be found at the end of the season in Denali.

He breaks the strange vibe with a question. "Would you and your friend like a beer?"

This is the right question, and she knows that this is her invitation to get to keep looking into his eyes, which for reason's she can't understand, is all she really wants to do.

He waves at his friend who is up at the bar. He yells; "Get two more!" He points at Liz and Denver, who had been trailing Liz a few feet away.

The guy nods back at them. While he is doing this, Liz remains unchanged, still just standing there; smiling and staring.

He takes two beers from his friend. Grateful for a reason to break the stare.

He calls one of his friends over, and says, "Mike, this is," he asks Denver's name, "Denver." He hands her a beer.

Denver and Mike start to visit. He passes a beer to Liz. She reaches to take the drink from him. He doesn't let go of it. "Hi." He whispers.

Liz's heart starts to thud, sending a tremor down her spine, around her hips, to her feet.

"Hi." If they could just do this, all night, it would be enough.

"I'm Ansel."

"I'm Liz."

His voice is like honey, so sweet and fluid. He gives her a bashful smile back, and then has to look away because her stare is just that uncomfortable.

At this time; Liz loses control over all her socialization skills and sense of personal space. She raises her eyebrows up, and takes a timid sip of her beer which is different than her usual mayor-gulps. The crowd grows, and with its help, she's pushed in again, she lifts her hand to place on his chest for balance. He leans in, letting her.

Unsure of what to do or how to react, Ansel deduces he'll act casual. To prove Liz isn't making him nervous at all. "I work on the river, I manage the Stampede Raft

Outfit. See all these men;" he points at the bullish group. "These are my river guides." Liz looks away from him, for only a moment, to examine the crowd of well-statured, seasonally sculpted men.

"After all these months, I've never seen you?" She complains over the noise from the crowd.

"I'm here now." He pushes forward a little, so her hands can press into his chest a little more. "The bar scene isn't something we're big on. We spend most of our time on the river or hiking out in backcountry. I went on an amazing hike today, actually. We traversed two canyons. Off trail. Where are you from?"

"Stockton, California".

"I used to live in Sacramento."

Liz gets excited, "You did? Will you go back? That's only an hour from me!"

"I know." He answers in amusement. "Sacramento . . . I'm not sure." Liz frowns. "Maybe." She nods with encouragement.

Ansel is looking better, and better. She likes the way her looks are making him smile, and squirm at the same time. He feels it too, she can tell. The crowd thins out, but they remain body to body close.

"Jace!" He waves to one of his raft guides. Jace comes approaches the two of them. He introduces Liz to a beach blonde surfer type, river-tan skin.

He whispers in her ear, "You should talk to him, you'll like him."

Liz steps away, crinkling her eyebrows together; shaking her head, and pointing to him. She whispers, "You."

Jace gives her a wave. Liz nods, "It's good to meet you." She slips a few inches away from both of them. She looks out at the crowd, processing Ansel's effort. She's unsure why he just did that. She's disappointed, and hadn't considered he would do something so mean; like pawn her off on some other man. She wonders if he thinks she's just drunk. He brought her romantic high down, which she finds immensely irritating. He can sense her disappointment, and tries to take it back. He steps close to her again and grabs her hand discretely. "Sorry, Jace. Just checking-in I guess.

With the touch of his hand, she's pardoning anything before. It doesn't matter. The season is passing, it's almost gone.

He smiles and becomes serious, brushing his finger along the top of her hand, "I'm sorry, forget I did that. Come on." He leads her over to a little table for two in the corner. She's not in the mood to talk. Instead she wants to just watch him. It feels honest and natural. He watches her too; trying to understand. She can almost read his thoughts by the expression on his face while he works hard trying to infer the strong "come hither" looks.

Ansel is older, somewhere between four and six years would be Liz's guess, and with his age, she can see his maturity, his responsibility. Once in a while he scans the bar, keeping tabs on his raft company. Liz is positive they're watching him too. They aren't talking much. Instead, they're counting minutes, moving closer, he's holding her hand, which she's slipped onto the top of his thigh just beneath the table. He's gently petting the top of her hand. They still look, open to the other, troubled by what it is they might have.

Liz hasn't spoken much, only answering short responses to questions prompted by Ansel. Her lack of words, this silent presence she's evoked communicates louder than her words. Her words would break down the meaning of the feeling. The honesty is right for both of them.

She asks him for what she wants. To steal him away. "Can we go somewhere?"

He looks at her and doesn't answer. He's contemplating, and she's happy to keep on doing whatever it is that they're doing, until he figures it out.

He lets go of her hand and looks down, exhales, looks up and confesses, "I have a girlfriend."

Liz has had this conversation before. The sting of the rejection still there. She's not going to hear it again. She won't relive the pain. Not tonight. So she tugs his hand, and responds with, "Let's just go somewhere and spend time together tonight." He can see something practically electric in her green eyes.

She has no interest in consequence or his past. Only a future. All she wants is this moment that belongs to Ansel with Liz, nothing else.

Liz silently watches him have some sort of inner struggle, figuring out a solution. She's not sure if he's thinking of ways to ditch her, of ways to take her away with him, or if he's just trying to talk himself into doing the ethical thing. These are all his problems, and she really doesn't care.

Liz's reasoning's are much more simplistic; she just wants to be near him. She waits for his decision. She's having the best time with him right now. Primal, aggressive, and all consuming.

All the time he's spent working on the river has given him stillness and wildness, which somehow reflects in his eyes. He has an unshaven look about him that adds to his burly, peaceful river-guide style.

He finally finds the answer, he's been searching for. "Let's go outside." His voice is heavier and slower; like it hurt to say it.

Liz dreamily follows him out the door of the bar. They're in the parking lot, continuing to walk to the furthest corner. It's dark and away from others. He turns to face her, this time smiling, he explains, "I have to think."

The night air, and stars in the sky only add to the pressure, and help her cause. It's a cool, romantic night, and they both look star crossed, bathed in the moonlight. It's so quiet outside the bar. Liz unintentionally finds herself holding her breath, afraid to make sounds. He pulls her close, bringing her into his arms. His hands move down to the small of her waist, his fingertips touching and seeking warmth. They haven't even kissed, but the energy between them is undefined. She rests her head against him. They breathe. She looks up at the sky. She watches a wispy cloud slowly move across the night above them. It's much higher than the usual clouds. She notices the strange way it's illuminated by the moonlight. Then, she realizes it's moving differently. She stands, intoxicated by his warmth and smell, staring and observing the sky and the cloud for many minutes. Finally, she's sure of what she sees. It's a very small, very faint, pale green Northern light. Her heart beats so fast. She's experiencing pure decadence in Ansel's arms, watching the light shift and lift, then dip down above them. They're quiet, watching the sky, hugging and staying warm. A few more people come outside to watch the Aurora Borealis.

She whispers in his ear, "Please, let's go somewhere."

He pulls her close again, looking at her hopeful expression.

"Okay." He answers in a seduced submission. "I have to give the raft guides a ride back. The van is completely full. After I drop them off, I'll come back and pick you up. Can you wait here for me for about a half an hour?"

This time he looks desperate, and hopeful, trying to secure their depraved plan. She's agreeable to his decision, but annoyed to have to wait. She can see that he's trying to be discrete, since he's potentially cheating on his girlfriend. He takes a step back, to look down at her, this time she submits to being the one watched and admired.

With a whisper in her ear, "I'll be right back," he's gone.

An hour passes, and he hasn't returned. Every quarter of an hour feels a little worse. The rejection is thick, sticking to her soul like gum to a shoe. Of course, her romantic night is only a fantasy. She knows she had to try. There was something about him. She goes outside to catch the two am shuttle. She looks up to find the pale wisp of light. It's gone. Liz goes home alone.

She enjoyed her night, and found it fascinating, but what bothers her is that she would like to know if he really intended to come back and see her, or if he was figuring out how to get rid of her the whole time. He seemed so sincere.

Her journal already tucked under her pillow, is opened for a new entry: *"A pattern unfolds before me. I seem to only have an interest in those who have girlfriends, Ryan, Aaron, Gabe, and now Ansel. Even my lesbian minute fling, has a boyfriend. Is it possible I'm only attracted to people who are unavailable to me because I fear intimacy? This whole time I've been forlorn, and lonesome, feeling so defective and undesirable. I'm starting to realize that my habits may be more complex than what rises to the surface.*

She's back in her room with solidarity. She pulls the covers around her, and buries the side of her face into the pillow.

She completes her entry, *"I'm happy that I met Ansel, and I'm still enchanted from our strange exchanges this evening. I also am sad, and hurt, because no one likes to be stood up or rejected. So with the bitter and the sweet I close my eyes, and let sleep come for me. Everything will be right in the morning"*.

Thursday, September 6th 2002

The darkness of night lasts longer with each day that passes. The temperature has dropped, and the cold is a messenger, urgently reminding her to eat. To feed before all the food is gone. She's now an efficient and deliberate machine, able to graze and chew for hours upon hours, into the late evening. When the dark falls around her, and the cold brushes against her tousled and shaggy coat, she's compelled to walk, climb, and smell her surroundings. One place in particular; she walks every night. It meets up with the strange river bed, which has no river. This waterless channel curves and bends into a large lake. This is the only lake she's seen in all her roaming. It's big, and has fantastic smells.

The shrubs that surround the lake are dripping with blueberries, and she usually eats as she walks through them. She does not remain here, and continues to move through this place when she visits, as other animals also use this area; including two other bears, and many moose. She's not concerned with the moose, even though there size makes her very uncomfortable. The other two bears are troublesome, bigger, and older than she. There is the very old, irritable she-bear, and the dominant very large he-bear. The best thing to do when she sees them is to submissively slink away, doing her best to make herself disappear. It is the male bear that follows her all those miles the other night. Eventually he stopped.

All three of them are consumed by one motive, and that is to eat and store fat. Running, fighting, and killing things, burn too many calories. So unless it's an easy meal, as hungry as they are, they will probably embrace even the most subtle opportunity. Here by the lake, she's killed rabbit and pika, and she even manages to take a dead ptarmigan away from a little red fox.

Backcountry

Sunday, September 8ᵗʰ 2002

It's eight fifteen at night, and Liz is listening to the echo of her own steps as she walks down the black painted stairway in the park visitor center. She's just finished counting and depositing the bookstore money in the safe upstairs above the theatre. Down the stairs, each step echoes, bouncing from wall to ceiling to floor. It's so loud in contrast with the silence of the quiet halls. She has three steps to go before she's out of the dark, narrow corridor. Something within inspires her to stop. She stands very still, three steps up, looking out at the empty space with the great vaulted ceiling. Everyone left only minutes before. She's alone. It's so quiet and serene, and she feels as if she doesn't belong. The sound of her steps are impossible to ignore. The empty stillness reminds her how alone and vulnerable she truly is. She gets a chill at the thought of herself in this place. This niche has become a hideaway for Liz, a shelter from the temptations and judgments of seasonal work, and more importantly seasonal workers. The season is almost over now and everyone starts to grow wild, risks grow bigger, and consequences seldom hold value.

In her hideaway, she studies the books which are all inclusive, concerning everything Alaskan, and everything Denali. These prints, and postcards, books and maps help summarize the idea of Denali. The names themselves are like beautiful one word songs, A-la-ska, De-na-li. They sound so persuasive and transcendental. The visitor center is an introduction to those who have traveled out of their way to come and see for themselves the expansiveness of a pristine existence. Here one can come and understand the heritage, the evolution, and the vision that makes Denali the treasure that she is. Here we come together in fellowship and praise of this tangled relationship between earth and spirit, life and death. The struggle here is constant, and should never be taken for granted.

She steps down, and her two feet make their way back onto the visitor center floor. She chooses a direct path straight out the big double doors. She gives them a single jiggle to make sure the building locks behind her. She can now make her way down the dark pebbled path to catch the last shuttle back to her property.

She's so cold, and so tired. She puts her hands together, to warm them. She lifts them to her mouth to blow warm air on them. She thinks about gloves. She has none. The chill in the air pricks and freezes, it torments her nerves. Paired with exhaustion, the cold creeps in, and she can feel it in her chest, and lungs, and down into her feet. It's this cold tired feeling that somehow makes her so deeply sad. She has a physical ache that penetrates right through her in a way that chills her soul. She thinks of herself. She can imagine herself so small and tired; outside, waiting for a bus in the interior of Alaska. She's so alone in the darkness. This image she has of how she must look; breaks her heart.

"What am I doing here, why am I doing this to myself? It must just be the exhaustion. My mind is weary, and the change in seasons is introducing different thought patterns in my mind." She exhales, to remind herself to breathe. Sometimes breathing is all one can do. She senses she isn't alone. Eyes are watching her from the edge of the forest that now casts long shadows over the empty parking lot. The final shuttle is late. She wonders if it's canceled now that the Season is changing. After all, no one is here. She is. She is here. Alone. Cold. Shadows dance with a breeze, grasses beyond her sight are being rustled. She slowly steps back. Again, until her back is against the visitor center. The visitor center she has locked herself out of. She slides two steps to the right. She picks up the receiver of the pay phone. A collect call or a long night hike through the woods. The choice is made. "Hi Mom, umm, yeah, I'm fine. I just need a favor. I'm kind of stuck. And, yes. Yes. Uh, huh. Mom, so could you call my property and let them know to send the shuttle. Uh, huh. Yep. Umm, no, I'm not all alone. There are other people with me. We're just a little stuck. Yes, it's night time. Okay. Yes. Uh, huh. Okay. Thankyou! I love you".

Twenty long, cold minutes later; she steps off the shuttle, making her way to the employee cafeteria to forage for some dinner. Her legs are tired and she's careful to navigate down the steep bank. She puts her hands together and breathes into them. So cold. Dinner is put away for the night, but she's able to find a cup of mint tea, a bag of chips and an orange. As she stands there with her less than impressive meal, again she begins to feel sorry for herself. The whole summer she's been battling apathy, only to have it show up and kick her ass tonight.

She's pulled from the depressed thoughts, by something that catches her eye on the bar side of the cafeteria; its dreadlocks; and he's watching her. He's sitting with Tom. It's Molly's boyfriend.

" *Oh, what is he doing here? Was he looking for me? Does he want to beat me up*"? She darts out the side door and takes the long way around the building and up to her room. Now, she's cold, tired, sad, and a little paranoid of a dread lock hippie guy. It must finally be time to go to bed. Once in her bed and food in her hungry stomach, with the covers pulled up, so warm; Liz closes her eyes. She turns to face Jane, who's lying warm in her own bed.

"Liz, when are you going to quit second job?" Jane is sensitive to her struggles.

"Don't worry Jane, I'll quit when the right time comes."

"Yes, but you don't need the money. What are you doing it for? It doesn't seem worth it. I think if you keep going at this rate . . . you'll hit the wall."

"I don't know. The work helps me focus. I stay out of trouble."

Liz loves their pre-sleep conversations. They could be twenty something's, or little seventy year old ladies the way they carry on, and chat.

She writes this down, "*We have three weeks left, before the season will end, and this will end, and everyone will go, and it will never be again, at least not with us, and the way we are together. So, we have these nights, and we hold them so tightly, so dearly in our hearts*".

Tired from the work and the cold temperatures that fast approach, they're ready to complete the task. But saying goodbye will be difficult, and going home will require great adaptation, as this life has become so good and familiar.

"*When the work is gone, what will I have to fill this emptiness within?*"

Thinking about the visitor center, and the park, Jane's inspired, and suggests a perfect adventure. She stares across the room at Liz's pack pushed up against a corner. "Liz, I like your backpack, but we haven't spent the night in the park at all this summer. What if we go backpacking for a night?"

Liz slams her journal shut. A pulse of energy shoots through her body; considering the new prospect. Here, Liz is focusing on tying loose ends and completion, while Jane choses to focus on starting new projects. "Really Jane, do you think we can get two more days off, so we can go together? Jane you would go backpacking with me in the park?"

Jane laughs. "Sure, we should do it Liz. You're stuck at the desk at the visitor's center all the time. Let's get you out into the actual park."

Liz is renewed and ecstatic, also a little intimidated by the idea of backpacking into the Denali Wilderness with Jane.

She opens her journal, *"You could say I'm a sucker for adventure, and it seems I harbor a weakness for risky activities. The proposition of the two of us roughing it in the park, is the greatest gesture I can think of to highlight the Alaskan ideal of adventure that I so longingly wish to embrace".*

Tuesday, September 10th 2002

At work the next day, Liz tells Lauren her story, "I was in the cafeteria last night, and Molly's boyfriend was there with Tom, he was staring at me. So I ran out the door."

Lauren looks confused for a moment.

"Lauren, is he going to beat me up, was he looking for me?"

Lauren can see the way it stresses her friend, and she giggles in amusement. "The dreadlock guy is good friends with Tom, and they were just hanging out." She continues; "He doesn't want to beat you up. Don't worry. The Mayor is safe."

Liz nods her head in relief, and is glad that Lauren has a way of making things better. Their friendship has definitely evolved over the season, and what she once thought was snobby and judgmental is now; understanding Lauren's different and often fascinating perspectives regarding how people interact, and the entertainment value from the decisions they make. She's an artist first and foremost, and she has taught Liz to look at things in new ways, to take away a more complete understanding of an idea or event. Like the art she loves, she herself seems to be a vision of well-defined composition, and balance. There are twenty days left, before everyone departs and completes their contracted work agreements.

It's now off season, and the volume of assholes has decreased. Instead of always running around two steps behind, they work steadily and have all the wrinkles smoothed out. Tips are efficient, the breakfast lunch crew are making sure to get themselves servings of halibut, salmon burger, and crab cakes, in abundance. Liz can be found any given afternoon, sneaking deserts out of the walk in freezer, to indulge. She's now officially using chocolate as a substitute for sleep. The days are long, but satisfying.

She writes, " *We are the burly and tough survivors, who have stuck it out. Yes, we are standing on sore, swollen, blistered feet, but here we remain, to see it to the end. I'm curious if there is some worthwhile reward for not quitting, or giving up, or fucking up. If at the end of it all, we we'll find something that will give it all meaning.*

The suggestion that our days are numbered, cannot be denied, even the weather and light echo the looming changes that must, and will take place. Denali is a place of change, and the change is always dramatic, tragic, and haunting. The fall light is more infectious than the relentless presence of the midnight sun. My mind turns to California, and it makes me feel frozen like the permafrost, stuck, not wanting to return and revisit old habits, and complacency. I like being a stranger, in a strange place".

Friday, September 13th 2002

Its morning in Denali, Jane and Liz are standing on the stoop in front of their work, clad in backcountry gear, with big eyes; anticipating their great adventure. They've just raided the kitchen at the restaurant and have their backpacks full of peanut butter, bagels, muffins, cheese, strawberries, yogurt, little cans of cranberry juice, and their Nalgene bottles full of water.

Liz is thrilled because she gets to use her new backpack, which she paid over four hundred dollars for. It feels incredible, and the waist strap hugs her round hips in such a way, that it takes all the stress from her back. They have their packs, their boots, cameras, and sunglasses. They both have bandanas in their hair. Liz is fully dressed for the occasion. She has her hair in braids, and red lipstick. She's sure she's not the first girl to wear red lipstick into the backcountry. She believes Denali will be looking gorgeous for her, so she wants to look gorgeous for Denali. She's wearing her jeans, a snowboard jacket, and a double layer of sweaters. She's so happy to be in her hiking boots. They happen to be her lucky boots, and are close to four years old. It seems that whenever she has these particular shoes on, she finds herself trekking in the most beautiful and inspired locations.

"These boots carry me to the places I dream of".

The visitor center shuttle stops in front of them, and the door folds open, Liz looks at Jane, "Here we go Jane!"

"Good morning." Jane greets the driver. The women climb aboard, walking proud. They can sense the bus driver, and the other two random people looking them over with interest.

An old woman sitting across from them, leans forward. "Are you girls going to spend the night in the park?"

Jane turns to her, "Oh, yes."

The lady shakes her head at her husband, then asks, "How many nights are you going to be out for?"

With this prompt, Jane gives Liz a mischievous look "We're going to be backpacking for six days."

"Oh my." Gasps the lady.

Liz bites her lip to keep from giving away the lie.

"Please girls, be careful!"

Jane answers, "Thank you, we will."

She begins to narrate her journey in her head, *"There are so many surreal moments here in Denali, but this experience is surely one that divides those who dream and those who do. To prove that she is worthy of greatness, and is not afraid to pursue her passions and convictions. To go out alone, only to discover likeminded creatures as indifferent and independent as they want to be. That is why we come, that is what we celebrate here".*

Soon Liz and Jane board the camper bus, heading deep into the park, arranging to go as far as the bus will take them. Jane and Liz each take their own seat with their faces pressed up against the window, content to look. It's autumn in Denali, and she now knows this is her favorite time to be here. The palette of colors that blend, and sweep through the hills and valleys are gold, copper, purple, turquoise, pink, and brown. All the metallic hues look as if Mother Nature herself harbored a special love for this place and decided to bedazzle it, with all the shiny sparkles and glazes. The sunshine is rich and bathes the whole landscape in deep tones, and saturated shades. Even the clouds seem to hang a little lower in the sky, as if to come down and get a closer look at the grandeur and elegance of the park, while it prepares to bow down in submission to winter's freeze.

All the animals are out, roaming and foraging for food. They remind Liz of the employees back at the lodge. Everyone is out for their last big thrills, to fill them and carry them through, until their next journey begins, before the chill of the season moves in and pushes everything back, and things grow sparse and slow down . . . stop. The moose with their velvety antlers, caribou, fox, ptarmigan, swans, otters, ground squirrels, and the grizzly, they are all out along the winding road. Liz has devised a mental catalog in her mind, where she files away the images of each animal, so that later she may go back and review them, and know that she was there. That she saw them, in there element.

They're coming to the end of the road after hours of twisting, climbing, turning, over loose gravel switchbacks. This is the end; the camper bus turns around and goes back to the beginning from this point. Jane and Liz are now making their way off the bus, and into a place called Kantishna. Kantishna is a very old abandoned mining town that hugs a deep gurgling creek. The actuality of their adventure is now crashing down on them as they watch the old camper bus roll back down the road and out of sight.

Now, they're alone, very much alone, with no life lines, in the middle of Denali National Park. The weather can be unusual in Denali, and today they've crossed through patches of sun, and clouds with rain. Kantishna is hidden within old trees, and rocks and a road that seems to rise up and twist on to a place they cannot see. Two women, one with bright red lipstick, stand together, doing a full three hundred and sixty degree turn, trying to pick a direction to hike too.

One of the rules with the backcountry permits is that you cannot use the road, or be on the road, and that you must go into the backcountry. So the pressure to pick a direction is definitive. The obvious choice is the old mining road. So Liz and Jane hoist up their packs, centering their core balance, and begin to hike along the lifted path. As they climb upward, a fog starts to close in on them. It becomes very cold, and the mist is so thick, it's wet. There's something about this fog that creates panic and distress. They don't discuss it. The women are too busy moving. Moving to stay warm and moving because they're not happy where they are. The fog is odd, because it's coming down the road approaching with a fast, broad coverage. Liz looks at Jane. With only their eyes, they agree that this place obviously isn't desirable for setting up camp, or even hiking in. So they back track, and within thirty minutes find themselves standing at the starting point, where the bus had left them.

Liz is starting to feel less badass, and wants to regain her confidence. "What do you think Jane?" She tries to sound brave and secure with her voice, projecting it clear and strong in the direction of her friend.

"I really don't like this area Liz." Jane's voice wavers, and she doesn't want to pretend everything's okay. Her doubts are starting to bind her clarity. Options constrict, and she'd like to find a spot to build their camp.

Liz understands, and the proposition of walking away from Kantishna is the most attractive option. "Let's go that way."

She points up the Park road where they can see sunshine and open sky. This is the first mistake the women make on their trip. When a backpacker applies for a backcountry permit, they have to mark on a grid with the park service where they'll be, in case someone goes missing or something happens. This way they can locate the missing people or person. Or at least have a better idea of what might have happened to them.

The women leave their square; and are now off their grid. "We go this way"! Liz keeps moving, she's already decided to where. Wonder Lake is the place people usually see in pictures, postcards, and books. It's one of the few large bodies of water out here and it attracts all sorts of animals; including Liz and Jane. The attraction; other than a gorgeous Alaskan lake, is that it sits in the foreground of one of the best views of Mt. McKinley. With one scooped valley that sits between the lake and the mountain, visitors find themselves so close; they can point out her majesty's glaciers by name.

Down the road, they walk until they reach their first view of the lake. It's brighter, and more open. At Wonder Lake they don't see any eerie fog. Wonder lake is one of the few places that is restricted for backpackers, and for reasons Liz isn't sure of. She ignores the rule. She reasons that this is a good option since both women are overwhelmed with where to go. After feeling scared in Kantishna, they want to find someplace less imposing, and more park-like. Wonder Lake is park like, and Liz feels better here.

Its late afternoon, and they wouldn't see any more busses until tomorrow. Liz is curious if they had seen a bus, if they would have been tempted to just get back on, abandoning the plan to camp out here on their own tonight. Without a good camp selected, and night fall growing closer, they officially decide to post up near the lake.

"Let's go this way." She calls to Jane.

They suck it up and try out their bear calls while tromping through tall bush. "Here bear, here bear, Heeeeeer beeaaar!" It's now time to practice all the techniques instructed at their backcountry permit class. They hike down a little stream outlet, that tucks them in between a dip in the hill, hiding them from the roads view. The women have a gorgeous view of the lake, and about thirty percent of the top of Denali is showing above the clouds. This is usual, and in all the months; Liz has only seen her completely revealed twice.

Camping at Wonder Lake is their second mistake. Earlier in the day, when they were on the bus, Liz observed two rangers in the area with a big antenna. She suspects they were tracking a problem bear that they had to collar. She quickly dismisses the thought, and refuses to let the threat of a problem grizzly ruin their fine adventure. Besides, they are running out of options. After exploring and inspecting, they find a soft patch of tundra for their tent. Next, they carefully put all of their food in the bear can and move it over fifty feet from their tent in the triangle formation they learned about at the mandatory course. The women are doing their best to be by the book, and it feels similar to a couple of little girls playing "house". As if it's all play, and they really are inexperienced and taking for granted the methods used for backpacking.

After all the days in the visitor center, Liz thinks she's fooled herself into thinking she would know how to do it. She didn't expect to feel afraid out here.

"Jane, I'm so glad we're doing this."

"I know Liz, it's incredible. I can't believe we're here." The women stop, and watch Denali, modest and covered by her draping clouds. Although it's unrealistic, Liz can't help but anticipate and expect the clouds to recede. With her camera ready, she fully believes the mountain will show for them. She can't shake the feeling that it will happen. She feels like this act of nature is owed to them, and she's here to collect their dues. The clouds still hang, and hide, teasing poor Liz. They spend several climactic minutes looking out at the lake, valley, and mountain.

Back to the bear can, they compile a light dinner, before removing any scents and remnants of food or food packaging back into the secured can. Out of all the places in the world to dine: For the two Tolkat servers, the meal shared together, surrounded in a decadent eco-system and sitting on the forgiving tundra; proves to be one of the best, and most memorable meals to be enjoyed in one's entire span of life. Cheese sliced with a pocket knife and miniature cans of cranberry cocktail juice.

Liz can no longer wait for the sun to set, the coldness is all around them. "Shall we retire my dear?" She whispers to Jane.

"It's been a day Liz, let's get some sleep. I'm pretty much ready for the morning." She shares, looking around and feeling intimidated.

Unspoken, they both feel a desire to hide in the tent before night completely takes over. The sensation of being out in the wilderness in the dark is one they hope to avoid. It has been a long day, and they're happy to finally be curled up in their sleeping bags, safe inside their tent. Both women are looking forward to the sun rising in the morning, and perhaps trying for another glimpse of the mountain. Everything seems fine, until the cold settles for the night. Jane has a pad under her sleeping bag, but Liz does not. Her sleeping bag is fancy, and ultra-light, but doesn't fit her well, and she can't get inside it entirely.

The chill is pure misery. Liz finds one method to help her through the night. She lies facing down on the ground. The side of her body that's against the floor of the tent can find warmth. Then, the topside. So every five to ten minutes she rotates herself to warm the opposite side of her body. She feels like a rotisserie chicken, turning and spinning all night, to keep from freezing. This is a cold that scares her and it's only September. She's a woman who loves the snow, snowboards, plays in it all the time back in California. She celebrates the cold. This time, things are different; this cold hurts, and sucks the energy out of her body. At some point, she must have fallen asleep, but only lightly. She's half awakened by the sound of Jane moving in the tent.

That's when she hears the whisper of her name. "Liz." Jane's hand reaches over and touches Liz's face.

Liz understands the meaning.

There they are lying beside one another, Jane's hand over her face, solemn and listening. She can hear it. Something is moving around outside their tent, then against their tent, pushing inward then releasing to let it bounce back into it's form. Then the sound of rustling near the brush up the hill from them. In her sleep mind: she's frightened it's a park ranger who sees their tent and is going to arrest them.

Frozen, and picturing the white ranger truck up on the road, she doesn't move. Imagining the ranger cautiously traversing a caribou trail down to their tent, brushing into bramble on their way. Only, too much time has passed. The ranger would have asked them to come out by now. She's struck by the discovery that it might not be a ranger. Only a moment before, dreading the ranger, she now wishes desperately that it is a ranger. If not, then who? Other visions orient her mind; a Kantishna ghost, a wolf pack, a grizzly? She sits up in a sudden spell of panic. When this happens they hear the something run, rushing through the brush, snapping twigs, and then it's gone.

"Jane, I thought it was a ranger!"

"Sshhhh ," She whips her head to face Liz. She's shaking hard. They're lying next to each other, not talking, not moving for at least an hour. It's very cold. Dawn starts to lighten the world again. Jane keeps her hand across Liz, they are closer, and Liz is thankful for the warmth of her friend.

Liz can see in Jane's eyes that she's more than upset. She's never seen Jane affected by anything like the way she seems tormented by the events of the night they just had.

"Jane (she whispers again). I thought it was a ranger."

"Liz, it wasn't a ranger." Her voice quakes, and sounds coarse. "While you were sleeping, I was wide awake. The bear was smelling me". She shivers as she speaks, "It was smelling me through the tent."

"Oh, hey. You're okay now."

"No Liz. It was breathing and grunting." Her hands tremble, speaking of the encounter out loud.

Liz can't think of anything to say, that would make this better for her.

According to Jane's story while she was sleeping, Liz had done one of her rotisserie turns, and it made the bear pull back. That's when Jane reached her arm out to get her to be still. Poor Jane was facing death, and Liz was beside her, completely ignorant to the danger.

"It's okay now, the sun is rising, the birds are singing, and the lake is sparkling." She does her best to try to convince Jane to put her fear in the past. The friends are in a position to see out a mile in all directions, and nothing is near that can harm them.

Liz volunteers to leave the tent first. She goes to unzip their little cocoon, when she sees mistake number three. They removed everything with a smell, and placed it far from where they slept, with their bear can.

Everything, except their hiking boots.

"Oh God, Jane."

"What Liz?"

"Our boots."

The smell of the sweat and leather was most likely very interesting to a bear. Liz flashes back to last night, "Liz, I'm putting these sweaty hiking boots out of the tent."

She's used to Jane's attention to detail, and didn't even consider stinky boots as an invitation to danger. Emerging from their tent, resembling an arctic ground squirrel, Liz timidly peers out scanning the unleveled terrain. She has to walk several steps in her socks to fetch their boots that had been scattered close to the tent. After grabbing the boots, she darts back into the tent, and they both put on their top layers of clothes and shoes quickly. Then again, she pops back out of the tent, viewing the tundra, looking for the bear. Jane comes out and stands close beside Liz. Jane's shaking, afraid.

"We're alive, and we're okay. We're going to get our things, and get to the road." Liz puts her arm around Jane, holding her with love and care.

Together they work quickly, folding the tent, grabbing the bear can, and hiking away from Wonder Lake.

Friday, September 13th[b] 2002

While the nights get longer, she finds her favorite trail to the big lake. So much activity is taking place, while the moon enchants the stars, whom all peer down to watch the display of transition that causes a frenzy of preparation in the wilderness below. The northern lights appear, then disappear, then reappear, but they don't concern her. They are all there; at the lake feeding and searching for food, and feeding again. Herself, the old she-bear, and the big strong he-bear, the two male moose with their velvety antlers, and the trumpeting swans who float with ease across the water, sounding their prayerful honks that resonate through the frigid night air. After building strength, growing, and gaining a healthy layer of fat, she's almost enjoying these days of feeding. The mosquitos are gone, and have been replaced with small, sugary blueberries, in every direction. She likes the blueberries, but would like to find meat.

This is why she's now following a scent; it's not meat or insect. It's confusing, and she's sure its food. She negotiates her way through the labyrinth of thick blueberry shrubs, down a graduating hillside. There is something over there; large and still. It doesn't move, so she's sure it smells her. It must be a very large bear. She should turn away. But, what if it's something else, something to eat? Her predator instincts take the rein, and she crouches down, treading upon the earth with the stealth of a fox. Each step brings her closer and fills her nostrils with the curious smell.

She's right beside it now, and whatever it is, it sleeps. Lying still in an open place, down low among the brush. It doesn't smell dead, but it's strange to be sleeping in a place that is so out in the open, in such a busy area during one of the busiest times of the evening. Her ears are back, and shoulders square. She steps closer to the animal. She cannot make sense of its form, and she cannot tell where the mouth and claws are on this beast. It is much bigger than she, nearly twice her size. Although she senses danger, her instincts insist to investigate the allure of the smell. Now, the scent is more complex, and she has locates very old pieces of carcass, which have bites that are fun, but barely edible. She moves the strange, carcass piece away, and inspects the other smells. Animal smells, mingled with the heat the beast creates around itself.

Prepared for attack, she makes her body big and strong. She bumps her shoulder into the beast, it does not stir. So she tries again, and it does nothing. Now that she's certain the thing is dying or in a deep sleep, she helps herself to exploring it. She smells it so hard, that her nose and snout are in contact with its odd skin. It has neither feathers, nor fur, nor flesh. She can push into it with her snout a great deal, and find no bones, or meat. It seems as though it is skin and air, but the smell tells her another story.

Somehow, deep within this creature, lies living, breathing meat. She can smell the breaths as they leave its lungs, she can smell its blood flowing through it, and can even smell the scent of the heat it produces. She pushes her long snout into the strange skin, and inhales long and slow, allowing the different scents to fall onto her palette to determine what course of action to take. Then, breathing out, and once more a nice long inhalation to figure out the best way to eat the beast; if she wants to eat the beast. Perhaps she can just open her mouth and take a big bite out of its airy, tangible skin, sinking further down towards the heat, and smells.

At this moment, the beast awakes. It makes a strange heavenly sound that strikes fear in her young bear ego. She jumps away, and the beast rouses once more, something big and powerful, hidden within this mass of skin. She does not want to confront this animal. She fears for her life. She turns and runs, long, hard strides, zig zaging through the brush, and back up and over the hillside. She will not return to the water again tonight.

Saturday, September 14th 2002

Jane is shaky, and as they hike up to a kettle pond vista. She's really starting to feel bad about the whole situation. One of their shoes was definitely carried a few feet away. Poor Jane was sleeping right next to the door of the tent. It's now obvious that they are novice backpackers, and have made some poor choices. Liz is confronted with the truth, deducing that Denali is not Disney Land, and she has to give this wild place the credit and respect it requires.

Later, having watched so many grizzly bear documentaries she can see the way they dig, pull, split and crush with their great paws to find food. They rip open logs, throw boulders, and shred with their sharp teeth. It's autumn and every bear in the park is looking for a meal as they prepare for hibernation. She's not sure how close they actually came to a bear attack, but Jane had a bear encounter that even the most experienced grizzly naturalist would have avoided at all costs. Liz is certain it's a grizzly, because the black bears and brown bears don't share habitat, and she happens to know that Wonder Lake is a brown bear area.

It's difficult to put into perspective how much danger they were in last night. All she knows is that she's so thankful to have the morning light, and to have her Jane safe beside her. They spend the morning picking wild blueberries, until both Nalgene bottles are stuffed full. A few pictures from the road and they are safely picked up, back on the bus, heading to the lodge.

On the bus, Liz leans over and whispers to Jane who's sitting in the bus seat opposite of her, "*I love that we went backpacking, two badass girls, brave and open to adventure. I'm even glad that it was scary and dangerous. We are going home with more than a backcountry tale, we have a grizzly story. Where we'll casually mention that we were backpacking in Denali, and our audience over the years will look at us, and think "Wow, she's really amazing", and they will be right*".

Jane pushes her head back into the seat. She closes her eyes.

That night, back home in their room, they each lay their head down, "Goodnight Jane."

"Goodnight Liz, I'm so happy to be back on property."

"We're okay now." Liz affirms with a sleepy voice.

"Yes," She yawns, and rolls over.

"I'm so happy that I can sleep without spinning like a chicken!"

Jane falls asleep immediately, but in less than a minute she gasps and sits straight up in her bed; she's shaking.

"Jane!"

She looks over at Liz, her eyes bewildered and fierce, her breathing fast and shallow. "The bear, it, it, it was smelling me!"

"Jane it was a dream." To see her friend suffering from her experience made Liz want to cry. "You're okay, we're here in our room, there's no bear."

It's starting to set in with her, how traumatic Jane's encounter was, and she hopes her roommate will be able to sleep without grizzly nightmares. She lies back down, and both women fade into sleep.

The week passes quickly, and Liz continues to keep herself constantly busy, going back and forth between first job and second job. This is her final week at the bookstore. She gave her notice, and scheduled the end of second job; a week before their season at the Tundra Lodge ends. Now that they are down to the final two weeks, people are optimistic and sharing plans for what they'll do when they go home. Conversations about what they are going to buy, and where they want to go out to eat are filling their hearts with anticipation. The hard fact that the goodbyes and disconnect are approaching are subjects saved for the final week.

She no longer has a desire to go bar crawling or tramping around. What's the point of meeting someone she might like, or love now? This takes a burden off her preoccupied mind, and she's no longer chasing anything, or searching for answers. It's not exactly what she had hoped to discover in Alaska, but none the less, she's found the things she needs, and she's able to appreciate them. She has good friends. She has a good job, and a good second job, plus she has turtle cheesecake from the Tolkat.

Tonight Liz wants a drink, but ever since Drew kissed her in Girdwood, she's been way too shy to see him back in Denali, thus avoiding the employee bar. So she decides to take the long walk to the pizza pub where Celeste is working. When she gets there, she finds a group of the dinner shift servers mixed with several of the actors from the dinner theatre. Chris and Amber motion to Liz to join. Liz loves this group, and regrets not finding more opportunities spend time with them. Still, she feels like she struggles to fit in with such a cultured group.

"It's been a long season Liz, and we've hardly spent any time together." One of the actors points out.

"I know Nate, but I'm stoked to be here with you now."

Liz pulls her chair closer into the circle, watching the sophisticated actors. They compete with outgoing personalities, kindness, and stewardship. Despite failing to be as poised as the rest of the members of the group with her understated style, it feels good to be included. She decides to revel in the experience, and pretend that she's as suave as her company.

"Nate, have you heard about Liz's bear story?" Chris contributes, the moment Liz crosses her legs.

"I don't know. There isn't much to tell from my point of view. I slept through most of it. It was scary".

All eyes are on Liz, a bit envious of her grizzly encounter.

"We heard. Everyone's so relived your both okay, and survived to tell the story. Employees come out here and have tragedies, you know. So tell us Liz, the Bear Charmer, has it been a good summer for you here in Denali?" The theatre singer inquires, before taking a long sip of his gin and tonic with a twist.

She leans back in the chair, crossing her legs in the other direction, catching a warm patch of sun that splashes onto her chilled skin. "It's been an amazing summer, Gavin".

He approves. The people at the table seem happy for a new face in their crowd.

Liz rises from the table to go into the bar for another drink. Thinking about what she's thirsty for, she makes her way into the warmth of the bar. She stops in mid step, hearing a voice call her name, "Liz!"

She swings around. Her jaw drops. She's struck completely in shock. More than the dawn at Wonder Lake. The last person she expects to see, ever, and there he is.

"Ansel. Hi."

Standing there, smiling at one other (even though she doesn't mean too), she's caught up in this undefinable attraction. But this time, she doesn't want to play that game. He left her at the bar, and she's not sure what to say to him. She's not feeling angry, because she can't deny his appeal, and he's giving her a very forward and flirtatious smile. But, she's not going to let him in. She gave him the chance. Her heart was wide open, and he declined. She's still curious, and can't ignore the weird connection to him.

She can't decide what to say, and he's not speaking. Her heart wants to know why, what happened to him, how he could leave her waiting, wondering if he imagined her their waiting like shad been, wondering how he could feel okay with that.

Eventually she chooses her words by impulse, "Would you like to come sit with me on the patio, with my friends?"

His reply: "Yes, I want to. But, I'm picking up pizzas for the river guides, and only have a few minutes." He looks down, disappointed to have to decline her invitation, yet again.

Liz shrugs, signals to Celeste to deliver her another drink, then turns around to go back outside. He follows her. She can see everyone at her table's eyebrows raise at the gorgeous, sweet guy following behind her like a puppy dog. She drags a chair and fashions it next to her own. She introduces him to the table.

"Everyone this is Ansel. He works for one of the river outfits."

The cocktail group stands to greet him with welcoming hospitality. Liz is pleased to watch him sizing up her friends. Learning and understanding more about who she is.

"Hey Ansell, glad you can join us." Nate says with encouragement.

He still looks incredible. After the round of introductions, he's now sitting beside her as if he's her boyfriend. She can't help but find herself flailing in a dangerous place. She's wide open again. The whole time he's beside her, she feels tingles and chemistry that makes her want to reach down and grip the seat of her chair, holding on; to control herself. After his drink, he turns to Liz, "I have to go pick up the pizza." He stays in his seat. Watching her.

She hesitates, "I'll walk you out".

They pass the bar. He lifts a few boxes of pizza as they walk. In the foyer, he turns to face her. He has something on his mind. She watches him working on a thought. She can't hold her position for much longer. She knows she'll say something. Something that will be for nothing. .

"Goodbye, Liz." He stops, and permits his eyes to drift over her slowly, looking guilty of a secret thought.

"Goodbye Ansel." She works to make her voice sound alluring.

He lingers for a single second, and then whatever he is figuring out in his mind is dismissed, and he's gone. She regrets not confronting him. She's desperate to know what happened that night. But, she feels defensive of her heart, and doesn't want to revisit the disappointment of their first exchange. She fears he'd project pity on her, and apologize, the same way Aaron had.

She thinks, *"I hate when guys apologize to me. Why can't they just eliminate the behavior that requires apologies?"*

She returns to the people at the table, and sips her cosmo. She's quiet, but laughs at the jokes and stories that are shared until the sun sets, and they all go in to find warmer surroundings.

Liz walks back across the property, a little bewildered. Seeing Ansel definitely tugged at her heart strings, and she's sorry for not getting to know him. She can't define their chemistry, but when she sees him, the energy is beyond any she's known. She wishes she had a chance to explore this more. It's impossible to suppress the attraction. She's glad she preserved her dignity, and didn't try to ask him to see her, or yell at him for leaving her at the bar. She was careful about it all, and this gives her the power, and he's still the jerk for standing her up. She lets out a heavy sigh because he's stirred up her emotions, and now she's going to have to spend the rest of the evening trying to stuff them back down.

Her housing building is in site and she imagines how nice it will be to just stay in bed for the remainder of the day. "Hey Bear Charmer"! It's Chris. "Wait a sec". He jogs his way to her. Liz looks behind him for Amber. She's not with him. "I have a question for you. I mean, I've been thinking about you. Remember how I was so mean to you in the beginning? I hope you don't think I'm a horrible person. It was horrible of me. I had hoped to make it up to you, and you know, I've been kind to you, try to buy you a drink when I see you out". He's rambling and they are moving closer to the building. Liz stops, she can see she's rushing whatever he wants to say.

"Thanks. Thank you for being nice to me". Her answer sounded terrible, and she realizes she's in an awful mood which probably isn't helpful while trying to sort anything out with Chris. But it's her mood and she wants it.

"No. No, it's not that. I'm not trying to get feedback or anything. Please don't thank me. We're good. I know that. I just feel bad about how we started, after getting to know how cool you are. I really don't like that I was so lame to you. I'm going to miss you". He opens his arms to give her a hug. She steps in, but isn't in a happy place to enjoy the connection. She's simply wishing for a quiet place and her bed.

He scratches his head, "I had just left some baggage behind. I was an angry person when I first came here. Amber has been helping me work that out. Who was that guy? Are you dating?"

Liz shakes her head.

"You know what, that's too bad. I watched how hard you've tried. I've seen you from the beginning of the Season to now. Trying every day to feel so passionate about what you're doing, where you are, and your friendship. You're sad. I get sad too. That's my anger. The things I had to work out. That guy . . . don't even stress about him. He's not worth it. There is someone for you. He's going to be such a lucky guy.

Liz looks at the ground, she shrugs and slides her foot through the dirt.

Nate laughs, "Okay. Believe me. I'm not being funny. You are so cool and you don't even know it".

"Okay". Liz mumbles.

"We're hanging out soon. Got it?"

"Uh, huh. See you in the morning". Liz continues to look down, feeling like a deflated balloon as she continues on her path up the stairs to her room. Chris watches her drag one foot after another.

Northern Lights

Sunday, September 22rd 2002

Her journal reads, "I *wish I could have just one positive experience with love here in Denali. This is the most romantic place I've ever been to, and I haven't been able to share that with someone*".

Liz is hanging out with Denver and Rebecca in Denver's new boyfriend's room. The boyfriend and his roommate are bell hops. The roommate is in the midst of describing to Liz what a bell hop actually does.

"No really, that's all we do. We work for like four hours a day, and we make a couple hundred dollars in tips."

"You're kidding?" Liz feels cheated. Here she's been slaving away at the restaurant, believing her job was pretty good, only to discover there's a faster and easier way to earn great tips.

"Yeah, we have to get the morning guests luggage to the train depot, and when we go to pick these up, they always give us five to twenty dollars. Then we just relax until the afternoon train arrives. This is when we unload and deliver bags to the rooms. We get tipped again. That's it, that's all we do."

"Oh." Liz feels humbled to learn how inferior her own job feels.

Today, the topic of discussion is the big party the Denali bell hops are throwing. It's the annual Bell Dog Bash. Every year at the end of the season, the bell hops from all the hotels combine money and purchase food and beer for everyone. The location for the Bell Dog Bash is just off the highway in the middle of a ridge that gradually slides down towards the Nenana river canyon.

A third bell hop who joined the leisurely group in the employee room describes the party to Liz. "The terrain is rough, and uneven, but it's open and big, and when it's filled with all the people, and vehicles, and music, it really is a crazy time. The best party of the season."

The bell hops are extra excited because this year they've collaborated with the dinner shift chefs to help dig a pit, and roast a whole pig on a spit. Liz isn't completely dazzled by the idea of going to some, super charged employee party. She hasn't committed to the event in her mind yet, but there is a small chance she'll go. She was never really comfortable at high school keg parties, and that is very much what she imagines this Bell Dog Bash to be, a big, over inflated high school keg party for those who suffer from arrested development.

After hanging out, Liz has a hearty dinner with Jane, and a restful sleep. Week two is coming to an end.

Today, she's headed over to the visitor center with Kyle, who has also been working second job. Kyle sometimes worked with her, and other times he works opposite of her. "Hey there cowboy, let's go quit our jobs!"

Kyle is much younger and more sheltered. "It feels like we've just started working there, that's so crazy." He replies.

The hard working duo decide it would be easier to quit together, and today they are going as a team to collect their final pay, thank Fiona their manager for giving them second jobs, and then congratulate one another on the completion of a challenging, and exhausting task. The entire idea of it causes Liz to want to celebrate. She's so happy, she could run straight up to the top of Mount Healy, and at the summit, just jump and down, screaming for joy.

"Kyle, I'm nervous for our final day."

"Your fine Liz, we both kicked ass, and you should feel proud of yourself. Enjoy this."

She's so grateful to have Kyle beside her.

The warmth and appreciation doted upon them when they arrive at the bookstore is unexpected. Their supervisor greets them with sincerity, "I have a little something special I picked out for each of you. I appreciate all your hard work and your reliability. If you ever want to come back, you always have a job with me". She hands Kyle and Liz a hand-selected matte print.

When she gets back to the property, she and Kyle exchange a friendly hug, before going separate ways.

Back in her room, she writes about the gift, *"My print is of the mountain herself, covered in white, and standing centered in the picture. It's an unusual picture because unlike so many Denali images, this one doesn't have anything in the foreground, nor clouds creating composition. Instead it's simply the mountain, honest and revealed. That is what I'm holding: a flat, wide picture, of one giant mountain, with nothing else to distract me from her. This photograph reminds me of myself now that I have completed the season. On my final day, I will be confronted with the reality of boarding the plane and cutting this life line, which attaches me to Alaska. I'll be alone again, with nothing else. To different to return to the same. Now that I've grown so much, I will be alone, a singular mountain, blank and distant with nothing else. At least until I get it all figured out".*

She's already promised herself she won't stay in Stockton, living at her parents' house. She's going to pursue her interests; which she's decided; lie in Lake Tahoe, with the snow and the snowboarding. With plenty of money to start out, she's going to find her place back in California. Thinking of winter in The Golden State, and snow, reminds her to feel displeased that she won't experience snow here in Alaska. She's been here for five long months. She's watched spring, summer, and fall come and go. If only it would snow and she could experience the park covered in white.

The nostalgia from ending her time at the visitor center has left her in the mood to go out tonight. It just so happens that tonight is The Bell Dog Bash. Jane and Lauren are going, but Liz decides to travel with her party partners Rebecca, Denver, and Celeste.

"Are you sure you don't want to come with us Jane" Liz says, hanging in their doorway striking a limber stretch with her arms.

"I'm sure. I'm going to ride with Tom and Lauren."

"Okay then my dear, I'll see you soon!"

The girls catch a ride with one of the bartenders from the Moose Inn down the road from them. In no time, they're standing outside under a purple sky, looking out on a stretch of earth covered in clusters of employees. Everyone has a drink in their hand and a smile on their face. They see Dave the bell hop, he greets them with hugs and cups.

"How are my girls tonight?"

"Thanks Dave." Liz calls to him raising up her cup for the keg.

"If you ladies need anything just come and find me. The bad news is that the keg itself is down a steep ravine".

In order to get beer, they literally have to dig their heels in, and slowly slide down a steep descent. The first time is difficult, but after more beer, it just becomes fun.

As social as a party can be, she works her way around from group to group, greeting and hugging, high fiving, and chanting stupid songs. The Turkish bussers are there, dressed really nice, and share with her some Turkish dancing. Then she stops and visits with the chefs from the restaurant that are babysitting there big roasted pig. The pit of fire and meat had attracted men from near and far. As for herself and the vegetarians in her company, she couldn't see the appeal.

One of Tom's friend's pulls up to them in his truck, and Liz, Denver, Celeste, and Rebecca climb into the back. About eight people are riding in the bed of the truck, while the driver takes them for a little joy ride along the ridge about three miles, only to turn around and drive them back again. Everyone's laughing and waving. She feels more drunk than usual.

The milling around, the people, this is her community. Down in the clearing by the kegs, Liz slips and falls. She thinks *"I'm too drunk, and too tired".* She can't properly gage the degree of her injury because the alcohol is clouding her ability to sense pain and common physical awareness. She limps up the steep embankment to the party above. It's dark and she's on the outskirts of a large mass of generic faces. She's lost track of all her friends, but every time she passes a figure in the darkness; a "hello" and hug are shared, before she moves on, unclear of her own destination. She's glad she's lost touch with those who brought her here. She wants to be on her own, like her picture of the mountain. Staggering and faded, and a little belligerent, she pulls back.

The night is going by sweetly and quickly, and Liz finds herself in the earliest hours of the morning standing in a drunken bubble, leaning up against Tom's friend's truck. She's looking out, happy to watch the charged up crowd, instead of participating in it. All these faces, they were her friends, she trusted and knew them all, they shared this place, and it brings them a little closer than you might find in some other similar circumstance. She closes her eyes, and listens to the murmur of the voices layered, rising and falling, broken by squeals of laughter and shouts. She tugs at her beanie, pulling it down around her ears. She thinks, in her own space, watching from the outside, "*This place, Denali, it whispers to us; and we're so eager to listen. Its suggestiveness is sometimes wicked, and we're enticed to act freely with little consideration of consequence. We're more wild, fluid and desperate, and we love the way this place gives us permission to be ourselves, to act on our impulses*".

The owner of the truck is now standing beside her, also leaning on his vehicle. They're both throwing in the towel, having mingled and drank, there is really nothing left for them here. She turns to him and remembers that she needs to find a way back to the lodge.

"Can you give me a ride back?" Not even saying hello, she tells him what she wants.

He looks at her, discerning her question and says, "Sure."

She can tell he's ready to go, and she would have been satisfied to go at any time.

They load up in his dark green truck. He shifts into drive and they pull out onto the highway. The ride lacks in conversation, and both of them enjoy the comfortable silence paired with the slow purr of the engine. He swerves twice. They're halfway back to the lodge, when she looks over at the clock in the dashboard. It's almost morning. She turns and gives him a renewed look, in an off the wall impulse, she has a rush of a second wind come on. She's feeling nostalgic and inquisitive. Curious about the driver, and deciding she isn't ready for the night to end so simply.

"Let's go to the park!"

He looks at her, uncertain and confused.

"Right now? You want to go to the park?" Other than the word "sure", this is the first time she's hearing his voice. She's fascinated by the sound of him, and this helps her with her inner debate, deciding if she likes him or not.

"Yes, absolutely. I want to go the park right now. With you." It's easy to tell him exactly what she wants.

This is the first time; she's actually noticing whom she's with. His name is Kurt, and he's a few years older than Liz. She notices he's dressed similar to her, in a hooded sweatshirt and jeans. She studies his unshaven stature, and wonders what he looks like under his black baseball cap. She wants features or qualities she can relate too. She left everyone she knew, she doesn't really know him. He hasn't smiled and is definitely quiet. Liz reaches to consider what she actually knows about this person. He's Tom's friend, and everyone knows Tom's story of how he came out here three years ago to work from Oregon, and has never left Alaska since. This guy is a local, and it's obvious he didn't fit in with the seasonal workers. He's too quiet and reserved. Liz decides she likes that he's quiet, and it's nice that he's taking her back to her Denali home.

He looks over at her sitting in his passenger seat, back straight turned towards him, trying to be provocative.

"The sun will be rising in less than an hour, if we go out to the park; we can watch the sun rise from there. Please?"

She's making up her plan as she says it. He shrugs his shoulders and agrees. So off they go, driving right past the Tundra Lodge, down the highway and into the park. When they reach the Savage River, he stops and turns off the car. It's a good thing the light is starting to transition a little into morning, because he's quiet and not entertaining, and they didn't bring anything to drink with them.

Her impaired thoughts wander. She's reminded of a similar circumstance. It was her very first week in Denali, when she experienced her first introduction to the park. It seems she's come full circle, now reveling in her final week, once again finding herself in the passenger seat of an Alaskan's truck, parked at the gate of the Savage River. She has to laugh; her soul's amused because life has a way of folding over, onto itself.

"I wonder if I'm ending, exactly where I started from . . . all those months ago".

They both get out of the car, and for the first time she notices how cold it is. There they are, Liz and her random stranger, standing against his car, just as they were back at The Bell Bog Bash. Choking on the silence, hidden in shadows, watching, as if waiting for something meaningful to happen. It seems no matter who she meets, or what she plans to do, she's always finding others to humor her, indulging her daring heart.

She doesn't have many questions for him, and he has none for her. She's leaving in a week; it would be pointless to even try. They just stand there, letting their drunkenness dull their senses, and relax the mood. It's so quiet she can hear the rush of the river as it maneuvers its way around sand bars. She can hear the wind gently moving the shrubs and fanning the willow.

She lets her mind mill over some final conclusions, *"Even though I'm next to Kurt, I am standing alone, on my own. I'm really unaware of him in this moment. This is my moment, for me, and I am still, and existing in it. Standing vulnerable and open to the possibility of the unknown, which can be found here, if it doesn't find you first.*

I just want to be here in the park, in my Denali. Concealed in my own experience. I want to remember her, and know her more than I have thus far. I want to take as much of her back to California with me. So all I can do is stand here in the dark, on the gravel road, looking out, not blinking".

It's so tranquil, and as the light starts to slowly illuminate the landscape, she moves closer to her escort. He's been so nice and she's grateful he's obliged her requests. She can see that he's growing restless.

She understands he's tired, but she wants to remain a little longer. Desperately wishing to see the sun rise up over the mountain range. So, she walks up to him, pushing her body against him. He's sandwiched between her and his truck. He isn't surprised, and responds almost mechanically. They hug, but it's not intimate or nice.

It's as if they're going through the motions, but are not truly present. Maybe she's too distracted by her surroundings. Maybe he really isn't into it, but it seems like it's supposed to happen, because what else are two strangers doing at the end of a road, parked at a gate, with no one for miles?

Then something changes. At first, the groping and touching suggests a sense of equality. But, when he opens the door of his truck and lifts her into it, pulling her legs around his waist, there's something new, a flash of dominance. His movements are rushed and unresponsive to her own. He unbuckles her belt, unsnapping her jeans; tugging them down a bit. Liz is stalling, addressing her own issues, assessing if this is something she wants to be doing, and if not, when she's going to say something to him. He's still not speaking, but he's touching, pushing himself on her, the same way she had just done, while they leaned against his truck, but for some reason, because it's him pressing into her, instead of the other way around, she's unwelcoming of the sensation. She can feel how strong he is, and she can't help but fear the hard fact that she knows nothing about him. He's kissing her, but it's not her. He doesn't even know her. She's nothing but a warm body, which frightens her. She's tense, and not reciprocating his advances. She pushes him away. He steps back and stops.

"What's up?" He's casual and eager to resolve her issue.

It's was so easy to tell him everything she wanted. Now she struggles to assert what she doesn't want. Her voice squeaks. "I don't want to have sex."

He shakes his head in disapproval, this makes Liz feel ashamed. "Why?"

She wants control back, maybe she can manipulate her way back into his good graces and coax him into taking her back soon, or to just relax and let her enjoy her sunrise. She slinks over to him with a sultry smile. "Just keep me warm. Can you just hold me Kurt?"

He steps back, and unhinges the tailgate of his truck. "Sure. Just don't be so misleading. Here, let's chill in the truck." He hops into the back of his truck, and waits for Liz to join him.

214

Only hours ago, she was riding back there with her friends, feeling so free and full of delight. Now she's terrified to sit back there. A discerning hunch is warning her, to stay away from him and his truck. She's caught. She's been trying to entrap him since she asked for a ride, making him do things he didn't want to do. She feels obligated to go to the truck now. She goes to him. When she steps up to climb in, she puts her weight on the injured ankle. She cries out from the sharp surge of pain. He grabs onto her forearm and pulls her in.

"What happened?"

"It's my ankle. I hurt it at the party."

"You should get that checked out. Here, let me see it. He lifts her tender ankle onto his lap and cradles it with care."

"I know, and I'm a waitress. I have to work on my ankles and feet all day long." A tiny tear swells in her eye, from the pain and frustration of her situation. The whole situation, being stuck in the truck with an unpredictable date, having to work on an injured ankle, and feeling so cold. She moves to him, and buries her face into his sweatshirt. He puts his hand on her back, gently rubbing her sore muscles. This is nice, and she feels better. She starts to touch him back. Then he grabs onto her hips, he slowly turns her hips in a favorable direction, while pressing himself on top of her.

"Hey. I, I don't want to do this." She sniffles.

He doesn't answer her. He's kissing her neck, and letting his hands explore beneath her sweatshirt. She drops her own hands, and tries to cross her ankles, since she can't cross her legs, because he has them pinned open by his own hips. He sits up, straddling her. He reaches down and grabs her pants to pull them down.

This is it, the moment she decides she has to commit to a decision. She can let him have sex with her. Or she can try to stop him. The more she loses control, the more she knows what she needs.

More tears come, and she cries, "Kurt, I'm not going to do this."

She takes her arms, and shoves him back. He counters her efforts with his weight. She now realizes he has her held down, and it's going to take more than just pushing him away to get him to stop. She tries to wriggle up. She's trapped. She tries squirming down. He has her hips angled in such a way, that she's completely at his mercy.

She screams, "Get off Kurt. I don't want to do this. I swear to God, if you do this to me . . . you'll be sorry. I'll go to the police. I'll tell everyone in Denali! Get off of me!"

He stops, and she lies under him, panting and starting to cry.

"I know you've had a lot to drink, but you're not making any sense here. You've brought me out here. Kissing on me. Now you're crying".

He lifts his pelvis off of her for a second to unzip his pants, she's able to slide herself over a little. She moves her hand along the bed of his truck, trying to find anything that might help her. She makes contact with the smooth glass of an empty beer bottle, from their joy ride from earlier. She flashes back; recalling having tossed an empty bottle into his truck back at the Bell Dog Bash. She wonders if it's her own bottle. It wouldn't function as much of a weapon, since she's pinned down, and has little leverage to hit him with it. She's going to have to anyway. It's all she can do. He raises up again to pull his pants lower, this is when she tries to bludgeon him. He sees the bottle gripped in her hand. He lifts himself off and away from her. "Really?"

She won't let go of the bottle. She knows she can't actually attack him. She doesn't want to hit him or anyone. He watches her put the bottle down, and retract her legs. She places a hand on the side of the truck and stands. "I'm going now".

"Yes, you are". He laughs.

She swings her leg over the truck bed and drops to the ground with a thud. Favoring her bad ankle, unsure, she walks into the thickets of willow, just off the road. He's not chasing her, and from what she can tell, he stayed in the back of his truck. She dashes through the maze of brush, trying to find a hiding place close to the water. She ducks under a bush, and curls herself into a ball.

She can hear movement in the brush, uphill from her, then it retreats. She can hear a car door slam, then another. She waits, listening for the truck to start in anticipation of it driving away. Tears stain her face, but she does not make a sound. The truck isn't starting. He's out there. He's planning something. She's trapped.

She's confused. Thoughts bounce back and forth in her mind. Was he drunk? Was she going to be raped? Will he find her? The truck starts, she hears it shift into drive. The sun rises over the ridge, breaking up the shadows and fears. She shivers, and presses her back against the trunk of an old Spruce. The trickle and gurgle of the stream outlet reminds her that she's in the wild. She searches for animals, the caribou she'd seen before, or a hungry grizzly. The threat of the beasts are enough to urge her from her hiding place, and back up to the road. She starts to limp the many miles back to the visitor center at the entrance of the park. Her mind races. Thoughts crash up against thoughts. Blame needs to be placed. Blame on herself, blame on him, blame for being a female. The word rape flashes and blinks in her mind like a seedy neon casino sign. Almost raped, raped, date-raped, not raped, are sweating and glistening in her thoughts. She was drunk. He was drunk. She questions how much of it was real? She's sorting out the details, unsure of what she did, what he did, and what she does now. She walks, she gets home. His threat and his power, convince her to leave it. She'll leave it on the road, and bury it in the park, like so many other secrets.

With a step on her weak ankle, she has to ask herself the most important question: Did this experience damage her? Is she hurt? Can she trust men? Can she trust herself? Will she ever take a ride from a stranger again? Will she drink at parties again? Was I actually going to hit Kurt with a bottle?

This is her answer: "I'm okay." She starts to laugh, and embraces a spirit that floods through her. She offers all the worry and doubt to the universe, letting it go. She had no idea how strong she really is, until this morning, when a sun rose for the day. Shining down on her transcendence, shining light as mountains come into view one at a time. Her ankle isn't as bad as she once thought. She's traveling down the road on both feet, one step after the other. She adjusts her beanie down tight around her ears and pulls the zipper on her jack all the way up to her chin.

She comes to a bend in the road, she can see something up ahead; it's quite large. She's still too distant to determine what it is specifically. She keeps moving forward, since her ankle is agitated and she's cold. Soon, the two creatures cross paths. Liz is more than seventy five feet from a great Bull Moose. He's standing right in the middle of the road. His antlers are so big, he towers high above the Sitka spruce. Moose are extremely dangerous and this is mating season.

"Exactly how many times am I going to have to save myself this morning?"

The vision of the massive beast standing in this spectacle of a park stirs courage within Liz. The moose is watching her, his ears flicking in irritation and interest. She backs off the road, and kneels down to let him know she's no threat. He takes a step in her direction. At first she only kneels to put herself out of harm's way. But, now that she finds herself kneeling before him, she's compelled to close her eyes and bow her head. She prays to God to deliver her home safely, thanking him for all the blessings that continue to make her whole.

The moose moves on, crossing the road and hiding somewhere nearby. She rises, and continues the long walk. Fifteen minutes pass, and a park service truck roars up the road. Liz's heart fills with gratitude, as she waves her arms in distress. The truck pulls up and comes to a slow stop. The door springs open, and a ranger jumps out. She runs to Liz. "Are you okay?"

Liz nods her head and smiles with joy for the young woman in the park service uniform. "I'm okay. I just kind of ran into some trouble, but nothing serious. I just need a ride back."

The ranger chuckles, "Let me guess, The Bell Dog Bash?"

Liz nods her head, feeling a little embarrassed.

"Okay, hop in. I can take you to the visitor center. You'll have to catch the shuttle back to your property from there, otherwise I'll run behind schedule. You're lucky I found you out here. This area is teaming with moose right now, they're all rutting and in rambunctious moods. It's not safe, you know? It's critical to make sure every choice you make, is a good choice out here. One bad decision can cost you dearly."

Liz considers telling the ranger about her moose sighting, but decides to keep it to herself.

Wednesday, September 25th 2002

The final week is passing slowly, and the tourism has slowed to a low trickle. Liz refuses to attend any more final parties. All of that is over, and she's focused more on Jane, and how she's using her time during this final week. She's made so many preparations for her return to Oregon. She has school and even a vacation with her boyfriend to The Big Easy. The roommates go to work together, go back to their room together, rest, think, and visit. The restaurant feels different lately, without the hustle and bustle of the assholes, and half of their breakfast lunch crew gone. The space seems tired, and empty. The slow days encourage thinking, and Jane and Liz have committed to working up to the final day. There are no more days off, or discussions of festivals, bands, bars, or road trips to Fairbanks.

In some ways, the end has already occurred for so many things. It reminds Liz of the Golden Oaks back home in California. *"Throughout the fall the tree will lose many of its leaves. We are the last leaves, still hanging on, reluctant to let go, with grips that are so strong, and yet we know that with one gust, we'll all be detached and scattered. Without the tree that connects us all, we'll be alone. I hadn't realized that the last days of a seasonal entity were so serendipitous and impeding"*.

She's now looking South in the direction of California. She can't wait to see the sights of home, the smells, and traffic, and populated areas. She misses spices and ethnic foods.

During more private times in her day, she reverts back to thoughts about her morning with Kurt. She's angry at herself for making extremely bad choices. She's not speaking a word of the incident to anyone. She believes his threats, and doesn't want him for an enemy. He's gone, and that's how she wants it.

In true Jane form, she's in the middle of one of her plans, and second to the last night, her dad will be visiting her. Jane has talked to their busboy Brennon about having Liz stay in the empty bed that's in his room. So her dad can stay with her, in their room. Brennon agrees, and Liz is happy to oblige, for it means something interesting and distracting to alleviate the anxiousness and wariness that surrounds them all.

Brennon is a doll, and kind of shy around girls. As aggressive as Liz can be, and he knows she can be, she's interested to see how uncomfortable they may both feel; spending the night in a room alone together.

She comments on their plan in her journal, "This is a perfect distraction for me. I love Jane; she probably asked Brennon because she knew it would be fun for me".

Saturday, September 28th 2002

In the afternoon Liz and Jane walk over to the Vista property to get their portraits taken. There's a portrait studio, called the Wolverine Studio. The roommates are going to dress up in fun costumes, and spend some quality time together. She's touched by the gesture, and looks forward to having a fantastic picture to remind her of their friendship. They dress up in frontier dresses with animal hats and fur stoles, complete with big shot guns. In true Fat City form, they stop and buy some fudge from the candy shop, along with espresso before heading back to Tundra property.

"How's your ankle today Liz?" Jane's acute to Liz's traits, and only she would have noticed the mild way Liz has favored her other foot.

"It's a lot better. I'm just trying to keep the pressure off of it, so I can make sure it's healing one hundred percent."

"The way you fell, I thought you broke it for sure."

"You saw me fall?"

"I saw you jump!" Jane starts to giggle. Then she saw the blank expression on Liz's face. "You don't remember do you?"

Liz shakes her head.

Jane sighs, shooting a worried look for her friend. "You lush! Remember the steep ravine we have to slide down to reach the keg. Well, Drew jumped from the halfway point, and landed in the clearing. You were hiking down behind him, and tried to copy him."

Liz's mouth gaped open, surprised she did that.

"You were chanting "Fat City", and you got a lot of other people down by the keg to chant for you. Drew ran over and picked you up after your crash landing."

"He did?"

"Yup. Hey Liz, I'm glad you're not drinking this week."

"Me too."

Jane's dad would be arriving soon, and she needed to move a few of her things, like her uniform down to Brennon's room. The two friends head up to their room. They see Brennon and step inside his employee housing room. This is her first time in his room, and it's nothing special. It looks similar to her own room. He has the two twin beds pushed together, so he has one big sized bed.

She has to tease him, "Oh Brennon, that's so sweet, you already pushed the beds together to get ready for our big night!" He blushes, and tries to laugh, but it's obvious the comment freaks him out. Actually, Liz is sure he hates the comment. She really likes Brennon. However, they struggle to relate to one another despite being the same age.

Jane's dad arrives, and she sits with both Jane and her father for an hour to visit. Jane's dad has just come from staying with her boyfriend, Orin. He's planning on driving back down the coast with Jane and her boyfriend in a couple days.

Liz is surprised that she's uncomfortable to go down to Brennon's room. She's not sure what to talk to him about for a prolonged amount of time. She thinks she would make him nervous, which would make her nervous. So she opts to go see Drew at the bar.

"Liz, how have you been?"

A visual image of her jumping from a cliff, and crashing to the ground, then being lifted up by Drew gives her goose bumps. She reasons, it's better to not mention it. "I'm good Drew, what have you been up too?"

He gives her a thumbs down, and says, "I'm fighting a bad cold."

"You should stop by my room sometime I have Echinacea that will help you out a ton."

The thought of Drew stopping by her room is enough to make her blush.

"Liz, you're so sweet." When he says this; he gives her a knock-out look, and her heart beats faster. Then he smiles, "Do you want a margarita?"

"Nope, I'll have a cola."

He walks over to her, puts his hand on top of hers and grins. "I totally get that."

Soon the bar gets busy. She writes down some poetry in her journal. Then makes the uneasy trek to Brennon's. He has the beds apart, nice and wide, and has cleared a space for her things. She has her ultra-light too-small sleeping bag and pillow. They visit for a little while, mostly gossiping. Thankfully Lauren and Tom come by and join them. Liz considers asking Tom about his friend Kurt. She also wonders if Kurt said anything to Tom about her. She doesn't dare bring it up. They lounge around talking about nothing, until ten or so.

Now it's awkward, just the two of them. Brennon turns the lights off and climbs into his bed. Liz squirms down into her sleeping bag, "Goodnight Brennon."

She can hear him roll over "Goodnight Liz."

Sleeping alone in a room with him isn't so bad, and sleep comes easily. Several hours later, there's a bang on the door, and some shouts. They both sit up and look at each other, awake and confused. It takes a second to process the knocking and shouts. Liz wipes some drool from her mouth.

Brennon looks at her and says, "It's the Northern Lights!"

With that, they leap out of bed. Liz grabs for her jacket. They both dash into the night. Thrilled, resembling two young children on Christmas morning, rushing to see if Santa had come, Brennon and Liz huddle together, raising their gaze to the sky.. Brennon's room is on the bottom floor, and in several steps they're in the middle of an open area of the property. Above them, they can see the most vivid, haunting demonstration of light and expression that will surely etch onto the canvas of one's soul.

The green light glows and dances, moving in so many unpredictable ways. It starts as a dot, and then draws a line across the sky; the line expands upward, creating a curtain of waves. Fading back to a dot before it dives. After swooping down, it shimmers to nothing. She feels glad to be sharing this with Brennon, sweet Brennon. And as she looks out across the property; she sees employees in pajamas standing in groups of two, staring up the sky, with their mouths open, almost as big as their eyes.

They watch for a long time, and even though the light would fade, they all wait, hoping, to see more in disbelief. The light resembles a being, with personality. The message and symbolism it evokes defies reason.

She's satisfied, *"The light puts everything into perspective, and I am certain I will leave my heart in Alaska, for nothing is as heavenly, or phenomenal".*

Brennon and Liz are just about ready to go back to bed, when two friends approach them. It's James the bartender from the Vistas, and Joe.

"Hey guys," James says.

She watches Joe squirm a bit as he stands across from her. All four people are nothing but smiles, still effected by the ethereal display in the heavens.

"It's Joe's birthday." James informs them.

Liz leans in and hugs James, she then walks over to Joe and gives him a quick kiss on the cheek. She whispers, "Happy twenty first birthday, Joe." She beams with happiness. "What a gift you have tonight!" She gestures to the heavens.

He looks alarmed and encouraged by her gesture. "Hey, do you guys want to come with us to a bonfire on the river?"

Liz looks at Joe and then James, "Who's going to be there?" She hesitates. Still separating herself from the deep sleep that came before.

"Mostly the dinner shift and theatre crowd." Joe answers.

She's so joyful from watching the lights, that there's no way she's going to be able to go back to sleep. She turns to Brennan, "Let's go!"

Brennon gives her his "responsible, boring guy look" and says, "I'm going back to bed. We have to be up really soon for work."

She nods, and tells him, "I'll be back later. You know, I just can't sleep. It's too exciting!" She puts on her work pants and grabs her jacket from the room.

With that, the twosome that was making its way across the property is now a threesome. The guys are thrilled about the lights, just like Liz. Their pace is quick. Partly because it's extremely dark and bitter cold. They have to keep moving to stay warm.

They leave the property and are now on the highway, walking over the concrete bridge. Soon she's sliding, and skidding down a ravine, towards the Nenana River, which she can't actually see, but can definitely hear. When she gets to the river, their brisk walk for warmth is replaced by alcohol for warmth, and a nice raging bonfire.

Many of the dinner shift servers are there. The stories and jokes are abundant. The actors are telling really great scary, river stories. The servers are telling dirty jokes, and everyone is wishing Joe a very happy birthday. Liz is truly glad she came here tonight. It alleviates some of her anxiety about leaving in less than 48 hours. She's also thankful to have a peaceful feeling between Joe and herself. Not that their falling out has been causing her stress lately, or that she even thought much of it over the last month. Still, it's good, to end things well.

She can't help but notice, while she stands among the group, that Joe seems to be standing near her more than not, and when different girls come up to give him special birthday wishes and cuddles, he isn't paying much attention to them. One girl in particular helps her realize this. She's seen this girl hang around Joe before, she was with them the night they ditched her at the pizza pub, with her striking red hair and curvy figure. She's definitely trying to get Joe's attention, and he acts as if he's not aware. He's been right beside Liz most of the night.

Down by the fire, she grows tired of the jokes and stories. She's more aware that she has to be at work in two and a half hours. She can stay and listen to more of the same, or just call it a night, and try to lie down for a few hours. She decides to think like Jane, and bid everyone a goodnight, thanking them for having included her.

Everyone stands up, and tells Liz goodnight, warning her to be careful walking back, in case of bears.

"I'll be careful. I've been told I'm a bear charmer." Liz promises.

Joe turns to her and says, "I'll walk you back, to make sure you're safe."

"I'll be okay," Liz gives him a genuine smile, "You stay and enjoy you're night."

"I want to walk you back." He says. He gives her a brief but intense look.

She can see he really means it. The gesture is so unexpected from him. She's not sure how to feel about the fact that he's willing to walk out on his own party. She had resigned to the idea of walking back alone, and had worked up all the courage to do so, only to not have to use the bravery, and instead focus on her present company.

The two of them climb up the steep terrain. Liz is in the lead, and Joe is following close behind.

The red head steps forward and shouts, "I'll go with you guys too."

Liz continues forward, grabbing hold of tree branches to pull herself up, while digging her toes into the layers of dirt and rock. When she reaches the top, right after the bridge on the highway, she turns to make sure all three successfully ascended the embankment. They did. She's out of breath and panting from the climb.

She steps out onto the highway, pointing herself in the direction of their property. It's getting to be so cold, her hands now hurt. Joe catches up and walks beside her and the red head shouts to Joe, "You aren't going back?"

He doesn't look back. But, yells over his shoulder. "I'm walking her back".

She shouts in an angry tone. "I hiked all the way up so you would have someone to walk back down with!"

Joe, shrugs his shoulders, saying, "I'm sorry."

The redhead turns around, disappearing into the ravine.

Now Liz and Joe are alone, and she's beginning to suspect Joe might want to have a private birthday celebration with her.

Liz thinks, *"Poor Joe, he just made peace with me, only to have another girl pissed off at him".*

Alone, on the highway, standing by the bridge, he slides his arm around her to get warm. He's not trying to kiss her or grab her, just pull her a little closer. He locks eyes with Liz, and this confrontation is deep. He's never looked at her this way before. His face is serious and sad. Liz's heart was beating quickly from the quick ascent up the river canyon. Instead of slowing, it beats fast in response to the unexpected way she finds herself on a bridge with a man who has caused her to both swoon and shout in anger, someone who brings out her honesty.

"I'm sorry I told your friends we had sex. I'm sorry I hurt you. I really like you."

Above the river, she thinks about his words, *"I believe everything except that he likes me. I never thought Joe was ever really that interested in me. He always seemed to be interested in Lauren, Denver, or the redhead, or my hostess at the restaurant who is my best RISK partner. All of them, but not me. I never thought he was interested in me, or even noticed me, except after I yelled at him. Then he looked miserable and tried to avoid me. I'm not sure if I should believe him, but I can tell he's sorry, and even, that it's been bothering him for a long time".*

She decides to listen.

"Why didn't you come and talk to me? I like you, too." A confession is easy when the river roars, and the night blends.

"You just really hurt my feelings, and I was embarrassed." His voice trembles and she can hear his sincerity. "I'm just screwed up, and I didn't think you wanted to talk to me."

Following the words, is a kiss. Entangled in emotion and touch, two seasonal beings, pushing out the cold, standing on a bridge between two places.

It feels nice, their arms wrapped up in one another, holding and squeezing. She understands now, that he's been trying to get her alone since he saw her shivering in her pajamas under the Aurora Borealis. She wants him too. He seems so vulnerable and alone. Clinging to the pull of attraction, they walk back to the Tundra Lodge.

He's talking to her, telling her about his feelings. She listens, and with each sentence; she knows him more, and he speaks well, and is thoughtful. He opens up, his birthday gift to her.

"Liz every time I saw you I wanted to go to you and talk to you, but I thought you hated me. I'm a loser. Liz, I'm so unhappy with myself, and if I could be a better person, more like you, maybe we could have been close this summer."

Liz smiles, *"It's his twenty first birthday, and I think he's maturing right before my eyes".*

"Joe, you don't want to be like me? If you knew me, you wouldn't say those things."

She's in shock, and only an hour before had figured she'd be making this lone trek back solo. Here they are, together, lost in the night with no one else to judge or interrupt. It's now okay to say whatever she needs too.

Frozen Blessing

Saturday, September 29th 2002

They go back to his room. Inside, it's warm. He turns on the light. The brightness in his room is a shock after walking in from the black ache of night. One lighted room within rows of dark rooms, they must be the only two people awake on property.

The spark between them could light the space all on its own. He still looks sad, approaching her with a heavy heart. It occurs to her, that she hasn't been the only one trying to connect, to navigate and struggle here in Denali. He reaches for her, again, the embrace is warm, gentle, and so nice. It's what she wants. It's what he wants. The bed is right beside them. They sit down. They lay down. Things slow. When her head rests on the softness of the pillow, her body urges her to seek out sleep. She shoves the need back, refusing. He pushes his fingers through the waves of her hair. Kissing her forehead. His blue eyes pierce. It's something of substance that they now hold. She can see he's overcome by the wave of emotions he's had to suppress all season; keeping up with a fast crowd, he was lost in them, used by them. Now he wants her to hold him and use him too. He wants to reconcile, and finally gain her acceptance. She's not concerned with his reputation or who he is here, it's who he is right now; that she wants.

Liz questions what she wants. She thinks about her fragile heart. She thinks about the end.

But, then there is Joe, and the way he's touching her, and looking so sweetly at her, and the way he wants to spend his birthday with Liz out of all the girls down by the river. With each touch she wants him more, but her convictions have to hold strong. So she finds herself lying in his bed, in the middle of an epic battle with herself; based on whether or not she should or shouldn't.

"Liz, you're so pretty." He whispers.

She pulls back slightly, wishing to hide, exposed in the bright light of his room. He pulls her back to him. Covering her like a blanket.

"Do you know how pretty you are?"

Jackets come off, then shirts. She reasons that this is the line. She won't go any further. But the closer he gets, the more she's tempted. Time is compromising and threatening their exchanges. There are no promises beyond this point. They have less than forty eight hours remaining, and very soon she has to leave him. Very soon she has to be at work. The attraction between them that ignited from the night they walked alone in the woods, is undeniable now. During the stretch of the long season, their desire has overinflated, and now threatens to pop.

She can see something in him when he looks at her, it's so serious and so sad. It reminds her of her own sadness. She wants to be close.

He could have been sad and lustful in this way with a number of the women down by the bonfire. Yet, she understood, that it had to be her. They reach for the other desperately, holding on, and staying close. He grabs for her pants, and tugs them off. She wants to be what he needs, to fill his emptiness, but as his pants come off, she can feel her boundaries disintegrate around her. She hears a voice in her head. It's Amber the bartender, Chris's girlfriend, and she can hear the echo of the warning she had made sure to tell Liz about.

She said, "Stay away from Joe, he's dirty."

It is this voice that brings her back into a reality of logic. She grabs her pants, pulls them back on. He stops, and lets her go. He moves sideways to the edge of the bed. She reaches for her sweatshirt and jacket. He sits up looking completely crushed.

"I'm sorry, I have to go to work. It's almost four!"

She pounces back on him, straddling his waist and steals one final kiss, which is less passionate than those that came before. She slides off of him and secures the button on her pants. She runs out the door, and rushes all the way back to Brennon's room.

She jumps into bed and hides under the covers for forty five minutes, until the time to work calls her to face her responsibility. Now feeling like a Northern Light deviant, she peels open her heavy eyelids, recalling how frustrating her life can be. Brennon gives her a look, curious and amused. Jane is used to seeing her slink back in from wild escapades late into the night, but apparently Brennon hadn't realized that she is in the habit of not sleeping.

She smiles and tells him, "I had fun last night. You should have come with me."

Tonight will be Liz's final night. Tomorrow she will wake up, serve breakfast to the last assholes who will all board a train by ten, and by noon all the employees will load onto shuttles; in route for Anchorage or Fairbanks; depending on which flight they've scheduled. Jane splits up with her dad, but will meet up with him tomorrow in Anchorage. Tonight is theirs. Liz doesn't want to go searching for Joe, or anyone. She just wants to be with her friends, the ones whom she's worked alongside all these harrowing months. The ones who know the punishment and pain of waking before the sun, and the way old people can be so nasty and rude during breakfast. Their evening is quiet and preoccupied with packing; which marks the end of something good. Every object, every article of clothing, put away. The only things that are out, are their terrible black and white uniforms, along with a sweater and jacket to put over their work pants for when they board the shuttles that will take them away from Denali.

With packing, came visiting. Friends stop in and hug. This evening they have Fat City gathered together in their room, eating a buffet of left over snacks that they foraged from all their rooms.

"I'm going to miss the Mayor," Lauren sighs lovingly as she pets Liz on the head.

"Lauren what will I do without you?" Liz stares at her gorgeous platinum blond friend, who consults her on all her strange social fallacies.

They snap photos, sing, and laugh. This isn't the time to revisit past memories of the summer, or a chance to make one last story to share. They don't talk about going home, or tomorrow.

Liz sets up the self-timer on her camera, and runs over to the bed where they jam Celeste, Denver, Rebecca, Lauren, and Jane, along with The Mayor.

Together they yell, "Fat City!"

Snap, the film captures them.

"As The Mayor, if I'm ever feeling hungry out in the real world, off Tundra Property, I'll hold up my donut in a toast to you ladies: The citizens of Fat City." Liz affectionately proclaims.

With drinks and food in hand, the girls hold them up and chant; "To Fat City."

Monday, September 30th 2002

The morning. As in the morning they've all thought of, during the relentless season; wishing, and praying, and faithfully trying to survive until the final day; when it would actually take place. They're all there; reporting to work, looking sharp in their black and whites. Faces are sparkling, smiles are cemented, and there are hardly any assholes.

She walks up to a middle-aged couple sitting in front of a big picture window, a carafe of fresh coffee tilted out, as her wrist bends with skill. "Can I warm up your coffee?"

The man and woman push their nearly empty mugs a few inches towards Liz, welcoming of the hot caffeinated beverage. She's interrupted their hypnotic gaze out into the park. The woman drops her eyes, and lets them set on the plain waitress. Liz can feel the woman's stare, as she pours the steaming liquid into the cups.

"So, is this your final day here at the lodge?" The woman asks in an inquisitive tone.

Liz brings the carafe up to her chest, hugging it in the crook of her arm. "Yes. I'm scheduled to go home in a few short hours."

"Where is home?"

A twinkle flickered in her eye, revealing to the guest the girl who's hiding behind the server uniform, and for a fraction of a second, the woman saw Liz. "California." Her voice couldn't hide the emotion attached to the name of "home".

"Did you have a good summer here in Denali?"

Liz stops, thinking about her summer. She's pleased with herself that the answer is yes. She takes her free hand and collects the emptied breakfast plates that sit on the table. "It was a really good summer, but I'm happy to be going home." She gives the woman a nod, and retreats to the cover of the server's station.

She may have had a total of five tables. They didn't matter at all. She spent more time just looking. She looks out the windows. She looks at the lawn outside, and the grey river rushing below. She looks out to the view of the taiga forest, and mountains beyond them. She looks at the back wall, with the bigger sized tables for the rare occasions when she had a large group. She looks at the carpet, and the stacks of glasses. She wants to remember every finite detail, and after having to stare at it for so many mornings, mornings where she cursed the sun, and held back tears of exhaustion. Now she just wants to look at them once more.

Jane and Chris join her by one of their favorite picture windows near the South end of the building. Chris breaks the deep meditation, "We've been so wrong".

"Oh, no, really, Chris. You already apologized. You weren't that mean to me, please don't".

He cuts her off, "Oh my gosh, no. I'm not talking about that. There is life happening beyond the scope of you, Liz! Chris rolls his eyes at her. Which feels the more genuine than any other conversation they've had since the time he got angry with her. This makes her smile. "We're wrong. All of us. They aren't assholes. They

232

are us. Don't you see it? So they get a little cross. Think about how far they've traveled. Oh, what? Can't. Just think about how far you had to travel. What it takes to come here. Girls, honestly, none of us, and this whole property . . . we are here because of them".

Liz lets out a deep sigh.

"Right. We are Ying, and they are Yang". He pats Jane on the shoulder and leaves them to consider his plea to redact the "asshole designation".

Ten came, and the old people left. Someone turns the lights off and the room illuminates by the daylight outside. The natural light is so soothing and overcast; complimenting their moods. They can take off their bowties, and put on their regular clothes. By then, their bags are being picked up by the bellhops and loaded onto shuttles. They have nothing to do but sit and wait. Liz has no idea where everyone else on property is, but here in the restaurant it's just them; the breakfast lunch crew. They sit with coffee and hot chocolate; legs propped up on chairs and tables, giggling, and patiently watching the clock. The ease of the day leaves Liz forlorn and internalized. She's politely sitting, but her friends fail to keep her in the moment. Her mind drifts aimlessly, unable to focus on any one thing. Then something magical happens, something unbelievable.

Something against the window catches her eye, and then another as it gently touches, and rolls down. Then more, in small delicate flurries.

"My wish," Liz exhales as quiet as the weather.

Her coworkers watch her jump up, pulling on a modest brown sweater. She dashes out the front doors of the restaurant. The cold wind jolts her cells, and the exposed skin on her cheeks and neck tingle. The snowflakes dance to a muted rhythm, before fumbling and falling around her. She catches them on her eyelashes and cheeks. She raises her hands up to the sky, palms facing up, grabbing at the spaces that take up everything. She's alone, just outside of the restaurant. It's Liz; and the soft white of the lodge's first snowfall of the season. She hops from foot to foot, hysterical from the joy of her good fortune. Happiness is hers.

A hand settles on her shoulder. She turns to see Jane, wrapped up in two polar fleeces, and a down parka. Her green eyes peering out in recognition. She pulls her hand back, and raises her own palms up to the sky, taking Liz's lead.

Liz smiles in delight. "Jane, this is what I came here for."

"This?" She asks, in a questioning tone.

"I can't believe it, now I feel I've experienced a small slice of each season Denali possesses. With this gift, I can go home. I have the Universe's blessing, and it is falling down around me."

She nods her head. "Yes. You found it, Liz."

Behind Jane, the front doors to the restaurant open, a mismatched group of tired servers trickle out. They rush to Liz and Jane. It was just them. They couldn't see a trace of any other employee on property. It was the breakfast lunch crew.

Marvin comes out last, and he has a cup of hot chocolate in his hands, he passes it to Liz. "Here you go my ice princess."

She takes a sip, and wonders how she possibly had felt lonely all these months, when she has friends like these.

As they board their shuttle, she takes a seat next to Jane. Per, Jane's plans. The women look fondly out the window of the bus; they see their manager Claire. She's standing in a line with the other department managers. They've gathered to wave goodbye and send off the last of the seasonal employees. She's waving her hands and jumping up and down to get their attention. She motions for them to come out. Liz and Jane make their way out of the shuttle and each give her a big hug.

Claire hands them five small boxes, she smiles and says, "It's for Fat City."

When they get back on the bus, they peer into the boxes: slices of turtle cheesecake and molten chocolate lava cake. The bus pulls away from the curb, and within minutes they are gone.

Sunday, September 29th 2002

She treks up to the top of a large mountain. She's so high she's in the company of sheep. She feels compelled to take the long, hard climb above the canyons and valleys to seek out refuge, a place to rest. It's so desperately cold in this land that her body is draining all her calories just trying to keep itself warm each day. The blueberries are picked over, shriveled, and more difficult to find. She's come full circle and is back to digging roots for nourishment.

The bears with cubs are gone now, and have respectfully taken their broods down into the earth for sleep. The more wild and hungry bears remain, and the spirit of competition has taken over this land. Moose compete with moose for mates, caribou compete to keep up with the herd, and the bears compete for food, with not only one another but with the ravens, eagles, and even the clever foxes. As if this time was scheduled, and wired into her being, she knows the time for feeding is coming to an end, and the search for sanctuary and meditation is now at hand.

Prolonging this act of receding back to a den is pointless, yet she's restless and uneasy.

The first winter without Mama, by herself. What if she is hunted, or cold? What if she can't sleep and she's alone in the darkness for all those months? What if she goes mad? As she walks and digs roots, the frozen air wraps her up. Her breath slows down; which make her eyelids heavy and her arms and legs lazy.

So here she is; too high for reasonable bears. You will not find older experienced bears using up energy to climb mountains so close to the arrival of winter's sleep. But it is her anxiety, and lack of direction that has brought her here. She stands alone on this mountain, decorated with white dust and slick rock. The wind is strong, and it howls in laughter from the discovery of a silly bear high upon this peak. Despite the lack of logic, she stands here, above it all. She can see all the miles she's traveled, from the wet taiga, to the desolate expanse of tundra. She can see the odd river bed, that holds no water, and she can see the piles of earth dug up from countless bears who've found abundant root systems. Looking down at the braided rivers, they look so small now, merely a trickle through time, they too, look like the last reserves of water are making their way through before the big freeze.

She is a Denali bear, and she has survived the long season alone, and she will go to sleep, and when she emerges from her den; she will be an older bear, a wiser bear, who will know where to get food and how to find food. She will be strong, and maybe secure a territory. She's no longer confused and fearful. This place, her home has sculpted her; forging her into the grizzly that she is. Standing out, scanning the great peaks, looking down on the luminous valleys. She knows that it is time. With one last forlorn look, she turns to seek her den. These images will keep her company in her dreams for the many winter months that will gently soothe her strong spirit.

Goodnight Denali.

"Goodnight Bear," the wind howls softly.

Afterward

Tuesday November 20th 2012

To many it was just a seasonal job, but for me it was extraordinary. It made me extraordinary as well as those I crossed paths with. We each came to seek out answers and to be brave. We all agreed on some level that we were called there. It was meaningful and significant to answer this call for whatever it means.

She whispered to me as I dreamed under her majesty, the secrets. To learn how to follow a wish, or believe in someone when they have nothing left. I hold in my soul a small fragile snowflake, it was sent to me from her, and it reminds me to live every day, like it's the only day left, because sometimes it can be the only day left, and once it's gone, you can never really go back.

When I think of the young girl, eagerly standing out on the Denali park road, gazing into the darkness, watching and waiting, counting on something to happen, looking for it. I know she is right. We have to stand out on that road, and look for it, wish for it, to find the moments that define us.

98802331R00143

Made in the USA
Lexington, KY
09 September 2018